WITHOUT WARNING

DEE LAGASSE

Published by Danielle Lagasse

Edited by Melinda Utendorf of M.Ute Editing Services and Kelli Spear.

Cover Design by Kat Savage of Savage Hart Book Services

Formatting by Alexandria Bishop of AB Formatting

To The Minis.
Dillon, Kallie, and Hunter,
Remember that time I told you that you could do anything and be
anything you want? Here's momma backing up her statement. I love you
the most.

ACKNOWLEDGMENTS

I know that, typically, these go in the back of the book, but you wouldn't be holding this book in your hands if it weren't for my village. If it weren't for the all the amazing people standing by my side, there's no way I would have even started writing, never mind publishing *Without Warning*. They deserve to be in the front.

First and most importantly, even though they got the dedication… Dillon, Kallie, and Hunter. My reason for everything. Thank you for not only giving me the best title I could ever have, but for also making me the *luckiest* mom on this earth. I swear, I struck gold with the three of you. Never stop chasing your dreams. Ever. I believe in you, always. Love you the most!

Jeffrey. Thanks for holding down the fort while I ignored you for so, so, so many hours, staring at my laptop screen with headphones in. *And*, for not making fun of me too much when I sobbed like a baby after writing "The End." And, *also*, for all the late night candy and caffeine runs when I needed an extra boost to finish "one more chapter." But, most importantly, thank you for standing by my side and believing in me. For knowing when

I needed a push, or someone to hold my hand. Thank you for never letting me give this up, even when I said I wanted to. You knew I could do it and your faith in me got me to "The End." Oh, and sorry for drinking all your rum while writing Chapter Eighteen. Love you, Cracker Jack.

My big, crazy family – all twenty-seven sides of you. Before I was a Lagasse, I was a Beagley. And, being a part of our family made writing a big, loud, crazy, in your face family so easy. From the very beginning every one of you, on every side, have supported me and this crazy dream of mine. But, especially my dad John, my mom Debbi, my sister Vanessa, and my brothers, Joey and John Christopher. And, just because, Jeremy, Lily, Nico and Emily, too. Being your daughter, your sister, and your childrens' aunt is my second favorite thing in this world, after being The Minis' momma. (Even though my sister's weird.)

P.S. If you're related to me, feel free to skip over Chapter Eighteen. In fact, I highly encourage it.

Bobby Wheeler. You're the Harry to my Hermione, B. Grateful doesn't even begin to come close to how I feel about our friendship. Thank you for believing in me and for pushing me when I didn't believe in myself. But most of all, thank you for putting up with me for more than half our lives, and for encouraging every crazy idea I've had since I was fourteen. It's not the "Behind The Music" spot you wanted, but I hope this will do, Vanilla. (You know I had to throw that in somewhere!) You're my fav.

Chelsea Davis, Aimee Lavoie, & Lindsey Batts. (Pay attention to a few of the names (both first and last) in the book, everyone else. It's relevant, I swear.) There is a reason Hollis has three close girlfriends, and they meet every Tuesday for dinner. When I told each of you I was planning on writing, none of you even batted an eye...you just wanted to know what you could do to help. Your support and your love mean everything to me. There's no one I would rather have horrific bachelorette party memories with than the three of you. LOVE YOU!

Kenny Wetherbee & Travis Soucy. There's also a reason two of Hollis' big brotherly figures are named Travis and Kenny. Life may have pulled us in separate directions and the story within this book may be fictional, but the two of you taught me everything I needed to know to write about (over)protective "big brothers." I will never forget everything you both did for me growing up. There wasn't anything one of you couldn't fix, and I know if I called you today, right now, this very second, you would still do all you could to save the day. I will spend the rest of my life being thankful I have you.

Chantal Patino. For reading every single version of this story… and for being the friend that's kept all my secrets since the eighth grade. We didn't become the rock stars we wanted to be, but I'm so glad we still have each other.

Abbi Glines. You have been the most gracious, most helpful, most patient person during my writing process and while publishing. Thank you for believing in me, for answering all my questions along the way and for being such a bright light in my life.

Kandi Steiner. You were the first person in the book world to know that I was writing, and I will go as far as saying that your reaction is what pushed me to keep going. I will never not be thankful to have someone like you in my corner. Thank you for making *Without Warning's* cover so pretty. I'll always be here to tell you, "I told you so."

Jerilyn Martinez, Julie Moss, Casey Decock, Sarah Simone, Cristina Bon, Vicci Kaighan, Mac Marshall, Nikki Gasca, Jessica Downs, Tammy Deviney-Roden, Suzy Danylko, Tricia Ciak, JoAnna Alsup, Jaime Moss, Tammy Gaudet, & Nicole Moore – BABES! You ladies were there every step of the way. Whether it was beta feedback, post sharing, late night hand holding as I was stressing pre-release…your love and support is what got *Without Warning* out into the world. Before there were any teasers, reveals, or even a synopsis, you ladies were there. That means more to me than you will ever know.

Stacey Allen. My seventh grade English teacher. If it wasn't for you pulling me aside, and telling me that my words "mattered," I don't know if I would be here today. Thank you for believing in me all those years ago. *Your teaching matters.*

Melinda of M.Ute Editing. Thank you for polishing *Without Warning* and giving Hollis and Chase their finishing touches!

Alexandria Bishop of AB Formatting. Thank you for squeezing me in, and then letting me change my dates 92746482046 times, and for making the inside of *Without Warning* as pretty as the outside.

Kelli Spear. I told you this before, but I was terrified for you to read this. Your belief in me, and in Hollis and Chase means so much to me. Thank you for being the last eyes on their story and for your friendship-it is absolutely one of my most favorite things about being a part of the book world. Love you!

Autumn Gantz of Wordsmith Publicity. Our friendship is one of my favorite things to come from being a part of the book world. Thank you for doing all you did to get *Without Warning* out there, and for all your support "behind the scenes", too.

All the ARC readers, the bloggers, the authors that let me pop in your groups, and especially my very own Capparelli & Co. group! I appreciate you more than words can ever say.

And to you. Yes, you. For taking a chance on me. By picking up this book, you are supporting someone's dream. Thanks for helping me make this a reality.

I got a little close and that is all it took. I was captured. Because sometimes that is what happens when the heart recognizes home.

-J.M. Storm

PROLOGUE

September 26, 2004
Sophomore Gym Class, Abbott Hills High School.

KARMA IS A TRICKY BITCH.

The only logical explanation for me having physical education at seven o' fucking clock in the morning is that I must have done something terrible in this life or one before it.

I mean, I suppose that I could just bring my running shoes and walk around the perimeter of the gymnasium to get class credit. You know, like all the other girls in the class do. And, when I say "all," I actually mean every single one of them. Except me. Doing things just because everyone else is has never been my style though.

Which is why I am currently the only girl standing in this damp, freezing locker room fully dressed to actively participate in class. I'm the one with no make-up on, solid black track shorts, and a loose hot pink racerback tank-top over a visible black sports bra. Twenty-two other girls are scattered throughout the rows of narrow metal lockers, each of them with full make-up and their hair done.

As I pull together large chunks of my thick, dark brown hair into a ponytail, I'm approached by three girls on a mission. The moment reminds me of the cliché scene in every single movie with teens: when a group of girls, usually in a cafeteria or a hallway, think they run the school, and come strutting in with purpose. With every strand of their hair perfectly placed, their outfits calculated and chosen carefully, each of them looks like they're prepared for an Abercrombie & Fitch photoshoot instead of gym class.

When they stop next to me, I make no effort to stifle my laughter or hide my dramatic eye roll. These girls made no effort to look like models the eighteen school days before today. But, that's because none of those eighteen days were today. None of those eighteen days were the first home game for the school's football team. Making today the first Rally Day of this school year.

Rally Day, an age-old tradition, somehow, has managed to stand the test of time. Today and every Friday we have a home game for the rest of the season, every member of the Varsity football team gets to pick one "rally girl" before the end of the school day. Every player on the team starts the day with clean practice jerseys over the dress shirts and ties they're required to wear. By the time lunch rolls around, they must give their jersey to a girl of their choosing.

If you're picked as a rally girl, you get the distinct honor of wearing a football player's jersey like a trophy all day. You also sit closest to the field on the bleachers, getting the best view of the game. After the game, the player is supposed to take you out on a date. Well, it may have started out that way when the school debuted their first Rally Day in 1965, but thirty-eight years later, it's used as a glorified hook-up tool.

The few guys on the team who have steady girlfriends always choose their girlfriends and the rest of the guys use it to their advantage, knowing most of the girls see it as a competition. Right now, there are only three sophomores on the Varsity football team. My twin brother Davis, my cousin Travis, and our next-door neighbor Kenny.

The craziness started as soon as Davis made the team last month. For about two weeks straight, there was a constant string of teenage girls coming to our front door with baked goods. Why cookies and brownies are the only thing that stuck from the beginning of Rally Day is beyond me, but I digress.

He tried to be nice about it at first. Accepting two trays of cupcakes, three dozen chocolate chip cookies, two batches of brownies and an apple crisp. But because no one was getting any hint of who he would choose, the doorbell kept ringing. That is, until about a week before school started and he started making it very clear to any girl standing on the front steps with a tray full of sugary goodness that he had every intention of asking Kinley Lavoie come game day.

Word spread like wildfire and everyone's attention shifted to Travis and Kenny. The stories they've come back with are insane. Girls have offered baked goods, homework help, and the desperate ones offered blowjobs. It's not just sophomores either, even Seniors have been making their way to the sophomore wing to try to get their attention.

"Stop looking at us with those judgey eyes, Hollis." Kinley sticks her tongue out at me as she puts her backpack into the gym locker she shares with her step-sister Cole.

"I don't know what you're so worried about," the third girl, my cousin Ellis, laughs in Kinley's direction. "Everyone knows Davis is going to ask you."

"Yeah, well, he hasn't yet. And, I don't know why you two don't just tell Travis and Kenny you want to be their rally girls," Kinley shoots back defensively before loudly adding, "I mean, it would make more sense for Kenny to pick Ellis and Travis to pick Cole than any of the other bitches trying to get their jerseys for the day."

"Hey Hol, did you hear the fellas talking on the way in?" Cole questions, ignoring Kinley's comment, as she closes the blue locker next to the one I share with Ellis. "Something about a boy that used to live here, moved away and now he's back? He used to play football with the boys. Do you know who he is? Is it anyone we know?"

"Nope. New dude is news to me," I tell her as I tie the laces of my green and white Nikes. "I'm surprised I didn't get the speech, though."

Once my gym bag is secure in the locker, I close the door and the other three take my movement as their hint to make their way out of this dreary, dark room. When we get to the heavy metal door separating the locker room from the gymnasium just a foot away, Cole pushes it open.

When the four of us are once again standing next to each other, she shakes her head and says, "You mean the 'Hollis, play nice, not everyone understands you're an ice princess with no soul' speech?"

"No soul?" repeats a redhead with a face full of freckles, from the bottom row of wooden bleachers that we have made our way over to. "Must be talking about Hollis."

"Good morning to you too, Kenny," I say, playfully pushing the boy that has been my next-door neighbor and my brother's best friend since we were five. "And, by the way, I have a soul. I'm just not sure if it's connected to my body or if the devil has it. But, it's around...somewhere."

"Well, Satan, your shoe's untied," Ellis points out, nodding down in the direction of the loose laces of my Nikes.

Bending over, I grab one of the laces and make the loop to start the process of tying my shoe. It's a task that's so simple I don't need to think about to complete it. But, before I take the second lace into my hand, I involuntarily freeze in place, not knowing what to do next. It's as if I've completely forgotten the last decade of tying my shoes.

My shoes and the wooden planks making up the gymnasium floor below might be what my eyes focus on, but I can feel it. Someone is watching me. It's not just the everyday, someone's looking at you as they pass by kind of feeling. This is terrifying. I feel naked. Exposed. Transparent. I know my soul is in place, right inside of me because, whoever is at the other end of this stare down can see right through me to the very core of my being.

Not knowing what to expect, I exhale and slowly psych myself up, giving in to the universal pull drawing me to the person on the other end of this stare down. Following the connection like a magnetic force, my eyes lock with a smirking teenage boy.

There's nothing out of the ordinary about him. Other than his perfect face and his apparent ability to look directly into my soul, he's just a boy in a plain white t-shirt and black basketball shorts standing in between my brother and my cousin Travis.

Breaking our connection, he turns to Davis and nods his head, agreeing to something my brother said. He must be the new, but not actually new kid that I'm supposed to be nice to. After a few minutes of back and forth, Davis begins to walk toward where I am standing with our little group of friends.

Continuing their conversation, New Dude walks alongside him, like he, my cousin, and my brother are old friends. Who the hell is this boy? If Travis and Davis both know him, why don't I have a clue who he is? And why the hell is he affecting me the way he is?

The intensity of the moment causes me to forget I have an untied shoe. Standing up quickly from the edge of the bleacher, panic and premature embarrassment surge through me when I'm certain my face is about to abruptly meet the floor.

New Dude must be Superman or The Flash because before I hit the ground, there are arms around me, saving my face and my dignity. Wincing, I brace myself for the humiliating first conversation that's about to happen. Instead of saying anything snarky, like most of the boys I spend any of my time with would, New Dude slowly begins to stand us both back up. His hands are still on my arms, steadying me, as if he knows my legs could buckle out from beneath me at any second.

"Oh my God," the words begin to flow out of me. Without control or restraint, I continue to ramble like a lunatic, "I am so sorry. Are you okay? Wait. Of course you're okay. Look at you. I mean, that's not what I meant. Just that I'm the one that fell, and you saved me. Not that I needed someone to save me but -"

Smooth. Real fucking smooth. He doesn't even know my name yet and I've already made myself look crazy. Good job, Hollis.

"I guess I don't have to introduce you to my sister," Davis's laughter bellows from behind us. "I still don't know how you guys didn't cross paths when we were kids."

"Well, actually, we haven't been introduced yet," New Dude chuckles, his hands still on my arms.

Awkwardly stepping back, I stick out my hand, stammering something about being "sorry again" while Davis goes around introducing New Kid, who, as it seems, does have a name and it's not Barry Allen or Clark Kent, so he's not The Flash or Superman like I assumed.

It's Chase…

Chase Merrimack.

Gah. Even his stupid name is perfect.

With the same amused smirk he started off with across the gym, he takes my hand into his. Holding it for longer than necessary, he chuckles while giving me a gentle shake. Without realizing, my eyes trail up and linger over his bicep. As if I suddenly have no control over my actions, I just stop. Distracted by the muscles causing his shirt sleeve to pop up, I make no effort to pull my hand back, even after Chase stops the shaking motion between our hands.

My hand still in his and my eyes on his arm, he clears his throat just loud enough to get my attention. Quickly pulling my hand away, I only stay in front of him long enough to see his slight smirk turn into a full, cocky smile.

Squeezing myself between the comfort of Ellis and Cole, I focus on an empty space across the gymnasium. Taking advantage of the few seconds of silence I have, I start counting to ten in the three different languages I know. A failed attempt to calm my racing heart and twisted nerves. There is no way Ellis, Cole, and Kinley missed the disaster that just happened, so it won't be long until they're interrogating me.

"What. Was. THAT?!" Kinley whisper squeals, as if on cue, looking around the front of Ellis to me.

"A better question would be who is that?" Cole asks from the other side of me.

"That is Chase Merrimack," I shrug, attempting to play it off like it's no big deal.

If I make it a big deal, I'll never hear the end of it from them. Especially considering I've never showed any blatant interest in a guy before. I mean, not to say I didn't have little crushes here and there, but nothing worth ever mentioning to the girls.

They don't need to know my stomach is in knots, or that my heart feels like it's going to beat out of my chest. They also don't need to know that right now, it's taking every ounce of willpower I possess to fight the pull to be near him. Instead of sitting on this bleacher with my friends, I want to be over with the guys, finding out everything I can about the boy who just came out of nowhere.

"Yeah, we got that. But, I've never actually seen you obviously check out a guy," Ellis states, making no hesitation on calling me out. "And you were not hiding the fact that boy got your attention, Cousin."

"I need to go line up because they're about to choose teams,"

I say, sidestepping her and the looks I'm getting from Cole and Kinley. "See you after class, slackers."

The two gym teachers, who happen to also be my soccer coach and the boys' football coach crack themselves up when they choose me and then Davis for team captains. My brother and I both make our way to front of the group. Laughing, I flex at him and he cocks his eyebrow, upping the ante by saying, "Loser does the other one's chores for a week."

Turning to face the twenty or so teenaged boys, I feel like I could throw up. Playing with "the guys" has never made me nervous before. Even though it drives me crazy, I know they all take it easy on me. And normally, I'm one of the first ones off the bench when teams are chosen, especially when we play soccer, which we've been playing for the last week.

It comes with being the only starting sophomore on the school's girls' soccer team. Athleticism is just something my family was gifted with, I guess. My dad put me in the city's soccer league with Ellis when I was in kindergarten. Ellis didn't make it through the first season; I fell in love with the game and have been playing ever since.

City league turned into playing on a travel league, which turned into my trying out and playing for the middle school team and then the high school team. Since the school team only plays during the Fall, I played indoor in the Winter and went back to the travel team every Spring. After spending most of my freshman season on the bench last school year, it just worked out that my coach for the Spring travel team is one of the assistant coaches for the school team. She got the right people to see a few games and I started playing midfield on the school's team during our first game last week.

A loud collection of shrieking snaps me out of my daze. While I kept walking to the middle of the gym after our shit talking back and forth, my brother had, apparently, held back and finally asked Kinley to be his rally girl. Despite the fact we all knew it was coming, I was just choosing not to give the fact that my brother and one of my closest friends were slowly becoming a thing any added attention. I'm happy for the two of them, but it's still weird.

With half the gym making a spectacle out of Davis and Kinley, only I notice Coach Lavoie quickly tossing Chase a practice jersey and then Chase dropping it on the empty bleachers behind the crowd. Dressed to participate in class, no one would suspect that Chase is a member of the football team. The second he steps out of this gym, presumably in a dress shirt and tie, it's over though.

Just like that, Chase Merrimack became one of the four most sought after sophomores. With Kinley getting Davis's jersey and officially becoming his rally girl, the pressure would be on for Travis, Kenny, and now, Chase to choose theirs.

So much for getting to know him, ever. He's going to have the attention of half the fucking school before lunch time.

When all the craziness of giving his jersey to Kinley subsides, Davis makes his way over to me, scrunching his nose as I shake my head. Without skipping a beat, he calls out Chase's name. Pointing to Kenny, I flash a wide smile and say his name. My brother will pick my cousin next, so I have a whole thirty seconds to come up with my game plan.

"You're going down, Davis Capparelli," Kenny laughs, pretending to glare at my brother, before laughing hysterically and high-fiving me before taking his place to the left of me.

After Travis, my brother will choose his teammates based on athletic ability. It makes sense why he would choose to do that. In theory, you want to win the game. I have a different plan for today though. Sure enough, Davis picks Travis for his team and then all eyes are on me.

With my second pick, I choose Adam Harper. By lame high school standards, he's probably the nerdiest and least athletic kid in the entire class. Every single week he's one of, if not the last, kids chosen for teams. Not today. As much as I would love to not have to do dishes for a week, I would gladly have to the trash for a week if it means that even if just for this class, I made someone's day easier.

Confirming my suspicion, Davis picks Tyler Douglas next. Tyler's a dick, but he plays soccer for the boys' division of the travel league I play for. There's no way Davis picked him because he thought he would add to the team in any way other than getting points for them.

Davis and I go back and forth until every person is chosen. Like I assumed, my brother picks each of his teammates by their athleticism, so I do the opposite. As I call out each of the names of the boys who are usually last on the bench, I have to continuously remind myself not to look over at Chase. Not that he's making it any easier on me as he watches my every move. The few times I do look over, his curiosity is written all over his face. Like, I puzzle him or I'm not who he expected. Which is crazy because we know absolutely nothing about each other.

As soon as everyone is assigned to a team, Davis and all the boys on his team start taking their shirts off despite having more than enough green and yellow mesh pullover pinnies for everyone to put on differentiating the teams. Damn show offs.

"Guess we're playing shirts and skins," I say, dramatically rolling my eyes at the group of now half-naked boys as Kenny and I lead our team to the cart with soccer balls, goalie gloves, and the orange cones to set up goals.

Being team captain, I assign each boy a position. Keeping Kenny up with me as a striker, I know between the two of us, there's a small chance we might make a goal or two. My brother and cousin might run the football field, but I can and have run circles around them with a soccer ball.

Stopping in the middle of the court, I find myself face-to-face with Chase, that cocky smile still plastered all over his face.

If I can get past my nerves to win a state championship, I can get past the one building up in my stomach now.

Passing the ball over to Kenny, it's only seconds before it's back in between my feet. Seamlessly, I weave in and out of the guys on the opposing team. Faking passes, I quickly make my way down to goal range. I hear my cousin Ellis yell, "You guys might as well accept your loss now" and the laughter of her brother, my cousin, Travis when he yells back, "Never!" in the background. But that's all it is to me, background noise.

With precise calculation, I get myself close enough to the goal, knowing the chance of scoring is in my favor right now. Just as I pull my foot back to shoot, I feel someone's arms wrap around my waist, pulling me down. There's no need for me to turn around to know that it's Chase as we tumble down to the floor below. I just know it. I can't explain how, but I do. The closeness between the two of us causes every single hair on my body to stand up.

Jumping off his lap as fast as we fell, I turn to the teachers who are both closely watching me cautiously. Rightfully so, because like a ticking time bomb, I explode.

"Holding is a fucking foul! Give him a yellow card!"

And with that, the teachers, my brother, my cousins, our friends, and half the class burst out laughing, only infuriating me more.

"Calm down, you little Hurricane, it's just gym class, you didn't lose the World Cup," Chase chuckles as he pulls himself up from the floor.

"It would have been a damn goal if you didn't cheat," I huff before turning to walk back to the center of the gym.

"If it makes you happy sweetheart, please take the kick," he laughs, winking as he walks past me toward the bleachers. "But, I'll only agree to my 'yellow card' on one condition."

"First of all, don't call me sweetheart. And what condition could you possibly have after knowing me for five whole seconds?" I ask, equal parts irritated, because that's not how the game of soccer works, and intrigued because I'm pretty sure he knows this after saying I could take a kick, implying he knows at least a thing or two about soccer. And, I kind of want to know what his condition is.

"Be my rally girl."

Without waiting for an answer, Chase jogs over to the spot on the bleacher he tossed the practice jersey on. A slew of gasps and whispers come from the girls on the sideline near us, none of them making any attempt to hide their surprise.

Coming back with his smirk still intact and a little pep in his step, that cocky bastard doesn't think I'll say no. And, truth be told, I don't think I want to. I don't know why I'm so drawn to this boy, but everything inside of me is telling me to fight my common sense and say yes. Saying yes would mean that I would need to break my rule of never getting involved with a boy that plays football.

There are three things I've learned growing up a Capparelli. One, is that family really is the most important thing in this world; two, loyalty should never, ever come with a price; and three, if a boy plays football, he loves that game more than anything, and probably, more than anyone.

Surprising even myself, I snatch the jersey out of his hand, pulling it over my head. As it falls to my mid-thigh, I drop the soccer ball in position to take my kick, motioning for Chase to move out of the way so I can take my shot.

Making the goal, the cheers come in from my teammates, and I do my best to replicate the smirk Chase has plastered all over his face, shrugging arrogantly.

"Whatever it is you're trying to do, might work on the girls wherever it is you're from, but it doesn't work here. Not with me. You really want my attention? Step up your game, Merrimack."

CHAPTER ONE

HOLLIS

September 15, 2017

"I SHOULD HAVE BEEN A FUCKING PIRATE."

All the girls I knew growing up had dreams of being a princess and finding Prince Charming, but not me. I was never the girl that wanted to be a lawyer, a doctor, or a teacher. No matter how hard everyone tried, there were no ballet classes or fancy dresses for me. I played soccer because chasing the ball was like chasing treasure, and if I wasn't on the soccer field, I was in a karate dojo, convinced I would need those skills if I were ever to become a real pirate,

For five Halloweens in a row, I wore a red bandana on my head, knee high black boots, and held a ginormous plastic sword, determined that one day I would make that my everyday reality. In high school, I burnt out not one, but three Pirates of the Caribbean DVDs. There's no one I crushed on harder than Captain Jack Sparrow.

I wanted endless, barefoot adventures and the only love I planned on keeping was one for the open sea. And, maybe, for a parrot I would name Kiwi. As life would have it though, New

England grew on me and I never ended up chasing my childhood dream of wreaking havoc in the Caribbean. If I had though, I'd be happily drinking rum on warm, white island sand instead of miserably contemplating drinking rum on freezing, white kitchen linoleum.

The glass of ice sitting next to my left thigh amplifies the cold of the floor, pressuring me to make my decision faster. On my right, sits a half empty bottle of my go-to, fail safe black spiced rum. But, next to that sits an incredibly intimidating wicker basket. Though, in all fairness to the basket, it's not the basket itself that's intimidating. The execution of deciding whether to open it, *that's* what is scary as fuck.

Within said wicker basket sits a bottle. A $4,000 bottle of British Royal Navy Imperial Reserve Rum, to be exact. A bottle that should have been saved for a celebration, a monumental moment in life. Not to say today wasn't monumental, but it sure as hell isn't a celebration.

But, you know what? Fuck it. It's time to go big. It's time to stop settling. Life is too damn short to be drinking cheap rum and crying over boys that don't know exactly what they have and who they have it with. So, the Hollis Capparelli Comeback Tour officially starts tonight. Right now, in this exact moment, actually.

Sucking in a breath, I slowly open the lid of the basket, carefully pulling out the ceramic jar that holds the gallon of molasses colored rum. Taking a solid minute, I admire the engagement gift from my grandparents before a heinous cackle escapes me. The irony isn't lost on me as I lift the bottle in the air, and cheers to nothing and no one.

The oaky taste of the rum lingers on my lips as I pull myself off the floor, setting the bottle back onto the breakfast bar it came from. It only takes one swig of rum to conclude that drinking by myself, on my kitchen floor, is a pitiful excuse of a comeback. Leaning on the cluttered breakfast bar, I scroll through the contacts in my phone, deciding to start with Kinley.

Not only is she one of my longest and closest friends, she's a professional party planner. If anyone knows where to go to start an epic break-up party, it's going to be Kinley. The added bonus of texting Kinley is that she'll take charge, because that's what she does, all the time. She would take offense to being called a "control freak," but as they say, if the shoe fits…

Knowing she would take the reins on the evening as soon as I let her know what happened takes some stress off me, so right now, I'm all for her executing her leadership skills, per se, and managing the plans for the night. I won't even have to text anyone else, Kinley will take care of it. Though, I should probably call or text Chase, too. Actually, I know I should. But, I also know that if I call him right now, he'll drop everything and come straight here. That's what he's done since we were teenagers. Chase Merrimack is my very best friend and the self-proclaimed one-man "Hurricane Hollis" recovery crew.

When he does get his phone call, he's going to give me such a hard time for not letting him know sooner. Like, three hours ago sooner. Or, really, three months sooner. That'll be a whole different battle to fight after the initial dust settles from this shit storm though.

The first thing that will come is the worry, and then the pity. The very last thing I want to be is the friend that ruins a perfectly good Friday night. Especially tonight of all nights. Besides, what doesn't scream "I don't care that I just wasted two years of life with a cheating scumbag" more than a night out with your best girls? Nothing, that's what.

It's time to get the ball rolling on this comeback of mine. Knowing she's scheduled a few event consultations and a catering meeting for this afternoon, I opt to text Kinley instead of calling her. Normally I would never tell someone something this important through a text message but hey, desperate times call for desperate measures.

Snapping a picture of my empty left ring finger, I attach it to a text to Kinley and quickly text out,

See something sparkly missing from my finger? We need to celebrate this shit. HELPPPPP.

Pressing send, I decide the next step while embarking on my comeback tour is to find an outfit that says "daaaaamn, girl." I'm not sure exactly what look I want to go for tonight. However, I do know everyone is going to see a side of Hollis Capparelli that they haven't seen in a long time tonight. That is for damn sure.

With my phone still in hand, I take the few necessary steps to get to my bedroom. My little apartment may not be much, but it's mine. Well, kind of. The space is mine. The apartment, however, is in the finished basement of my father's house.

Oh, my dad. My sweet, overprotective father. He's another one I should probably call. He's another one that is going to lose his fucking mind when he finds out. My dad, my brother, my cousins, my uncles. Fuckity, fuck, fuck, fuck.

There are times being part of a large, crazy Italian family has its perks. Like, every Sunday when we get together for dinner at my Nonna and Nonno's house. To say that there will never be a lack of love in my life is an understatement, to say the very least. But, because of that, this situation I'm in won't just go away on its own.

A pulsating vibration from my phone, signaling an incoming call, brings me back to the present. A rage that could give a certain green superhero a run for his money fills me, but I fight the urge to "Hollis Smash" my phone. Slamming my fingers on the red decline button, I hope I can block the number before a voicemail comes through. Before I can get to the block option, three texts in a row come up on my screen.

One: Call Me!!!!!!!!!!

Two: Hollis, it's not what you think.

Three: Baby, please, please, please call me before you talk to Chase and Davis and the rest of your family.

A full belly laugh leaves me knowing thirty-two-year-old, big shot marketing executive Noah McDougal is worried right now. Serves him right. Douche. Picturing him stressing about the possible repercussions of me telling my twin and my best friend that he's a complete scum bag gives me more pleasure than it probably should.

It doesn't matter that I went there to break up with him. It's what I found when I went to his office, unannounced. It doesn't help matters that Davis and Chase both tried warning me about Noah from the get-go. All it took was a quick scroll through his ex-girlfriend's social media to find out that Noah had cheated on his ex... more than a few times.

Given Noah's history, I might have listened to Davis (probably not) based on the merit of brotherly intuition. Chase, on the other hand, has found an excuse to not like any guy I've ever shown any kind of interest in since I was sixteen. So, I brushed it off. Like every woman who thinks they can be the reason a guy changes, I thought it was different with me and Noah. Joke's on me, I guess.

My fingers fly over the keyboard, furiously typing out directions on going directly to hell in response to his texts and hover over the little blue arrow to press send. Instead of sending it though, I backspace and block the number. He cheats on me and thinks I'm going to take anything he has to say into consideration?! I might have missed a page or two in the "how relationships work" handbook, but I'm pretty sure that's not how this works.

Now that I've temporarily handled Noah, it's time to focus on what really matters. Music. Giving this comeback a solid soundtrack and finding an outfit for tonight, that's what I need to focus on right now. Over the next ten minutes, I flip through the double stacked black milk crates that line the wall of my bedroom. Finally settling on Dropkick Murphys' *The Warrior's Code*.

If there's anything I'm certain of, it's that a girl's favorite band can fix just about anything. And, just like some form of voodoo magic, the bagpipe and piano introduction to "Your Spirit's Alive" hype me up. By the time the fast-pace of the guitar starts up on "The Warrior's Code," I've almost forgotten about What's-His-Face.

With a little too much gusto, I open my closet door. The doorknob slams into the wall behind it, leaving a small indentation in the paint. Sliding a dozen shirts on hangers to the opposite side of the closet, nothing jumps out at me. Come to think of it, I should probably wait to hear back from Kinley to figure out where we're going to end up tonight. I wouldn't want to be overdressed or underdressed. Despite my original idea to go all out, I find myself hoping we end up somewhere that ripped jeans and Converse are acceptable.

The bright red digital numbers on the alarm clock sitting on the wooden whiskey barrel used as my nightstand read 4:47PM. Which means, in the real world, it's only 4:27PM. The love/hate relationship I have with the snooze button requires setting my clock twenty minutes fast. Over time I thought I might adjust and not need the snooze button, but the only thing my groggy ass is thinking about at 4:30 in the morning is getting a coffee in before my brother comes strolling in at five for our daily morning run. Sister or not, Hell hath no fury like a retired Marine waiting on your ass when they're motivated.

Only a half hour stands between the current calm and the impending phone call from Kinley, freaking out, needing every little detail leading up to the text I sent. Not that I blame her. If I got a text from one of my oldest friends like the one I sent her a little while ago, I would call her back freaking out.

Taking the vinyl off my record player, I put it back in its sleeve and scroll through my phone's music library until I find Devin Dawson's "All On Me" single. Not everyone can go from Celtic punk rock to California country, but my love for good music knows no prejudice. With every song that plays, I feel myself relax a little more, sending me crashing from the adrenaline high I've been on.

After convincing myself I'll only lay down for five minutes, I let my body fall onto the queen size bed. As the memory foam molds to fit me, spending the night at home, specifically here, in this bed, hidden from the rest of the world starts to sound like a solid plan. The lavender scent heavy on my recently washed bedding sends a soothing wave over me as my head hits one of the twelve decorative throw pillows taking up half my bed.

I'm not sure what the point of having a dozen decorative pillows on your bed is, but my grandparents insisted on buying every brown and tan pillow they could find when I moved back home after college. The second I told my dad I was coming back to Abbott Hills, everyone in my family stopped what they were doing and got ready for me to come home. And, while I know that might make me sound self-important and spoiled, that's just how my family is. It's not just me.

Four years of an empty house had been more than enough for my dad, and me being hours away had been more than enough for the rest of my family. Before I even had the chance to look for a place of my own, my dad and my uncles renovated the entire basement of his house into a little in-law apartment for me. I told him over and over that I would have been more than happy to take my old bedroom on the first floor, but he wouldn't hear of it.

My aunts and cousins chose paints and decorated. Both sets

of my grandparents furnished everything. I came home needing to do nothing. At first, I had been resistant to move back home, back to all the Capparelli craziness, but now, the thought of leaving the comfort of my own little corner gives me anxiety.

It's why after two years together with Noah, I never once pushed moving in together. It makes sense now why he didn't either, but even if he had, I wasn't ready to give up having my own space. That alone should have been a clear indication that being with Noah wouldn't last forever.

I loved him, especially in the beginning. But, I never needed him. It was fun, we were fun together, but our relationship was never all consuming. And all it took was the security of putting a diamond on my finger for Noah to feel he didn't need to be as present.

The first year was an amazing whirlwind of fun. We met at a private charity event hosted at Capparelli & Co. just over two years ago. As a bartender, the weekend singer, and granddaughter of restaurant owners, I was working. That night I was on entertainment detail. It was just me and my guitar, singing an acoustic set on the second-floor lounge area of the restaurant. At the end of my set, he asked to buy me a drink, which led to him asking for my number. A week later, we went on our first date.

We spent weekends in New York City, San Francisco, Dallas, and Las Vegas while he met with clients…and that was just the work trips. We spent my birthday weekend on Martha's Vineyard, his in Myrtle Beach. He proposed to me in front of Cinderella's Castle at Disney World, a trip we took for our "one year" anniversary. No sooner did our plane land back in New Hampshire—without any sound reasoning, at least not any I can make sense of—he started with the excuses.

He always had some reason why I couldn't come with him anymore. Not that I had ever asked to go in the first place. It was his job. He was working, and I understood that. I never got mad at him for working. I got mad because he was lying. After going on multiple trips with him, I knew he didn't spend four or five days holed up in a conference room negotiating deals. He spent the first day and maybe some of the second working, while the rest of the trip was used to explore and have fun. More so if he and his partner managed to secure the contract they were trying to score.

The final push that sent me over the slippery slope that began the end of "Hollis and Noah, the super happy couple" happened eight months ago, only four months after he proposed. When my grandmother invited me, my aunt, and my cousin Ellis on a "girls' trip" to Italy for her sister's birthday, there was no hesitation in my decision to go. Giving him a month's notice, I texted Noah letting him know I would be out of the country for a week.

And, he lost his damn mind. It started with three phone calls, being hung up on each time. Then, him blowing me off for dinner the next night. When we finally saw each other face-to-face about a week after, he ended up leaving the restaurant before appetizers were even served because I refused to change my plans. He had the audacity to say that he was upset I didn't "check" with him, when so often the only way I found out he was going out of the state was an email with a forwarded travel itinerary.

In hindsight, I should have just ended it right then and there. There was no coming back from that. I went to Italy with my family and didn't speak to him once while I was gone. When I let him know I was back, after two weeks of not speaking to each other, it took him three days to even answer my text.

But, it's not like I didn't at least try to fix things. When I came home from my Italy trip, I tried to make lunch plans, dinner plans, plans during the week, and on the weekend. It didn't matter when, there was always an excuse and usually a personal dig thrown in for good measure.

"I know you don't understand, but some of us don't have a father that lets us live in their basement and grandparents that just hand us a job right out college, Hollis."

"We can't all just work for only four hours in the morning."

At first, I would defend myself. But after a while, his words just became incoherent babble to me. From that point, instead of growing together, we grew separately, as individuals. The more time that passed, the further we drifted from each other and the stronger I felt without him.

He didn't understand how I could be happy using my business degree "just" to talk on the radio and why I wasted so much time handling the social media platforms, the website, and answering the e-mails for my 85-year-old grandparents that owned Capparelli & Co. He looked at my Friday night of bartending and my Saturday night acoustic gig as a hobby. I had spent so much of our relationship trying to justify my career and my passion to him, and the more time we spent apart, the more I realized I shouldn't need to.

It was cool for me to get him and his friends front row and backstage at concerts, but when I did a radio promotion at a sports bar or a business opening, I was just "out flirting with everyone." It didn't matter that I worked six, sometimes seven days a week. Or, that I put in more hours and made more money than him. No matter how much I did, nothing was good enough or considered a real job to the lead marketing strategist at Brady Branding.

Eventually, I stopped going out of my way to plan something, anything, with or for him. Instead, I just worked. A lot. (Go figure.) Days turned into weeks, weeks turned into a month. Out of the blue, he would ask me to meet him for lunch, never dinner. Each time, I went, bracing myself, expecting, and if I'm being honest, hoping for the break-up, but it never came.

Today had been three weeks since we had seen each other and that wasn't out of the ordinary for us. You would think that the space and time apart would give us more to talk about, but the last lunch it had been a stretch to exchange small talk and simple, casual conversation. There was nothing of substance or meaning anymore. It was just a lunch of bottomless margaritas and empty conversation.

Never mind the fact that I hadn't had sex in six months. Half a fucking year. Being given the impression that he was a workaholic, I assumed he was just too busy with work to care about not getting anything from me. And I didn't need the attention from anyone else.

Beyond the lack of everything substantial needed to make a relationship last, my family hates him. When I say "hate," I don't just mean that they strongly dislike him. I mean the very rare presence of him makes everyone around me turn into different people. My warm, loving, embracing family becomes cold and rigid.

Noah's adamant refusal to come to my family's Sunday dinner, when it was the only day, every week, we could have certainly seen each other spoke volumes to them. I tried for a long time to make excuses for him. At first, in hopes things would get better, and then eventually just because I didn't want to get lectured about wasting my time. Because what rebuttal would I have? I knew it was true. There was no reason why I didn't end things with him. I just didn't.

My family was "too loud" and "gave him anxiety." How he intended to spend the rest of his life with me and avoid Sunday dinners at Nonna and Nonno's baffled me. But, like everything else, he had an excuse.

"I asked to marry you, not your entire family, Hollis."

He made the mistake of saying that after I very specifically asked him to come to dinner because it was my grandfather's birthday…with both Davis and Chase in the room with us.

Noah had called me on a whim, asking me to go to lunch. Anticipating a break-up, I called Chase and asked if he wanted my ticket for the matinee Red Sox game Davis and I had planned on going to later that afternoon. Chase got to the house forty-five minutes later and somehow, he and Davis had convinced my dad to drop them off at the train station, taking "the T" into Boston instead of driving. They were both three beers in when Noah came strolling in, a half hour later than he'd said he would be there.

My brother kept it as nice as possible by only calling him a "fucking idiot," but Chase burst out laughing. I'm talking big, loud, holding-your-stomach-because-it-hurts uncontrollable laughter. Taking the bait, Noah asked him what was so funny and I braced myself, knowing the conversation was about to take a turn for the worse.

Sure enough, without skipping a beat, Chase reminded him that if you "marry a Capparelli girl, you do in fact, marry the whole family."

That might have been the end of it, but Chase had to go and add, "What do you seriously think is going to happen, buddy? Do you think you're gonna marry her and she's going to stop being a Capparelli? HA! I'm just the best friend though, so what do I know? I'm just there every Sunday and every single fucking time you decide Hollis isn't worth your time."

The wink in my direction that followed his tangent was the nail in the coffin, closing any chance of Noah and Chase ever getting along. The fight that came next from Noah's, "Maybe you should marry her then, dickhead," response was one of epic proportion. I ended up calling them both assholes and storming off. Grabbing my extra set of keys from the hook hanging by the front door, I made damn sure to slam the door behind me.

Without looking back to see if anyone was following me, I got in my Jeep, stopped for an iced coffee and then drove around aimlessly for hours. Over the blasting music, I couldn't hear the constant vibration of my phone sitting next to me in the passenger seat. It wasn't until my gas light came on one-hundred-sixty miles from home in Augusta, Maine, did I realize exactly how far I'd driven and how long I had been gone. At the first sign of gas, I pulled off the highway to look for a gas station and possibly a coffee shop to give me a boost for the ride home.

While I was pumping the gas, I finally checked my phone. The only people that texted or called me were my dad, my brother, and Chase. All of them worried because I hadn't been heard from in three hours and was nowhere to be found. I was about to group text them all letting them know I would be home in a few hours, when I looked over and saw the cutest little bed and breakfast across the street.

So, instead of going home, I checked myself in for the night. It was only early evening and on a whim, I decided instead of coffee to get home, I was now on a mission to find some lighthouses and eat some lobster. Because when in Maine, what else do you do? If my boyfriend wouldn't take me out on a date, I'd take my damn self.

Or so I thought. By the time I texted my dad, Davis, and Chase to let them know I was okay and planned on staying put for the night, Chase and Davis were on the way home from the baseball game. Chase persistently asked where exactly I was, to the point that I knew if I didn't tell him, he wouldn't leave me alone all night. Once he got an answer from me, he made me promise not to go eat anything until he got there.

I had stared at my phone for ten minutes, making sure I read his text correctly before answering him. Sure enough, three hours and twenty-eight minutes later, Chase showed up with a bag of full of my pajamas, my toothbrush, face wash, and a change of clothes for tomorrow in one hand and a bouquet of sunflowers in the other.

He apologized in the form of lobster rolls and hand-churned blueberry ice cream. After dinner he started to say his goodbyes, but I asked him if he wanted to stay and go lighthouse hunting the next day. He rented the room next to mine, which was never used because we both fell asleep watching a movie.

The next morning, I woke up to coffee, blueberry muffins, and a note saying he went to go buy a change of clothes. He didn't even a bring a change of clothes when he came up. All that mattered to him was making sure I knew he was sorry. I didn't hear from Noah for a week.

"Ugh," I groan out loud to myself. My little trip down memory lane abruptly interrupted by the reminder that if I don't text or call Chase soon, shit's going to hit the fan. "Fuck."

The thought of having to explain what happened today makes me sigh. He's going to be upset I didn't come to him with exactly how sucky things were with Noah. He's not an idiot. He knew things weren't leading up to a happily forever after, but he has no idea how non-existent Noah was in my life.

My family is going to be upset I hid it too. For all they knew, everything was fine and dandy in the world of "Hollis and Noah, the couple." The impending look of disappointment from my brother hangs over me like a cloud full of guilt. We haven't kept a secret from each other our entire lives.

Instead of figuring out how I'm going to tell everyone, I do what I do best. Pushing back my emotions, I procrastinate having to put myself out there, deciding I'll deal with it later. I reach for the scrapbook sitting on the pillow next to me. The blue book with "Memories" written across the cover sits in the spot I tossed it to after looking for a certain picture to make a cheesy happy birthday Instagram post for Davis this morning. I knew the picture was in the back, so I had flipped right to the last page this morning, leaving the rest of the book untouched.

As soon as I open to the first page, a sudden, overwhelming sense of nostalgia hits me like a ton of bricks. Looking back at me is the fifteen-year-old version of myself. The cream-colored visor on my head, the magenta puffy vest, and flared jeans make me cringe. A decade ago, I was certain they were the coolest articles of clothing I could possibly own.

My make-up is very minimal except for an obvious thick strip of white eyeliner drastically outlining my upper eyelid. The most noticeable detail of the picture is the pure, genuine happiness on my face as I'm wrapped up in the arms of a sixteen-year-old Chase Merrimack. A slight, half smirk on his face doesn't convey much emotion, but the excitement of the moment is completely captured in the lightness of his bright green eyes.

In the background is a football field, the lights shining brightly above us. The scoreboard reading VISITOR: 24, HOME: 28. Less than five minutes before that picture had been taken, with only 39 seconds left in the game, Chase had run 42-yards for the game winning touchdown. He was, at the time, only one of four sophomores on the Varsity team. He had worked so hard through the entire season to prove himself, and was *the* reason our high school's team not only went to, but won the state championship.

Seconds after he made it to the end zone, I remember running through the bleachers, skipping rows as fast as I could. One of the first to arrive on the field, I pushed my way through 40 football players and coaches. For the rest of my life, I will never forget the sound of his laughter when he saw me come through the crowd of people surrounding him.

"Soul mates." Those two words are the ones our friends and family, to this day, constantly throw around when it comes to the two of us. Our response—separately or together—has always been an eye roll, maybe some laughter or a shake of our heads, but we never agreed with them. At least not out loud.

Though in all honesty, in the beginning, I secretly allowed myself to get swept up in the thought of it. The concept that in your lifespan you will meet hundreds, if not thousands of people, and two people can be so connected that they "belong" together makes even me, the self-proclaimed black-hearted ice queen, sentimental.

And there's the fact that if we denied the connection between us, we would be lying. Whenever we are together it's as if we have this incredible inside joke that the rest of the world is just dying to know. It's been like that since the very first day we met. Of course, there's a catch though. There's always a catch.

Our souls may be "meant" for each other, but souls don't understand the concept of timing. They don't have calendars with the ability to pencil in the perfect date, or clocks with snooze buttons for when you're not quite ready. When fate, the universe, or whatever God or gods you believe in decide it's time to turn your whole world upside down, they just send someone crashing into your life.

It doesn't matter if you're prepared or not. There are no written directions or instruction manuals. Without warning, that person comes crashing into your life, and you're completely on your own.

I wasn't ready for my world to turn upside down. But, oh man, did it turn that September morning when the "new kid" walked into my sophomore gym class. Thinking back to the first day I met Chase makes me chuckle to myself and smile a dopey, cheesy grin. Unbeknownst to me, the day before he started school, my brother and my cousin Travis were called down to the guidance office and were told that Chase, a boy that played football with them during rec football days, was moving back to Abbott Hills. Out of all the people he played with, Chase remembered Davis and Travis. My brother and my cousin took him under their wings before he even stepped foot into the school, even going as far as securing him a late in the season football try-out.

I knew I was a goner the second our eyes locked. I pretended not to care when the guys caught up at the lunch table later that day. Instead I hung onto every word as he told me how he had only lived in Abbott Hills for two years when his dad's job relocated his family to New Hampshire from Washington. His mom had loved New Hampshire so much that as soon as Chase's parents' divorce was finalized, she packed up Chase and his little brother Tucker and moved them back to Abbott Hills.

Despite what you're probably thinking, it wasn't love. I don't care what anyone says, that "insta-love" crap is just that— complete crap. No, it wasn't love, but meeting Chase felt like coming home. That we were meant to be in each other's lives and something inside me knew we always would be. When we're together, everything in the world feels safe and right.

I can't tell you every exact detail of some of the most important, most memorable days of my life, but if someone were to ask me about the entire day I met Chase? I could tell you everything. All the way down to the cereal I ate for breakfast. (It was Lucky Charms.)

But I wasn't the kind of girl Chase wanted. At least not sixteen, seventeen, eighteen-year-old Chase. I had plain brown hair and freckles. I wore ripped jeans and band tees. I didn't care that he wore a football jersey for our school, but I understood the game he played and loved so much. I had morals. I cared about my grades and my future more than fitting in and the latest fads. I didn't need his attention constantly like the girls (he still tries to deny) he was getting "attention" from after practice. I had a lot of friends, in a lot of circles, but I was good being left in my own company too.

When Chase looked at me, he saw a girl that was dependable. The kind of girl that you tell all your secrets to—and over time, he did just that. Before long, he wasn't "Davis and Travis' friend, Chase," he was "Hollis' best friend, Chase."

We were thick as thieves and did everything together. Every week, for three years, during football season, he chose me to be his rally girl. He became an extension of my family and shortly after, so did his brother and his mom. Mischa Merrimack became the mother figure I turned to so many times as both a teenager and as an adult.

There were so many times I went over to their house to make cookies or watch movies with his mom. Every time I went over, I got the scoop on who was trying to be the next girl that slept with Abbott Hill's beloved wide receiver. Every one of them hoping to be the girl that got to wear his jersey to school on game days. But much to their chagrin, that honor always went to me—his best friend. The fact that he was Chase, the football God of Abbott Hills High didn't faze me. Student government, select choir, and being an assistant captain of the girls' Varsity soccer team kept me worrying about my own stats.

I would be lying if I said there wasn't a time or five that we almost crossed a line we never would have been able to come back from. Without fail, one of us always pulled back before it became something more. Each moment never spoken about again. As if it never happened. That was, until the day I decided I couldn't live on a "what if" or a "maybe" anymore. The day I pushed the idea of anything more than friendship and the mixed feelings I had for Chase aside, a new world opened to me—a world full of boys.

As it happens though, I should have kept walking past the next two fellas to grab my attention. The first one was Alex Hinsdale, a dumb seventeen-year-old boy that still wanted to be my boyfriend after he tried to dump me for just one night to take his ex-girlfriend to the prom. And then there was Noah. Not to say there weren't a few drunken hook-ups in college and a couple dinner dates after and in between Alex and Noah, but nothing that lasted long enough to be considered something serious.

Maybe I was just meant to be alone, to still live in my father's basement when I'm fifty. I should probably get a cat or six, and start extreme couponing, really embrace the forever single lifestyle. Shaking the thought, I look at the photo of me and Chase for a moment longer before turning to the next page.

Polaroids of me and a tall brunette are scattered over the next two pages. Her olive skin looks a few shades darker next to the pale, porcelain-like tone of mine. Every one of them are captioned within the white film underneath the processed photograph.

Reaching for my phone to send the "KINLEY & HOLLIS – SISTERS FROM OTHER MISTERS" pages of me and Kinley to her, I see that it's 5:23PM.

…and I never turned my phone off silent.

Notifications are stacked one on top of the other on my lock screen. Two missed calls, a voicemail, and three texts from Kinley; two calls from "Twin"; a call from my dad; and a text from my cousin Ellis. Ugh. There's no need to open them. Every one of them will be about the text I sent to Kinley.

Thinking rationally had not been my top priority earlier. Had I been thinking rationally, I would have realized what and where she would be walking into reading the text I sent. Right about now, Kinley's townhome, the one that she shares with my brother, is filling up for Davis's annual birthday poker night.

My dad, uncles, cousins, his friends that have known me most of my life, and a slew of off-duty police officers will be witnessing Kinley freaking out over the text message I sent an hour ago, one that I haven't responded to, in addition to all of their calls.

And Chase. Shit. Shit. Shit. Chase will be there by now too. So much for holding off. Before I get a hold of Chase, I need to text Kinley. Maybe if I can convince her I'm okay, she'll pass along the message and the guys will let it go for the night. It's wishful thinking to say the least, but I don't have a Plan B right now.

Quickly scanning through the messages from her first to see

if there is a question I need to answer immediately, I stop when I see, *"I'll head over in a few mins but, Chase was here. He wasn't waiting on an answer...he's on his way over."*

Putting my finger on the H in the box below the text window, I start to respond back, freezing in place when I hear, "I will fucking kill him."

Looking up, I am greeted with a set of bright green eyes that I'd know anywhere. Despite the shit show that's about to take place, I would have to be both blind and crazy to not appreciate Chase Merrimack standing there—distressed jeans, white t-shirt, and backwards black hat— looking like he's ready to take on the entire world for me.

It takes him seven seconds to make his way to over me. Five seconds for him pull me off the bed and into his arms. And two seconds for me to completely fall apart.

CHAPTER TWO

CHASE

I HAVE NEVER CONSIDERED myself a weak man.

I've been in my fair share of fights, both off and on the field. There's a whole long list of concussions, strains, tears, fractures, and broken bones, and I've been on the receiving end of more than a couple slaps in the face from females who didn't believe me when I said that I didn't do serious. But there isn't any injury in existence that could have prepared me for what I just walked into.

I still don't know exactly what happened to get me here, in Hollis's bedroom, in the first place. Twenty minutes ago, I had just walked into Davis Capparelli's for his annual birthday poker night. While grabbing a Sam Summer from the fridge, I overheard Davis's girlfriend Kinley frantically reading Davis a text from Hollis.

All it took was hearing, "She's not answering my calls or my texts, Davis. Doesn't your sister know you cannot send someone a picture of an empty ring finger with a text that says 'help'?" for me to abandon all reason and rush out the door.

Acting on instinct, there was no time for goodbyes. Leaving the open beer on the counter, I ran out of the house without a word to anyone. In retrospect, driving thirty miles-per-hour over the speed limit across town to her house probably wasn't the safest or the smartest thing to do. In the back of my mind I think I knew if I got pulled over, all I had to do was let them know I was checking on Sergeant Davis Capparelli's twin sister and I'd have ended up with a police escort with flashing lights, sirens and all.

The sight of her black Jeep parked in the driveway as I pulled onto her street allowed me to exhale the first real, deep breath since I left her brother's townhouse. That sudden sense of relief would be gone as fast as it came though. Sitting up cross-legged on her bed, I found her staring at a scrapbook in her lap. Her foot tapped along to some country song while a sad smile lingered on her face as she looked down at whatever was on those pages.

All it took was one look at her to tell she was just pretending to be okay. She's good at masking her emotions. Over the thirteen years I've known her, I've only seen her cry a handful or so of times and they were during Harry Potter movies. And then once before our Senior Prom when her date bailed on her last minute.

Well, to be more exact, she didn't shed a tear because her douche boyfriend at the time Alex Hinsdale tried to break up with her "for a day" to take Brooklyn Barrington to prom, solely based on the promise of making it "worth it" afterwards. Alex didn't care that Brooklyn had already offered the same promise to me, Travis, and half the football team before making her way over to the baseball team. I had learned my lesson with Brooklyn already and none of the other guys were dumb enough to take the drama that always came attached with doing anything with Brooklyn...Except the douche dating the girl who was, at the time, planning on holding onto her V card until marriage.

Spreading like wildfire, like most gossip and drama does in

high school, it didn't take long for my phone to start blowing up with people "concerned" for Hollis. Just like today, she refused to answer her phone that day too. But instead of me coming to her, just as I was about to walk out the door of my mother's house, there was a short knock and then it opened.

She was, and still is, the only person that can just walk into my mother's house and no one bats an eye. She didn't wait for me to ask what happened, she just started spewing obscenities, calling Alex every name in the books. I will never forget the disbelief and shock on my mom's face when she heard her sweet little "adopted" daughter call him a "pussy ass piece of shit."

Without skipping a beat, she went right into her plan to work at her grandparents' restaurant to pay her dad back for the money "wasted" on a prom she wouldn't be attending. Like most things when it comes to Hollis, before I knew what I was saying, I asked her to be my date. I hadn't even wanted to go to prom. It would have made sense to go if I had a girlfriend, but I didn't. And I didn't see the point in taking a girl I wouldn't be talking to a year from then.

That was until a bunch of the guys from the football team convinced me to go a week before. "One last hurrah for the Wolf Pack," they said. I had a tux from being in my aunt's wedding earlier that Spring, so I said fuck it and bought the ticket. I figured I'd spend a few hours at the hotel, take some pictures, and then we'd head up to one of the guys' family cabin on Lake Winnipesauke.

She was calm and collected when she asked if I was sure, but the hope in her eyes would have had me moving mountains if necessary. When I promised that it was exactly what I wanted, she burst into tears, and then apologized a hundred times for being emotional.

That's how it's always been though. Since the very first day I met her. To everyone else, Hollis Capparelli has perfected the art of putting up walls and pretending everything is fine.

Despite having a small army's worth of people behind her always, she doesn't want to be an inconvenience to anyone around her.

I've always been the only one that could easily call her bluff. Her poker face is solid, but it's not about her facial expressions or body language—it's all in her eyes. That's why as soon as I spoke, and she jerked her head up to look at me, I swear I died a little inside.

I made a somewhat joking comment about killing the, I guess, now ex-fiancé of hers. At first glance, you wouldn't have known she was on the brink of losing it. But when she looked up at me and I saw the complete hopelessness in her eyes, I was certain I felt the world crumble beneath me.

I didn't consider myself a weak man.

Not until my favorite person on this Earth completely fell apart in my arms. It's been a few minutes since she clung to me, holding on as if my presence was the very last thread keeping her together. There's not a single word said between the two of us as she leaves puddles of black mascara all over my white t-shirt.

It's not for a lack of trying though. Everything I play out in my head just sounds ridiculous. I could tell her that it's "his loss," but I guarantee she already knows this. I could say that she's "better than him," but I hope she knows that too. God knows I thought it the entire time they were together. This isn't the time to be charming or try to make her laugh, so I just stand there like a fucking idiot while she sobs into my chest.

"I don't even want to hear it, you know," she sniffles, breaking the silence, slowly pulling herself away just enough to look up at me. "I know it's coming, but right now I can't handle the 'I told you so' speech."

Squinting her eyes and scrunching her nose, she attempts to give me an evil glare. Which might be intimidating if her smeared black make-up didn't make her look like a cute zombified Munchkin of Oz.

"I know," I tell her, while leaving a short kiss on the top of her head, in the hopes it gives her reassurance. I'm here because I'm worried about her, not to be a dick. "I don't know what happened, to be honest. I was at your brother's and Kinley was freaking out. I didn't say bye to anyone. I just left. I wanted to make sure you were okay."

"They knew you were coming here. Kinley texted me that you were on your way. I'm sorry I didn't tell you. I just knew if I did, that this would happen and I really didn't want to ruin your night."

"You have nothing to be sorry for, and you didn't ruin my night. Being your best friend always comes first, Hol. So, are you going to tell me what happened?" I ask. "Or do I go beat the hell out of him without knowing the reason?"

"We," booms the voice of Davis Capparelli, Hollis's twin brother, from behind me. "We will beat the hell out of Noah."

Davis and Hollis may be twins by birth, but you would never know it by just looking at them. The only things they have in common are their deep brown eyes and the natural color of their almost black hair. Davis is the spitting image of their dad. Both Lorenzo and Davis Capparelli stand tall at six feet, have natural, year-round olive-tinted tans thanks to the Italian heritage they get from Lorenzo's side of the family. Both always have their hair styled in a clean, faded, "high and tight," more than likely courtesy of years in the Marines.

Hollis is an entire foot shorter than her dad and her brother. Her pale skin is covered in freckles, presumably from the Irish half of her. Her natural dark, brown hair is completely covered up by a bright blonde that sits just below her shoulders. It's the longest it's been for as long as I've known her.

For a long time, she kept it short because it was easier for soccer and to be honest, it suited her. She is one of the few girls

I know that I genuinely prefer having short hair. But, Noah McDougal lived up to his nickname McDouchegal by telling her that not only did he hate short hair, but that she'd look "better" with blonde hair too. McDouchegal is an idiot.

"Jesus, Mary, and Joseph," another voice adds from behind Davis. "What did Noah do?"

"Jesus has nothing to do with it, Pop," Hollis chuckles, pulling herself away from me before wiping the last of the tears from her face and snapping her attention to her brother. "And you especially will not be beating anyone, Sergeant Capparelli."

A small bout of laughter from the three of us earns a small but genuine smile from Hollis. She might be feeling a little low right now, but Davis and I have both been on the receiving end of a pissed off Hollis. We know better than to push her buttons right now. I wouldn't be surprised if he pulled me aside later though. We weren't kids anymore and we couldn't go fighting this dude for breaking Hollis's heart. But this wouldn't go unanswered.

And yeah, like she tells us, she could absolutely fight her own battles. Hollis is, without a doubt, the toughest woman I know. However, if the situation was reversed and it was me? She'd already be coming up with a game plan. Just ask Brooklyn—the one girl I dated in high school.

Yep. The same Brooklyn that Hollis's boyfriend dumped her for the night before prom. We'd been hanging out, mostly screwing around, a lot the summer before Senior year. When school started, Brooklyn all but begged me to make us official and I kind of felt obligated.

Well, a few days into the school year she made the mistake of boasting to an entire girls' locker room that the only reason she was dating me was to boost her chances of making Homecoming Court. The story everyone outside of the locker room got was that Brooklyn got hit in the nose with a volleyball when one of her friends tossed it to her. Hollis's cousin Ellis confirmed my suspicions though when I asked her if a certain five-foot Irish-Italian Hurricane named Hollis had anything to do with Brooklyn's broken nose.

Two days after I broke up with Brooklyn, I got accused of putting an open brown paper bag of hardboiled eggs in her locker. I laughed it off, taking the blame, because all it took was one glance across the hallway to a wide-eyed Hollis to know it was her genius at work. She took credit for the eggs later that day, but to this day, she still denies that she broke Brooklyn's nose defending me.

So, Noah McDougal would get his. Maybe not today. But I would make sure he got his "rotten eggs." As I begin to play out the ways I could torture the douche that broke my best friend's heart, Kinley Lavoie—Davis's girlfriend and one of Hollis' closest friends—squeezes herself through Lorenzo and Davis.

Before she makes her way to her, Kinley grabs a small white plastic tub from Hollis's vanity, opening it as she shoos the men surrounding Hollis away. Wiping the makeup from Hollis's face, her voice is laced with concern as she asks Hollis what happened. Since there was no vocalized threat to Noah's life in Kinley's question, Hollis couldn't sidestep any longer like she had with me, her brother, and her dad.

"I don't even know where to start," she shrugs, suddenly looking unsure of herself.

So, I look at her and say that only thing that makes sense in this moment, "Well, how about the beginning?"

Taking a seat on the edge of her bed, she begins to tell us how despite promising her last month that they would "absolutely" spend tonight together, Noah texted her at 5:45 this morning to break their dinner plans for the night. A dozen red roses delivered from the local florist and the excuse that he had a big project to finish at the office was all she got instead. My scoffing at his flower choice gets a knowing smile from Hollis. She doesn't like roses. The smell of them makes her nauseous.

Her favorite flowers are sunflowers. He was with her for two years and he doesn't know this?

She continues by saying that despite his shitty flower selection, she didn't think twice about it. He works in Boston at one of the largest marketing firms in New England, so she assumed he was on a deadline. I feel my blood boiling, my anger rising as the most selfless woman on this Earth talks about how she decided no matter what day it is, she would make the extra effort. She made that bastard a dozen red velvet cupcakes—his favorite. She spent an hour and a half straightening her hair, doing her make-up, and forcing herself out of her comfort zone to wear the "stupid fucking jumpsuit" she still had on.

The more she tells us, the stronger she becomes. Her body slowly begins to straighten, and she alternates between looking us all in the eyes instead of keeping her focus on the floor below her. None of us say anything as she tells us about the hour and a half drive into Boston to his office, strolling right into the building. My stomach dropping, already knowing what was coming next.

And, sure enough, she blurts out, "That asshole was there, sitting in his chair with his back to me. But there was no mistaking the bright red heels on the floor in between his legs."

Most women would have caused a fucking scene, made themselves known. But Hollis left him there to get his dick sucked. Emptying the cupcakes onto his desk, she shoved her diamond engagement ring into one of the few upright cupcakes. Leaving the door opened wide when she left.

When she finishes telling us, a deep sigh leaves her body as she exhales. Immediately she seems lighter. But that's not everything. There's something she's not telling us. If I know anything, it's when Hollis is hiding her emotions. There's more. With absolute certainty, I know we didn't just get the whole story.

CHAPTER THREE

HOLLIS

"ALRIGHT, SO WHERE ARE WE DRINKING?" I ask, quickly adding in, "I do not want to go to Capparelli & Co. I can't deal with that tonight. It'll be bad enough tomorrow and Sunday at Nonna and Nonno's."

My dad and my brother might not need every single minor detail, but my cousins and aunts will. And I'll beg them not to involve her, but somehow, they'll get my grandmother involved too. Hell hath no fury like an Italian grandmother who knows someone did one of her grandbabies wrong.

Cue being checked on every hour of my life, the lecture from my grandfather about how this would have never happened if I dated an Italian boy, and my uncles constantly—hopefully emptily—threatening Noah's life. I know there are worse things in life than having an overprotective family that are in your business because they love you. I just wouldn't mind a little bit of time in between the break-up and my family's infiltration. Thankfully, there is never a shortage of wine on Sundays.

"If you're cool with keeping it low-key, we can go to my

house?" Chase offers. "I have beer, a full liquor cabinet, and a few bottles of wine."

"And an outdoor fire place," Kinley adds, suggestively wiggling her eyebrows and nodding like a lunatic.

Four pairs of eyes are now looking back at me, anticipating my response. The sound of my dad chuckling from the doorway breaks the pause of silence. He's going to worry about me regardless, but if I stick with Davis and Chase tonight, he knows there will be someone to keep an eye on me tonight.

"Alright, I need to be up at 4AM to head down to Cambridge for a job. I'm going up to get settled for the night. Stay at Chase's if you drink too much," he says to me before turning his attention to Chase. "And you, take care of our girl."

Taking a step to where I'm standing, my dad leans over pulling me into a bear hug. My father is a man of very little words, especially when it comes to me. There's no doubt in my mind that he would move Heaven and Earth for me, but he tends to let his actions speak for him instead.

Growing up, he taught me everything he taught Davis. I know how to change a tire, and he taught me how to use every tool he owns. For our fifteenth birthday, he bought us both five speed Volkswagen Jettas, telling us they were ours, no strings attached, if we learned how to drive them.

But even though I know how to check and change my oil, I've never had to. My favorite tea is always stocked in the pantry upstairs. Every week when he goes grocery shopping for the house, there's a white laundry basket left on the landing leading to my area of the house with toilet paper, paper towels, my specific brands of laundry soap and fabric softener, and snacks for me to leave downstairs in my space. And despite me offering all the time, he refuses to take a penny for rent.

"I'll be okay, Pop," I assure him. "I am your daughter after all."

With a small, tender squeeze on my arm, he makes eye

contact with all of us and reminds us to behave by saying, "Stay out of trouble, you four."

Before he makes his way upstairs, he shoots us the look of warning he's been giving us since we teenagers, and funny enough, it has the same affect now as it did ten years ago.

"Alright, well, if we're backyard drinking, I need to change out of these clothes," Kinley says, not wasting any time as she glances down to the tan dress slacks and white blouse she's wearing.

"You live right next door to Chase, you weirdo. Why do you need to change here?" I ask as she begins to shoo Chase and Davis out of my bedroom.

"Because your closet is closest?" she shrugs, quickly adding, "And, I kind of want to steal that jumpsuit once you take it off?"

"Always kicking me out before the good stuff," Chase scoffs, winking at me as Kinley continues to guide them toward the door.

"Man, shut up and walk," Davis says, shaking his head as he further helps Chase out the door by giving him a little shove. "That is my girlfriend and my sister."

"Yeah, well, she isn't my sister." Chase's burst of laughter carries as Davis quickly pulls the door closed behind them.

As fast as I try to look solemn, Kinley catches the ear to ear grin spread across my face. Shit. Raising her eyebrows, pointing back and forth between me and the now closed bedroom door, I know I've been caught.

"Don't even go there right now," I warn, shaking my head the exact same way my brother did as he left the room.

"You're single. He's single. You guys are meant to be together—"

"I've been single for like six hours, crazy." I interrupt her before she can finish whatever she's about to suggest. "Cool your jets."

"But you don't deny that you guys are meant to be together though…"

She doesn't attempt to hide her disappointment when I shut her down. Being the self-proclaimed captain of Team Chase & Hollis, I knew Kinley would try to push the idea eventually. Even when I was with Noah, if there was a chance to bring up the possibility of Chase and I being more than friends, Kinley never missed the opportunity to take it.

Kinley was always my friend first and then my brother's girlfriend second. At least to me.

But when she started dating Davis, she became part of our family too. Which meant that she always had a spot at the dinner table on Sunday, and she used it often. Bringing her sister Cole with her most Sundays. It only took one Sunday of seeing Chase and I together with my family for both Kinley and Cole to decide that we "needed" to be together. Nothing, and no one, has been able to sway either of their minds otherwise since.

Knowing she won't get anywhere with me tonight, Kinley drops the thought quickly and dips into my closet. Less than a minute passes before she comes out, wide-eyed, holding a white and blue floral romper.

"Oh my God, Hollis Grace!" she exclaims. "One, I was shocked as hell when I came in and saw you in that jumpsuit, but you own a romper? And two, it's from Abercrombie & Fitch? When did you step foot into Abercrombie? I'm so sad I missed that experience."

"Ha, ha, ha. No," I deadpan. "Nonna took Elisabeth back to school shopping last week and she bought that 'for me.' Pretty sure Elisabeth instigated that purchase. I thought I'd left it in the bag with the half-naked dude on it."

"Oh, you did. I'm surprised it even made it down to your bedroom," she laughs before adding, "And, how did I get screwed out of back-to-school clothes shopping in college? I thought I was spoiled. You Capparellis are spoiled as shit."

"You can have it if you want," I shrug before warning, "But, if you tell Nonna I gave it to you, I will physically fight you."

Turning she disappears back into the closet and comes out thirty seconds later wearing the romper, holding a pair of white canvas shoes in her hand. I almost make a crack about her being able to get out of clothes so quickly, but I know her comeback will have something to do with Davis, and just no.

I've always been okay with them being together, I'm just not the friend she can go to when she needs to talk about, well, anything within their relationship. The day they started dating I officially became Switzerland. I do tell her that she looks amazing and the romper looks a thousand times better on her than it would have on me though. Her summer sun-kissed skin looks a few shades darker next to the light color of the fabric. Tossing her a pair of socks, she catches them one-handed and slides them and then the sneakers on.

With nothing else to do but wait for me to change, she takes a seat on my bed…right next to the scrapbook that inspired my trip down Memory Lane earlier. Pulling an elastic off her wrist, she pulls her hair in a top knot and rubs her hands together excitedly like she knows she's about to get into something good. Picking it up and pulling the scrapbook onto her lap, she opens it. Recognizing the photo immediately, a grin spreads across her face. Her smile turns into an evil, sly smirk as she reaches over to the spot on my bed where she dropped her phone when she first got here. Offering no explanation, she snaps a picture of the photograph of Chase and I on the football field. She doesn't make it any further than that before she closes the book, as if with purpose.

"I'm going to bring this out and look with the guys," she says, standing with the scrapbook tightly secured in her hands.

"I'll be like five minutes. Ten tops," I tell her. "I just want to get out of this jumpsuit and do something with the rest of the make-up all over my face."

"Oh! Why don't you just toss it in here, so I can take it with me?" she asks, laughing as she hands me the Abercrombie bag now holding the clothes she just changed out of as she leaves the room.

As she leaves the room, I realize how thankful I am for not only her, but Chase and my brother, too. Without hesitation, they dropped what they were doing for the night to be here with me. Davis had a house full of people that he had to have asked to leave to come here. People who were there to celebrate him. I honestly don't even want to think about what would happen if they weren't here with me tonight. Alcohol poisoning or tire slashing both sound like probable situations though.

As I peel off the jumpsuit, I wonder how chicks even go to the bathroom with these things. Ugh. Right in the bag with Kinley's other clothes it goes. I certainly won't be asking for it back. I don't care how cute they are, they're so far from practical. Making a mental note to ask her how she plans on going pee tonight in the romper, there's no question in my mind—she can keep both outfits.

This stupid, uncomfortable strapless bra needs to go next. My most used, most comfortable cotton white bra sits right on the top of a pile of clean clothes. Almost instinctually, I reach for it but stop, the lingerie never makes its way to my hand. Digging a little deeper, I search for the red lacy push-up bra I purchased last week at Victoria's Secret. No one is going to see it tonight, but as I hook the clasps, I feel a small boost in my ego. My c-cups look two sizes bigger. The red makes me feel a little sexy and a lot sassy.

Choosing an outfit for Chase's house doesn't require much thought. Quickly settling on a fitted V-neck, I slide the shirt over my head. Ending a few inches below my hips and hugging my curves, the solid black shirt showcases my hourglass figure. The elbow length, three-quarter style sleeves and longer length giving me a casual, but cute look. Next, I grab my most worn pair of ripped skinny jeans and shimmy back and forth until they're up on my hips. They'll loosen as I wear them but right now they stick to my skin like a denim suction cup. Satisfied with my outfit, I step into the closet, grabbing my favorite pair of black Converse All-Stars.

Remembering I still have half a face full of smeared black eye make-up, I sit down at the white vanity my dad built for me for my 16th birthday. The reflection looking back at me causes me to roll my eyes. If tonight was Halloween, I could have just gone as the undead. Waterproof mascara, my ass.

Taking a small cotton cloth full of make-up remover, I scrub my face clean. I don't reapply any make-up, instead choosing to leave the face of freckles staring back at me uncovered. Some people tan in the summer, but not me. My fair, light, Irish skin usually alternates between "Casper" and lobster. The only thing that changes with the seasons is the number of freckles on my face. Being that it is the tail end of summer, they are currently in abundance.

Even with my dad's plea to crash at Chase's, I don't plan on ending the night anywhere other than my own bed tonight. Grabbing only my phone and the bag with Kinley's clothes, I open my bedroom door, eager to forget about the day and move onto the next part of this night. Stepping right out into my living room, I find Chase, Kinley, and Davis squished together on one end of my brown leather couch. Opening my mouth to make a comment about "getting this show on the road," I close my lips as fast as they opened, a word never leaving my lips. Instead, I freeze in place when Chase points down to something on the page they're looking at and says that he's "never told me but he's glad Alex bailed on me that night."

Prom. It must be a senior prom picture.

Hanging back, I still don't say anything. Though, I'm not sure why. Maybe a part of me is hoping I'll catch Chase make another admission. My attempt at staying in stealth-mode isn't as smooth as I imagine though, because Kinley notices me lurking in the doorway almost immediately.

Nudging my brother with her elbow first, she stands up and gives me the same evil smirk that came right before the "Chase and Hollis" comments she made in my bedroom as she passes me. Davis hands the book over to Chase and stands up, taking his girlfriend's not so subtle cue to leave the room. Surprisingly, Chase makes no effort to move off the couch. His face is down, but I imagine his expression matches the one I had when I saw the first page of the book. When he looks up his eyes trail, slow and calculated, from my toes to the top of my head.

"Speaking of the prettiest girl in Abbott Hills."

Pre-Noah, it wasn't out of the ordinary for Chase to say things like that. Before I really knew him, I lived for those comments. If I was the kind of girl that wrote in a diary, there would have been multiple entries that started off with "Today Chase called me _____."

All it took was watching him talk his way out of a detention with our high school English teacher—who was old enough that she probably taught Shakespeare himself—for me to realize he's like that with everyone. Not just me. Chase Merrimack is the damn king of smooth talking.

As I dramatically let my eyes roll to the back of my head, I take a spot on the couch next to Chase. Following his eyes, which now are fixated on two pages full of pictures of me, him, and our friends from the night of our high school senior prom. Just like I thought.

"The twenty-four hours leading up to this night were the most stressful ones of my life," I remember out loud.

"I never would have known. You seemed so cool with it." Chase shrugs, looking over and grinning before turning back to the scrapbook. "I can't say I'm sad about the way things turned out though."

There are two professional photographs on the left page.

The top photograph is a group shot of nine teenagers lined up, each one linked in arm with another. Scanning the line of five boys and four girls makes my heart happy. Each of the four girls in the photograph is wearing the same all black, lace-bodice ball gown with small tank sleeves and a full, pleated satin skirt. The four boys all in shiny dress shoes, a tuxedo, and a black bow tie.

The line starts with my cousin Travis and Kinley, who is also linked to my brother. It's crazy to think Kinley and Davis had only been together for a few months at that point. Kinley's step-sister Cole stands next to Davis, her other arm linked with Kenny Finnigan, Davis's best friend. My cousin Ellis stands on the other side of Kenny, arm in arm with Tucker Merrimack. Wrapping up the line on the right-hand side are me and Chase.

Any time these pictures resurface, Tucker and I go back and forth about who got the better spot in line. He'll say it was him because he got to stand between the Capparelli girls, but I know it was me in between the two Merrimack brothers.

The photographer had been surprised when we told him we had the same dress on purpose. While most girls were trying to find something that would make them stand out, Kinley, Cole, Ellis, and I chose to pick something that would unify us instead. Despite begging and pleading from my aunt, Zia Kat, for each of us to do something different with our hair, we all agreed on the same simple halo braid, textured bun up-do too.

Prom was a big deal for the Capparelli family that year since there were four of us going. My dad even took the day off from work, which is something I can honestly say I had never seen him do before that day. Even when he takes sick days, he's on the phone making sure orders are in and setting up appointments with future clients. My aunt closed her salon at three that afternoon, despite having desperate pleas for afternoon appointments.

"Everyone else can make an appointment before then. It's

not every night your only daughter, your God-child, and their best friends go to prom," she had said when she invited me, Kinley, and Cole to come with Ellis to get our hair done.

When she flat-out refused to take any money from Kinley's mom for doing Kinley and Cole's hair and nails, three oversized chocolate covered fruit bouquets were delivered to the salon. My adorable father stopped in shortly after we got there with a pallet of sparkling mineral water and corsages made with roses from my grandfather's garden for each of us. My grandparents decorated the banquet room in the restaurant and had a three course dinner prepared for us and the fellas before we left for the dance in a stretch Hummer paid for by Kenny's mom. Thinking about how spoiled we were that day makes me smile and it doesn't go unnoticed.

"What are you so smiley about over there?" Chase asks, interrupting my thoughts.

"Just how everyone treated me, Kinley, Cole, and Ellis like princesses that day. Don't tell anyone, but I kind of loved it."

"If I remember correctly, you were the princess of prom," he grins, pointing to a snapshot on the next page.

His finger hovers over the tiara that sits on top of the candid, completely baffled face of a seventeen-year-old me. We all know he pulled some serious strings to get us named Prom King & Queen. As far as I knew, my name hadn't been in the running the entire month the senior class had to vote. God knows I certainly didn't put in for it.

It was no surprise when Chase's name was called. Everyone knew it would either be him or Alex, since Alex was the captain of the baseball team. The very last thing I expected was for my name to follow Chase's and that is very clearly seen in every photo taken.

Since prom, I've asked him a hundred times how he pulled it off, but he never lets on that it was anything other than pure luck.

No matter how many times he denies having anything to do with it, I'm certain his "luck" must be like how a volleyball "accidentally" found its way to his ex-girlfriend Brooklyn's face after she made the mistake of loudly bragging about using him. If he didn't fix the Prom Queen election, then I didn't punch Brooklyn in the nose after I found out she was using him to gain social status. And for the record, I absolutely punched Brooklyn in the nose.

As if he can see the wheels spinning in my head, he closes the book, leaving it on the couch next to him. Offering his hand, I put mine in his. With a pulling motion he "helps" me off the couch, neither of us making any effort to let go once I'm upright. When he asks me if I just want to ride over with him, I begin to tell him that I'll take my Jeep since I want to come home anyway, but I stop myself when I see the hopefulness in his eyes.

There's nothing to say Chase can't bring me back home later too. The truth of it is that Chase and I haven't been able to hang out, just the two of us, in a very long time. I know this has nothing to do with me spending the night or drinking, but everything to do with being able to just be the two of us again. Even if just for a little while. So I tell him yes.

The synchronized pattern of our steps comes to a pause as I stop us to grab my clutch and keys off the breakfast bar. The wooden door leading outside was left open from Kinley and Davis walking out a few minutes before.

"What do you think the lovebirds are talking about?" I nod toward where they're standing outside. Standing side by side, they're squished up against each other, purposely speaking in hushed voices.

"Probably arguing about how I told them if we get dinner, or well, anything, under no circumstances were you to pay for yourself or for them to pay for you tonight," Chase shrugs. "Your brother seems to think I'm acting like a caveman. Kinley thinks I'm a gentleman. So, yeah. It's probably me, and well, you."

"Chase Matthew! I don't need you to pay for me," I start to argue, but he cuts me off before I can give him more reasons.

"Hollis Grace," he smirks, mimicking my tone, before continuing, "I know you don't *need* me to. I want to. You just spent two years with someone who didn't make you a priority. It's just dinner. And I know I'm just your best friend, but I think, at least tonight of all nights, you could use a solid reminder of what it feels like when someone actually gives a damn about you."

And there it is, folks. The moment we've been waiting for. Chase's watered down version of the "I told you so" speech. As much as I want to be angry, his words hit me like a blow to my chest. Because dammit, he's right. I spent the better part of the last year being the one making all the plans and footing the bill most of the time because one of Noah's many excuses for not making plans with me was money. If it wasn't his insane car payment—because you know, it makes perfect sense for someone who commutes to Boston for work daily to be driving a brand-new BMW—it was his need for not one, not two, but *five* different Armani suits for work. Funds were always "a little tight" when it came to planning date night, but he had no issue ordering a $1,500 brief case from Barneys New York.

When a few seconds pass and I have no response for him, Chase turns to face me, his voice softening when he all but pleads, "Just let me do this tonight, Hol. I don't know what else to do to make it better."

"You're here," I tell him. "I just need you to be here."

Not waiting for an answer to that, I step down onto the porch, holding the screen door open for him. Pulling the old wooden door shut, I put the key into the doorknob and turn it, locking my apartment behind us. The moment I turn around, expecting to only see Chase, my brother, and Kinley, my stomach drops.

Before any of us can stop him, Davis pulls away from Kinley's arms, clearing every step between my porch and the short concrete path that leads to the driveway. Looking back only to tell me and Kinley to stay on the porch, Chase follows him. Both my brother and Chase stand tall, with arms crossed, as if they're the force fields separating Kinley and I from evil. And to be honest, that's not much a stretch from the truth.

Separated only by my twin brother and best friend, I brace myself as the white BMW X5 that had pulled onto my street comes to a complete stop in front of my house. This night just officially turned into a shit show.

CHAPTER FOUR

CHASE

IT TAKES a whopping twenty seconds after me telling her not to come off the porch for Hollis to mimic her brother and clear the handful of steps in between the porch and the pavement. I guess I should have expected it though. Telling Hollis to do anything is pretty much asking for her to do the exact opposite.

Brushing past Davis standing with his arms crossed, she strategically places herself in between Davis and the car. When she turns around and demands he step back, pointing toward where Kinley is standing behind us, I realize this has nothing to do with Noah, but everything to do with keeping her brother out of trouble. Knowing it's going to take more than Hollis's demands for him to step back, I place my hand on Davis's upper arm, patting three times. Nodding reluctantly, he steps back, acknowledging my silent reassurance that I'll keep his sister safe.

As soon as she sees Davis step back, Hollis turns back toward the street. The patter of her feet rapidly tapping against the concrete below us is the only sound surrounding us as we wait for the driver of the BMW to cut the engine and step out. Right now, I need to dig deep, shut off my emotions, and focus on getting that car and its jackass of a driver to leave.

Davis won't do anything to put Hollis in jeopardy, but he had promised Noah that if he hurt his sister, he would kill him. Granted it was weeks after they started dating and we were all drunk at the Capparelli's annual Labor Day weekend barbeque, but I've never known Davis to not follow through on his word.

So, as much as I would love to see that bastard face down in the dirt, the last thing that needs to come from this night is Davis reaping the repercussions of hurting a hair on Noah's head. Hollis adores her brother and if anything happened that resulted in Davis losing his job or worse, she'd blame herself. I'll be damned if I let him get to her though.

Before he even steps out of the car, I can already tell you what's going to happen. He's going to spew out a bunch of bullshit excuses and Hollis will let him try to justify it. That saint of a human I call my best friend believes the best in everyone. I've seen it so many times throughout the last two years. And like every time before this, she'll hear him out. Not everyone deserves a second chance. Not everyone deserves to prove themselves. Noah is one of those people.

Glancing back to make sure Davis is with Kinley, he quickly nods his head up, urging me to take the last few steps next to his sister.

"Damn it, Hollis. Do you ever listen? To anybody? Ever?"

I expect her to fight with me, to tell me to fuck off, that she can handle herself. She shocks the hell out of me when she faces me and pleads not only with her voice, but with those big brown eyes, "Please stay here. I can handle Noah, but you know Davis isn't about to let me fight this battle alone. Please stay here with me and don't let Davis touch him."

I feel my body loosen for a split-second, exhaling a deep breath; the tension and her protective stance coming back immediately after the breath leaves my body. The look on her face is one I've never seen in the entire time I've known her. Her eyes are dark and once again, focused ahead of us.

"I'm not going anywhere, Hurricane," I say, my tone softening with my promise.

The corner of her mouth creeps up in a slight smile when I call her the nickname I've had for her since the first day we met. It disappears as fast as it came when the engine of the BMW shuts off. Hollis's body quickly goes rigidly straight next to me. When she grabs my hand, I pause, taken back by her need for reassurance. Giving it a little squeeze to let her know I'm here, I rub my thumb against her index finger. The pulsating motion of her shaking hand in mine causes my blood to boil.

I've never seen her like this.

"I'm right here," I lean over, whispering down to the top of her head. "You give me the word, I'll handle it."

The slam of the car door causes me to snap my head back up. The man my best friend agreed to spend the rest of her life with calmly adjusts the jacket of his gray striped suit before even looking over at the woman he threw away. His face is void of any emotion as he runs his fingers through, and messing up, his perfectly styled volume of black hair.

"I should have known you'd be here," he sneers at me, not even acknowledging Hollis once he starts walking over to us. "Chase Merrimack, swooping in like Prince fucking Charming."

Not an "I'm sorry." Not an explanation. No words that implicate that he's here to fight for her. He's seriously using this opportunity, his one chance at potentially redeeming himself, to pick a fight with me, of all people? He's more of an asshole than I thought.

Fighting the urge to call him McDouchegal to his face is harder than I imagined. Little does he know Davis, Travis, Kenny, and I have been calling him that since we found out his last name. From day one, everything about him has always screamed douchebag. Every time Hollis managed to get him to come out with all of us, he was the asshole who made everything about money.

He had to buy the most expensive steak, the most expensive bottle of liquor. He barely ever joined in on conversations because everything was a pissing contest. We could be talking about football and he would turn the discussion into how much money his company bought out a sports brand contract for. He even walks like a douche. With his shoulders back, he sways his arms back like those assholes that brag that they have "swagger." But, if being surrounded by the Capparelli men for half my life taught me anything, it's that money doesn't make the man and that swagger is all about what you do, not what you say.

What makes him the most douchey, is that we all know the only time he threw money around was when he had an audience. He didn't use it to spoil Hollis behind closed doors. In fact, Mr. Big Shot had Hollis paying for everything when no one else was around. She would never have admitted that to me or any of the guys, but she did mention it to Kinley, who told Cole, which led to it getting back to the rest of us. I love our friends, but you can't tell any one of them anything without expecting the "telephone game" effect to come into play right after.

"What are you doing here, Noah?" Hollis demands, pulling her hand from mine.

"Oh, come on, baby," Noah croons as he reaches out for her. "It meant nothing. Put your ring back on so we can put this behind us."

"Keep your fucking hands to yourself," I snap, sidestepping in front of Hollis to keep him from touching her.

The very idea of his hands on her makes my skin crawl. Getting in between them was me acting on instinct and the second after I do, I regret it. Hollis will see it as me stepping in, thinking she can't handle the situation by herself. She asked me to stay with her to act as a barrier between Noah and Davis, not because she wanted me to help her stand up to McDouchegal.

She's stubborn about her need to take care of herself. I guess that comes with having her brother, cousins, my brother, and me in her business, trying to do our best to protect her all the time. I'll apologize after, but there's no fucking way I'm letting him touch her right now.

"I don't care what it meant," she says, as she places herself at my side again. "You have your ring. I have my dignity by walking away. There's nothing more to say, Noah."

Thinking back to why Hollis asked me up here in the first place, I glance back. With a puffed chest and crossed arms, Davis stands a few feet behind us. Kinley's face is full of anxiety as she holds tightly to one of his arms. It's as if she's keeping him in place, but she couldn't stop Davis if Noah gets out of line. His eyes are transfixed on Noah. All it's going to take is one wrong word, one movement that's too assertive, for Davis to snap. If he feels like his sister is in danger, not even I'm going to be able to stop him. I'm just thankful Travis isn't here right now too. There's no way I'd be able to stop the two of them.

"You know, this never would have happened, if you weren't such an uptight, prude little bitch," Noah spits when he realizes Hollis is not only not taking his bullshit, but she's done.

As if my body is acting on its own accord, my hand forms a fist. Before anyone has the chance to stop it, my knuckles hit his cheek. Sliding over his face and finally connecting with his nose, a loud pop fills the air. Dark red blood immediately gushes from his nose as the blow of the hit sends him stumbling back.

The sound of the front door opening behind us causes every one of us to turn. Lorenzo Capparelli steps down and that's all it takes for Noah to quickly continue in the direction of his car. I've never seen an angry Papa Cap, but that's also because I wouldn't want to be on the receiving end of his anger. Hollis and Davis are everything to him, and though he doesn't have a favorite, he's just *different* with Hol. Twenty-eight years old or not, that's his "bambolina" and Noah would be smart to make his exit now.

"Fuck this," Noah laughs menacingly, wiping his lips and spitting as the blood from his nose continues to stream down his face. "She's all yours, bro."

Despite knowing it's better that he's leaving, I don't know why I'm taken aback by his reaction. There's no way he came here thinking he could just smooth things over and everything would be fine. He might be business smart, but either he has no common sense, or he thinks so lowly of Hollis that he thought she would let it go.

"Deuces, McDouchegal," Kinley yells from behind, her voice getting louder with each syllable.

Pushing me further from Noah's car, and in the direction of a wide-eyed Hollis, Davis points to my truck and looks back to his dad, the sheer panic he feels emits from his presence.

"Dude, go," he demands. "You need to get Hol the fuck out of here. She needs to leave before Noah says anything else and my dad snaps. I got Dad, just get my sister out of here."

Grabbing her hand with one hand while I rummage through my shorts pocket for my keys, I lead Hollis to the black Silverado parked behind her Jeep. Unlocking the truck with the key fob, I open the passenger door for her. After letting go of her hand, she uses the grab handle and the frame to boost herself up and into the black leather seat.

"I'm sorry, Hurricane," I start, stepping into the space left between the open door. "I didn't think, I just..."

"Stop," she demands, pulling the seat belt from behind her, waving it off like I hadn't just punched her ex in the face like a psycho. "It's done. Just get me out of here."

Sighing loudly, she curses under her breath and points across the street. Ethel, her 78-year-old neighbor and her grandmother's best friend, is watching from a big bay window in her white nightgown. The base of the green landline telephone sits in the palm of her left hand as she clutches the handset with her right. When she realizes she's been spotted, she gives a quick wave to us and makes her way from the window.

"So, how does it feel knowing you're the talk of the Abbott Hills Canasta Club, right now?" I laugh, trying to make light of the situation.

"Fan-fucking-tastic," she retorts, shaking her head. "I'll be hearing from Nonna within the hour. Can we go eat s'mores and get drunk now?"

CHAPTER FIVE

HOLLIS

MY MIND IS GOING in a million different directions as Chase settles into his seat. The sound of his seat belt clicking and the roar of his truck starting are just muffled background noise to my thoughts. Chase's hand on my thigh causes me to jump and stops me from thinking about how I'm going to explain to my family on Sunday that there will be no wedding next Spring.

"Hey. Earth to Hollis," Chase chuckles as he takes his hand off my thigh and waves it in front of my face. "Did you hear anything I just said?"

"I'm sorry. Got a little lost in my head for a sec," I apologize. "What's up?"

"I said, No One Else Knows?"

A small smile escapes me when he mentions the game we started playing together the summer between our sophomore and junior years of high school. Kinley, Ellis, and Cole convinced me to go to a house party on the lake, even though I didn't really want to. At that point, I wasn't drinking yet and I didn't hook up with guys, so those parties had no appeal to me. Ellis was trying to get the attention of one of the guys on the football team, so she had begged me to go under the argument that there's no way she'd be able to handle our brothers in her business all night.

So, I went as her wing-woman and I regretted it about a half hour into being there. She found the guy she was looking for and managed to disappear when Davis and Travis were playing beer pong. A house full of jocks drunkenly hitting on anything with vagina had irritated me a lot sooner than I had imagined.

Knowing that none of my cousins, friends, or my brother would want to leave after being there for less than an hour, I snuck out the back door. After a few minutes of aimless wandering, I found an empty boat dock and took a seat. I was only there for five minutes tops when Chase sat down next to me and said, "Tell me something no one else knows."

After that night, we played every time we found ourselves in a situation where one or both of us needed a distraction, to tell each other a secret or to brace each other for a serious talk. He told me he was retiring from the NFL by starting a conversation like that. I told him my mom left like that...

"You first."

"Okay," he starts, "No one else knows, I'm glad you realized Noah is a scum bag. I knew it, but I had nothing to stand on and didn't want to be that asshole friend."

My rebuttal is easy.

"No one else knows, I'm glad Noah is a scum bag too. It's been pretty awful for a while now, Chase. Halfway into my drive to Boston, I decided I was going to end things with him when I got to his office. I don't even know why I still brought the cupcakes in with me. Like, hi, I'm here to break up with you, but here, have some cupcakes."

"Hold that thought," he says as he pulls into Dunkin Donuts. "We're definitely coming back to that."

Our game of truths is put on hold as he stops at the menu and the little speaker box to place your order. Raising his eyebrow like he's working hard to think of whatever he's about to say, he recites my coffee order the way I've been drinking it since high school. Giving him a little round of applause and nod of approval, I try not to show how impressed I am right now.

A snappy woman takes our coffee order and Chase pulls up to the window. Lifting my ass up off the seat, I stretch just enough to reach into my back pocket for the cash I had shoved in there just in case we grabbed food or chose to venture out for drinks. Just as I hold out the folded bills to pay for our coffee, Chase pulls out his credit card from his wallet and hands it to the cashier inside the window. She's maybe sixteen and makes no attempt to hide the fact she's checking him out. A snort escapes me as she giggles when he says, "thank you, ma'am" after she hands him our coffees.

Not that I blame her though.

Because no else knows I've been slightly jealous of every single girl that's held Chase's attention since I was fifteen.

As he cuts the wheel to pull out of the drive-through, he stops, waiting for a clearing in the oncoming traffic. "So, back to 'things have been awful for a long time?' Awful, how? And, why is this the first time I'm hearing about it?"

"I don't know," I tell him honestly, because the truth is, I wanted to talk to him about it so many times. There were so many times I picked up my phone to call him and texts that went unsent because I needed my best friend, but I didn't feel like I had the right to ask for his help anymore. I chose to push him away when Noah made it clear that he didn't like the closeness between me and Chase.

Opening the flood gates, I tell him how Noah and I haven't been much of a couple for the last year, that every time we got together I was hoping we would break up, even admitting that it's been months since I've had sex, which gets him to turn to me, shocked.

"What?" I ask. "Does it blow your mind that sweet little

Hollis actually has sex? And oh my God, actually misses it when she doesn't?"

"I wouldn't go as far as calling you sweet, Hol. You forget I know you better than anyone," he winks, taking a long sip of his iced coffee. "But it's not like your sex life is a typical topic of conversation for us."

Before it gets awkward, I decide to change the subject by continuing our game of No One Else Knows, admitting, "So, no one else knows I stood next to Noah's car in the parking garage and I seriously toyed with slicing his tires after I walked out of his office. I had my knife in my hand. The only thing that stopped me was noticing the stupid security cameras."

With that, Chase laughs, shaking his head in disbelief. "Hollis Grace! Remind me never to get on your bad side. And do I even want to know why you have a knife with you?"

"You could never," I assure him before explaining that when I started closing the bar at Capparelli & Co., my father had given me a small knife to keep in my purse. "I have a pepper spray key chain from Davis, too."

Nodding in silent approval, he doesn't say anything as he turns onto Spear Circle—the cul-de-sac both he and my brother live on—pulling into the driveway of the only detached condo on the loop. Why Chase decided to take the only three-bedroom single family home on the street is a mystery to me.

After a career-ending football injury he came back to Abbott Hills, and I think I'm the only one that knows he's only touched his signing bonus to buy the condominium outright. He said that the moment he saw the navy-blue shutters on the cream-colored house, he just knew it was "home."

Six months after Chase moved in, the left side of the split townhome next to Chase's went up for sale. My brother and Kinley put in an offer the day it went on the market and moved in less than three months later.

Carelessly whacking the garage door opener on his visor, Chase pulls into the garage and puts his truck in park.

"I'm going to go grab my mail," he says as he hops out of the truck. "Just walk in through the white door. It's unlocked."

Unbuckling my seat belt, I jump out of Chase's truck and let myself into his house. The moment I step foot inside, I'm awestruck. Noah hadn't "felt comfortable" with Chase and me being so close. So even though we never stopped talking and I had spent plenty of time next door at my brother's house, I hadn't been inside Chase's house since shortly after he moved in two years ago. There hadn't even been furniture at that point.

"Make yourself comfortable, I'm going to go change really quick," Chase says from behind me. Goose bumps travel all over my arms as he places his fingertips on my hips, gently moving me to the right and dropping his mail on the kitchen counter, before disappearing into a hallway off the room. Shaking off a shiver, I step all the way into the kitchen, twisting and turning to take it all in.

Matching stainless-steel appliances and marble countertops shine in the light. My eyes pause when I see the enormous fridge covered in pages torn from coloring books. My heart stops when I see a candid, Polaroid photo of me and Chase in the corner. Taken at his mom's house, a tall Christmas tree sits behind us. My hands are full of ornaments and my body is wrapped in white tree lights, courtesy of Chase. We're young. Maybe seventeen or eighteen. But we're happy. Genuine, unmistakable joy is written across my face as Chase looks at me with a goofy, amused grin on his own.

"My mom found that about a year ago. I just didn't know if it was appropriate to show you, you know, given the circumstances. I figured it was safe up there."

The sound of Chase's voice next to me startles me. As I turn to profusely apologize for letting things get weird between us while I was with Noah, I find myself staring at the man in front of me. How is it possible that he never looks unattractive? How had I pushed aside noticing for so long? And why the eff am I noticing it now? I've only been single for a few hours. And I would never make a move on Chase. Because, no. For so many reasons, I just couldn't.

Words fail me as I gawk at him standing there. All he did was change out his mascara-stained white t-shirt for a plain black one and his plaid shorts for a loose pair of Adidas basketball shorts.

His hair is tousled and messy from being inside the hat he was wearing. The sleeves of his shirt are wrapped tightly around his biceps, which, I swear are as big as my head. Oh my God. I need to stop. Hoping I haven't been caught, I quickly avert my eyes to Chase's face.

I'm greeted with a knowing, cocky half smile and curious, raised eyebrows. It's the exact same expression he gave me the first day we met. I couldn't keep my eyes off his arms that day either. I never knew arms could be sexy until the day Chase came strolling into that gymnasium, and the reminder, right in my face, catches me off guard.

Fuck. Before he can say anything about my gawking, his phone rings from the pocket of his shorts. A few "okays," a "that sucks," a "well, tell her I hope she feels better. I got Hol tonight," and a "no problem man, talk to you later," grab my attention. He's talking to my brother. His words are so calm as he responds to Davis on the other line, but the look in his eyes as he watches me is so intense that I need to look away before I let myself get caught up in a non-existent moment.

Ending the call, he says, "I'm sure you figured out that was Davis. I guess Kinley isn't feeling well. She started feeling sick on the ride over. Davis thinks that it's anxiety, she thinks it's the sushi she had at lunch. So, Plan B? We can totally still have s'mores and get drunk, but what do you think about a Chase and Hollis movie night? You can even pick where we get food from and crash in the guest room for old times' sake."

Chase and Hollis movie nights had become a thing when Chase was playing football professionally. His training was rigorous, and he wanted to do everything he could to avoid getting his face plastered in the media for being out drunk and partying. So every Friday night, I would drive the little over an hour down to his house in Foxborough, Massachusetts. We ordered a ton of takeout and watched whatever movie was newest On Demand. It was usually late when we finished and there was usually alcohol—at least for me—so most Fridays I just crashed in his guest room.

Once I started dating Noah, we began making plans together and my Friday movie nights with Chase became more sporadic, until they became non-existent. And then, when things with Noah became non-existent, I started picking up the Friday night bartending shift at my grandparents' restaurant.

Chase was right. It had been a long time. And we were way overdue.

"Okay," I start. "But, I'll need to borrow a pair of sweats. I didn't plan on staying over and I figured if we *did* drink too much and I absolutely had to, I could go next door and steal something from Kinley. But I don't want to bother her if she doesn't feel good though. And, I want food from La Mesa."

We had driven by my favorite Mexican restaurant on the way here and my stomach had grumbled at the thought of tacos and chimichangas.

Without skipping a beat, he says, "My bedroom is upstairs, last door to the left. Sweatpants are in the bottom drawer. You can grab whatever you want, whenever you want to change. And I am always down for Mexican food. I think I have tequila and mixer. We can make margaritas before the food gets here."

"Margaritas sound amazing," I sigh, happily. I feel... content? Safe? I don't know. I can't place it, but it's something I haven't felt in a long time. "Why don't you show me around a little before we order food?"

Leading the way, I step over the threshold into the dining room. The open concept of having the two rooms connected feels so homey. It reminds me of movies and TV shows when the mom character is in the kitchen making dinner or cookies for her kids, talking to them about their day while they sit at the dinner table doing their homework. Something I was always so envious of.

Pushing my mommy issues aside, I make my way to the floor-to-ceiling French doors overlooking a fenced-in patio and a huge yard. Swooping in beside me, Chase opens the door that I'm not standing in front of, holding it open for me to walk out ahead of him.

"Chase, this is gorgeous," I gasp as I step onto the blue stone patio.

He doesn't say a word as I run my hands over the four oversized wicker chairs sitting in front of a built-in stone fireplace. Weaving in between two of the chairs, pausing to admire the small cedar table sitting in the center of the chairs, I take it all in. Sitting on the table are navy blue coasters that match the cushions on the chairs, a citronella candle, and a small box of matches.

"Your dad made me that table as a housewarming gift," he says breaking the silence. "I would have invited you to the housewarming party, but I figured you wouldn't come unless Noah was with you and I -"

"I know," I sigh, not needing him to finish his sentence.

He didn't want Noah here, in his home. Which I completely understand. Chase had tried to be nice to him in the beginning, even going so far as inviting him to the annual Labor Day weekend camping trip all the guys take. After being looked down on and treated like they were less than him, all the guys stopped trying to be nice. Every time Noah decided to grace us with his presence, it ended in a fight between him and myself because he couldn't get his head of his ass for more than five minutes to be a decent human being.

Regret floods me when I think about how much I've missed out on because Noah didn't want me hanging out with Chase. We still saw each other all the time within our circle of friends and every Sunday dinner at Nonna and Nonno's. Because, you know, Chase didn't mind my big, loud, obnoxious family. I never ignored him, but I pushed him away little by little. Our daily texts became weekly, then they only came when something specifically worthy of telling each other happened.

Eventually, I started making excuses to not go to brunch on Saturdays at his mom's, something I had been doing since high school. I let Noah's insecurity dictate my friendship because I thought I was respecting our relationship and I hated myself for it.

As if he's reading my thoughts, Chase steps forward, bending his knees so we're eye level and says, "Stop. Whatever is going through that pretty little head of yours? Just stop. It's fine, okay? We're good."

"How?" I ask. "How do you not hate me right now? I did everything I made you promise me you would never do. You are my best friend, and I pushed you and our friendship aside for him. For that piece of shit."

Rolling my eyes, I'm annoyed with myself. It was my choice to even slightly alter my friendship because of a guy. I *could* have told Noah to fuck off. I *should* have stood up for our friendship and what Chase means to me. I always swore I would never become "that" girl and, low and behold, I did just that. I became *that girl*.

"You're being dramatic. First of all, Noah is a fucking idiot. He didn't like me because he knew I could see right through his bullshit. Why do you think even when he did make an appearance he never hung around me, Tuck, Kenny, Travis, or your brother? We all knew it, Hol. But you're so damn stubborn that talking to you about it would have made it worse," Chase says, before placing his beer on the stone wall behind him. "And, I could never hate you. I didn't like that I couldn't call you up and ask if you wanted to grab a cheeseburger or a beer, but you were never not there when I needed you. No phone call or text ever went unanswered. Don't beat yourself up over this."

"Speaking of cheeseburgers, that little set up you have over there is pretty bad ass," pointing out the grilling island, I change the subject, hoping to lighten the mood.

Walking over, I pretend to admire the grill sitting in the same gray stone as the fireplace. A stainless-steel refrigerator is built into the stone below a black granite counter. Matching the fridge is the grill's access door and a sink with a faucet. A wooden handled grilling set hangs from little hooks on the side of the mini-fridge. I hadn't come over here with the intent on being impressed, but sure enough, here I stand, impressed.

"Well, how about our next friend date, I'll make cheeseburgers?" he grins as he looks up to the clear sky. "You know, we can eat out here tonight and have a fire before the movie, if you want."

"That sounds amazing and so do friend dates. I'm in."

"Just tell me when, Hollis. I'll take you out on," pausing as if he's contemplating whether or not to finish his statement, "a date, anytime."

CHAPTER SIX

CHASE

TWO ORDERS of guacamole and chips, chicken chimichangas, beef enchiladas, espinaca dip, both steak and fish tacos, veggie tamales, pineapple sopapillas, churros, and two slices of flan cover every inch of the patio table.

"Wow, Chase. I don't know if you ordered enough," Hollis teases, trying to find a spot to put the plates and silverware she has in her arms.

"Hey, how about you shut it?" I shoot back, sticking my tongue out at her. "I didn't know what you wanted Miss 'I don't care, just nothing with refried beans.'"

Tipping the last of my beer back with ease, I toss it overhand into the trash barrel approximately six feet from us. A breath of relief leaves me as the glass bottle clinks, hitting something inside of the barrel. A loud cheer and applause from Hollis catch my attention, and I laugh as she brings her fist to her mouth, using it as a pretend microphone.

"Ladies and Gents, Abbott Hills High School football legend, two-time Super Bowl winner, and my best friend, Chase "Mack Daddy" Merrimack, just sank the winning basket and the crowd goes wild. *Clearly* someone missed his calling as a basketball player."

"*Clearly* someone missed her calling as a sportscaster," playful sarcasm dripped from my weak attempt at a comeback. "Maybe you should talk to your boss about taking over the sports segment of the show."

Despite a playful shove and a dramatic eye roll, the genuine smile on Hollis's face is one I haven't seen in a long time. Her calm, carefree, playful demeanor since we walked through the door of my house is the Hollis I grew up with, the one I haven't seen in a while. I hate that it took her walking in on Noah cheating on her to get her here tonight, but I would be lying if I said I wasn't glad she was back.

I would never tell her. Laying guilt on her wouldn't help anything, but the truth was, I did miss her while she was with Noah. I didn't lie when I told her I understood it, because I did. But I sure as fuck didn't like it. I know that life happens, and all good things must come to an end, like our reign as partners in crime. But in the back of my mind, I knew they wouldn't last. I knew that he was a douche. I knew that she was better than him. And she knows and believes that she's worth more than being the girl in the background. And that's all she would ever be with him, background.

Noah might have weaseled his way into her life, but he never got all of her. If she had let him in all the way, I would have walked away. I would have stepped back and let her have her happiness. She deserved it. But while we weren't constants in each other's lives the last two years, she still came to me when she really needed someone...when she felt she couldn't do it on her own. It was never Noah. It has always been, and still is, me.

Over the next forty-five minutes, we stuff our faces with plates full of Mexican food, effortlessly playing catch up on everything. We talk about my family and hers. I tell her about the team I put together this year. It's still crazy to me that I'm the head coach of the school that started my football career.

I was so pissed when I found out my mom was making me move back to New Hampshire. But if it wasn't for being in Abbott Hills and the Capparelli boys convincing their uncle—the head coach—to give me a shot when two of the starting players got injured mid-season sophomore year, I would have continued to be some punk ass. Just like everything else in my life, it all comes back to Hollis or her family, in one way or another.

After talking her ear off about the stats of a bunch of kids she's never met, I catch myself, realizing this is probably what it's been like with Noah for two years. Every time I was around the dude, it became a pissing match about money and status. She engages with everything I say, but I can tell she's bursting at the seams, trying not to be rude, but waiting, hoping, I'll ask her about her job. So, I do.

And man, am I glad I did. Her face lights up like she was just told she was getting a free puppy. She talks about the morning show first. She repeats my thoughts about coaching by saying that it's crazy to her that she's one of the voices everyone listens to on the way to work and school. She is a small-town celebrity just being a Capparelli, but when she started as a paid intern at 93.6 – The Ranch, Southern New Hampshire's country radio station the summer in between her junior and senior year of college, she almost instantly became a regional sensation.

Like everything else, when Hollis shows up, she gets everyone to notice her. Never with the intent to draw attention to herself, but the world can't help but notice her shine. I've read the story—more like stalked—from her tab on the radio station's website so many times, I could recite it in my sleep.

Showing up for her first day in a Beastie Boys t-shirt, Hollis grabbed the attention of Max Mariano, one of the morning show hosts. Not knowing Hollis was in the sound booth dropping off coffee, he was talking about how it was summer break, the new interns were there, and how the kids of today treated good music like a fashion trend.

"One of the girls here, is 21, 22 maybe…wearing a Beastie Boys t-shirt, interning here at a country music station. Just because it's on sale at Target doesn't mean you should buy it, kids."

Anyone else would have been embarrassed, but Hollis took it as an invitation. She cleared her throat and started dropping album names, songs, and even rapped a few lines. After laughing, Max apologized on the air and told Hollis that when she graduated, he would make sure she had a permanent job at the station if she wanted one. And he held true to his word.

After graduation, she moved back home and started working as a full-time promo girl for the station. About a year into Hollis working there, Casey Quinn, the other half of the morning show went on maternity leave for three months. The station offered the open seat to Hollis temporarily, but when Casey decided not to come back to the morning show after all, Hollis became a permanent fixture of the station's morning show.

Over the last few years, she's become such a staple of the station. Her voice is heard on thousands of radios every morning. Her social media alone is a testament of the region's love for her. Her Facebook is capped out at 5,000 friends and her Instagram has 23,000 followers. Not that I check her stuff often though.

She tells me about a few upcoming concerts she gets to go to for work. And though she's constantly rubbing elbows with some of the biggest names in country music, she lights up the most when she starts telling me about her Saturday night acoustic gig at her grandparents' restaurant.

It was supposed to be a one-time thing about a year ago. If

Hollis doesn't have an event for the station, she works in the second-floor lounge as a server and second bartender on Friday nights with her cousin Ellis. The lounge is always packed and the bar is always full when Hollis and Ellis are working together. They're both gorgeous and have the best personalities, especially when together.

Hollis had stopped by the restaurant to grab something to eat because she didn't feel like cooking one Saturday and she overheard her uncle, the manager, freaking out because the lounge musician called out five minutes before he was scheduled to be there. I knew she was doing Saturday night shows, but I never knew the story of how they came to be. And I hadn't gone. Not once. Even though I wanted to. Assuming me being there would cause her to catch some shit from Noah, instead I made sure to support her in other ways, like commenting excessively when Ellis went live on Capparelli & Co.'s Facebook page during Hollis's performances.

Though, come to think of it, I don't think I've ever seen any pictures or mention of Noah being there ever. That bastard. After that realization, I hear myself telling her that I "think I'm going to catch her acoustic show tomorrow night."

I would have sold my soul to the devil if it meant I would get to see the smile that came from making that promise. At this point, both of us have stopped reaching for more food, so I stand up and begin to stack the black Styrofoam take-out boxes. Hollis follows suit, standing and attempting to help, but I tell her to sit and relax. That crazy girl thinks I forgot what day it is. Like I'm going to let her clean up. It was hard enough convincing her to let me pay for dinner.

"It's your first time here, so you're a guest tonight. Next time you come, I'll let you clean up everything and I'll just sit here. But tonight, you just sit there, looking pretty."

"Fiiiiiiine."

With an eyeroll, she redirects her hand to grab the still half full pitcher of strawberry margarita. Refilling her glass, she happily sighs before sliding off her shoes and socks and sitting back down on the cushioned wicker loveseat. Seeing her so content gives me a weird satisfaction I've never felt before.

That is, until I can feel her eyes following my every move. Any other girl, I would try to use that to my advantage. I can almost guarantee any girl would end up in my bed, not sleeping in the guest room two doors over. But if anything is going to happen with Hollis, it won't be tonight and it won't be a rebound fuck.

Instead of harping on the fact she is currently like a moth to the flame, I choose to use this as an opportunity to remind myself that I had my shot. So many fucking times.

Everyone knew Hollis had a thing for me. It was the worst kept secret between our friends and families. Though, I don't even know if it could even be considered a secret. She never told anyone, I don't think, but we didn't do a very good job of hiding the fact that we were more than just the best friends we claimed to be. Not to downplay our friendship, because, we were—we are—best friends. She is my favorite person on this Earth. But when Davis sat me down our junior year of high school to not give me the "stay away from my sister" speech that everyone else got, but to tell me that if I "ever broke her heart, he'd break my face," I realized things were different with us. And not just for me and her, but for everyone around us.

I was sixteen years old when Hurricane Hollis came barreling into my life. The mindset of not being ready for any kind of serious commitment with the backlash of hurting her stopped me from pursuing anything with her in high school. It wasn't until college when I really understood how badly I screwed up by not stepping up and being the guy that she wanted me to be for her as teenagers.

When Hollis started asking me for advice about a few of the guys she was dating, I knew I had lost my chance. And I felt jealousy for the first time when she called me drunk, crying, eventually spilling that she'd had sex with the guy she was "kind of seeing." I knew I was in over my head when I instantly hated a guy I'd never met. Some asshole named Luke. No last name. No backstory aside from the fact they met in English class and he took her out for sushi for their first date. I drove from Boston to Rhode Island at two in the morning just to make sure she was okay.

"Just Luke" was a dick. For no reason, other than he got that part of Hollis no one else ever would. But it was too late to say anything at that point. We were living in two different worlds, two states away from each other. And now she's here, chugging strawberry margaritas on my patio because her fiancé cheated on her. The one constant in all of this was that I was — I am — her safe place. And while I love being able to be that guy for her, there will always be a small part of me that wished it was more.

My internal pity party for one is interrupted by the sound of my phone ringing in my pocket. Dipping into the house with the last armful of take-out containers, I roll my eyes. That ringtone means it can be only one person on the other line and I'm honestly surprised it took as long as it has for me to get this call.

"Hello, Mother," I chuckle, knowing damn well why she's calling. "Yes, Hollis is here. And you can tell Zia, Aunt Grace, Ellis, and Cole that she's okay."

"What?!" The voice on the other end gasps in a poor attempt of astonishment when she realizes I'm onto her. "Can't a mother call her favorite oldest son, on a Friday night, just to say hello? But since you mentioned it, is she really okay?"

"I think she will be," I tell her, not wanting to give her too much information. I love my mom, and I know she's calling because she's genuinely concerned, but it's just not my story to tell.

Over the years, Hollis became the daughter she never had. It was no surprise to wake up on a Saturday morning and see Hollis in the kitchen, helping my mom cook breakfast when we were growing up. In fact, I would be lying if I said I wasn't disappointed on the Saturdays I woke up and she wasn't there. Hollis became just as much a part of my small family as I became a part of her big, crazy one.

As if she understands what I'm not saying, without skipping a beat my mom comes back with, "Well, why don't you see if she wants to come to breakfast tomorrow? I can run to the farmer's market on Main Street and get fresh blueberries for pancakes in the morning."

Chuckling, I put the last take-out container in the fridge and make my way up to my bedroom. Mischa Merrimack is playing dirty right now. That evil genius knows her blueberry pancakes are Hollis's favorite. As we're talking, I make my way upstairs, only staying in my bedroom long enough to grab a medium sized gift bag off my dresser and two hoodies from my closet.

Apparently, the "okay, I will" in response to inviting Hollis over for breakfast isn't a good enough answer for my mom, the impatience obvious in her voice when she says, "Well, I mean, if she's there, just ask her right now, Chase Matthew."

It only takes me a minute to jog back down the flight of stairs and through the first floor. Purposely, I wait until I open the door to roll my eyes and say, "Alright, alright. I will ask her right now, Mother."

Hollis's eyes light up and instantly an ear to ear grin slides across her face at the mention of my mom. The adoration has always been mutual.

"Hol, Mom wants to know if you want to go over to her house for breakfast tomorrow. She said to tell you she'll make blueberry pancakes," I very loudly say, before covering the mouth piece with my hand and whisper, "You can say no."

"As if I could pass up Momma Merrimack's blueberry

pancakes. Tell her I'll be there, with or without you," she winks at me. Or well, tries to, after finishing off the last of her margarita. She closes her left eye for thirty seconds, scrunching her now rosy cheek while her body shakes with laughter. Pink cheeks only mean one thing. Hollis Capparelli is tipsy and well on her way to drunk.

"We'll be there, Mom," I tell my mother, grinning and nodding when Hollis giggles at the extra emphasis I intentionally put on 'we.' "I need to go though, okay? I'm being rude to Hollis."

My mom and I exchange a quick exchange of "I love yous" before we hang up, and I slide my phone back into the pocket of my basketball shorts.

"I haven't been to your mom's in..." she trails off as if she's trying to figure out when she was last at my childhood home. Dread fills her eyes when she realizes how long it's been.

"A year. Since Tucker's graduation," I finish for her, knowing saying it is too much for her right now. "Don't feel obligated to go to brunch. I know I kind of put you on the spot. I can bring you home in the morning before I head over there."

"Ha!" She scoffs. "You're out of your mind if you think I'm going to pass on your mom's blueberry pancakes."

Remembering the bag in my left hand, I hand it to her. Her puzzled expression indicates exactly what I assumed. She thought I forgot her birthday.

"I know today's been a little crazy, but don't think I forgot it's your birthday too, Hurricane."

Bending down, I place my lips on the top of her head, staying a few seconds longer than I probably should have. The coconut scent of her shampoo infiltrates my nostrils, the scent of her lingering as I lift her legs—which are stretched out on the wicker loveseat—and place them back down on my lap as I take the empty space beside her. I could have taken any of the three other open seats on the patio, but I just can't seem to get close enough to her tonight.

Every crinkle of the gold tissue paper as she slowly pulls out a sealed envelope and a black square jewelry box feels like pins and needles in my stomach. Second guessing my gift choice, I worry that maybe I did too much. Maybe I presumed this would be a good idea.

"Chase!" she gasps before lowering her voice to a whisper. "What is this?!"

"Just open it, woman."

Placing the box on her lap, she carefully tears the seal of the envelope and pulls out the card. A silver tiara is the only thing on the outside of the card. She opens the card and immediately a small manila envelope falls from the inside. Catching it between her fingers, she opens the smaller envelope containing the gift card for "The Sound Garden." Handwritten on the card is the package the receptionist had easily talked me into. Twenty-five hours of studio time with an in-studio sound engineer.

There are pools of water building up in her eyes, as she looks over the inscription written inside her birthday card. I'd been planning on giving it to her Sunday at her family dinner, so I had kept it simple.

"Go chase your dreams.
Happy birthday, Hurricane.
- C"

CHAPTER SEVEN

HOLLIS

GENTLE SHAKING on my arm wakes me from the best night of sleep I've had in, hell, probably ever. Swatting the hand doing the shaking, I flip onto my stomach and bury my face in the fluffy white pillow. Right now, I'm not even sure how I got here. Everything after opening Chase's present is a scattered blur of moments.

If I was anywhere else, I would panic, worrying about any bad decisions I could have made while being under the influence of an entire pitcher of margaritas. But I wasn't just anywhere. I was at Chase's. I know I'm safe.

Despite my still closed eyes, the longer I lay there, the more I wake up and begin to piece together last night. My head had started to feel heavy and I remember being dizzy, so I had laid my head down in Chase's lap. The last thing I can picture was him playing with my hair. I must have fallen asleep outside by the fire. I know I didn't walk up here, so Chase must have carried me up. Per usual, there's Chase to pick up the pieces when I become a mess. God knows I earned my "Hurricane Hollis" nickname.

Thankfully, other than the possibility of snoring or drooling in his lap, both of which I'm sure I've already done at some point in the past, I don't think I could done anything embarrassing. Unless I said something. The possibility that I could have spilled my heart out, admitting more than I should have, courtesy of some liquid courage is pretty high though. I don't even know how I'll be able to face…

Chase. He's here. Feeling his presence in the room sends my stomach in knots and somehow, calms me simultaneously. It's the most contradicting feeling. After mumbling something that was meant to be, "So comfy, go away," the soft fleece of the blanket covering me slides down my legs as if it's being pulled from me. Goose bumps cover my bare legs the moment they're exposed to the cool air.

Where the fuck are my pants?! The realization that I'm also wearing one of Chase's t-shirts hits me like a ton of bricks. I don't know if it's the hangover or my nerves, but suddenly I feel like I could throw up. The tight, bright red boy shorts hugging my ass are all that separates my naked butt from Chase's eyes.

In a panic, I reach behind me hoping to grab the blanket back. With no luck, I blindly stretch my arm, reaching over to the side of the bed that the blanket slid off. Instead of fleece though, I grab a handful of Chase. And, when I say Chase, I mean, Little Chase. Which is not actually little. So far from little.

Any normal person would let go the instant they realize they're holding onto their best friend's penis. But, me? Oh, no. I panic and freeze.

I. FUCKING. FREEZE.

With my hand on his dick. For a good, solid minute. I just lay there, face down in the pillow with my hand stuck in place. When I feel it twitch and harden, my brain suddenly starts working again. If my life was a cartoon, a big light bulb would have popped over my head when the brilliant idea to let go of his damn penis finally comes to me. Letting go like I am dropping a hot potato, I bring my hand up to cover my face as I turn to look at Chase. A hot flush fills my cheeks and I'm sure it's a thousand different shades of red when I finally get the nerve to peek up at him.

He's in only loose gray sweatpants. Opening my mouth to apologize turns into me losing words and sitting up silently gawking. What the fuck is with me and suddenly becoming tongue-tied these last twenty-four hours? If you asked me right now, I wouldn't be even able to tell you what animal he has tattooed on his chest. Despite it being the exact same lion that I have tattooed on my shoulder. You know, the tattoos we got together on my eighteenth birthday.

Because right now, I'm stuck on his V line. I don't know what it's really called. It's the abdominal lines leading to well, lower areas…But if you ask any girl what a guy's V is, she'll be able to tell you. Chase has one. And it's fucking beautiful.

Holy fuck. I need to put my hair up. It's not just my face anymore. The whole room must have risen fifty degrees in temperature in the last five minutes. Suddenly, it's hot as Hades in here. Or Hell, because Hades is a person and Hell is the place. And, oh my God, I can't even fucking think straight right now.

It's the hangover. It's gotta be the hangover. It's the frickin' hangover, I repeat to myself over and over again. Maybe if I keep lying to myself, I'll be forced to believe it. Because there's no way it's the guy I've known since I was a fifteen, my best friend on this entire Earth, and his stupid, perfect V line.

Instead of the mortified look I was anticipating, plastered across Chase's face is an amused, shit-eating grin. He looks so proud of himself. Cocky bastard. If I didn't know better, I'd think he could have read my thoughts while I was frozen there. Great. Just what he needs. Another female to stroke his already inflated ego.

It's not necessarily all his fault though. Since we were

teenagers, girls—and now women—have thrown themselves at him, eagerly. He's gorgeous. He's charming and funny. He's athletic. And kind, and genuine, and loyal…shit. I'm supposed to be apologizing for grabbing his dick, not making a list of what makes him worth throwing myself at…I mean, women. How I can understand why women in general throw themselves at Chase. Because, I wouldn't do that. Nope.

Shit. What was I doing? Oh, yeah. Apology.

"I'm wicked sorry," I start to ramble. "I was reaching for the blanket. I didn't think you were so close. I didn't think. I just, I, Jesus Christ, Chase, I didn't mean…"

He cuts me off with wave, like it was nothing, like it was no big deal I just had my hand cupping his not-so-little Little Chase. "I hate to be the guy that wakes Sleeping Beauty, but if you want to stop at your house to shower and grab clean clothes, we should probably head out soon."

Head out? To where? What did I agree to?

My confusion must be written all over my face because he immediately follows with, "After a few margaritas, you agreed to going to my mom's for breakfast this morning. If you're not up to it though, I can just bring you home. I'll tell my mom that you weren't feeling well. Though I have it on good authority she got up early to get fresh blueberries to make a certain someone —"

"Sold," I laugh. "All you had to do was say, 'Mom's making blueberry pancakes,' and I would have been up and ready to go."

"But, then we would have skipped over the last ten minutes," Chase smirks, looking down at me one more time before tossing the gray fleece blanket back to me.

"Yeah, how do we go about a redo?" I ask, shaking my head, covering my legs. "I would like to take it back, please and thanks."

"Oh, no, Hurricane. There's no take backs here."

CHAPTER EIGHT

STILL HOLLIS

IT TAKES me an hour to shower, throw my hair in a side braid, and pack everything I could possibly need for tonight. I don't think we'll be at Chase's mom's all day, but just in case I don't have time to come back here before my gig at Cap & Co. tonight, I would rather have everything together. Nothing is more frustrating to me than feeling like I don't have everything under control.

The second I lose control, I feel overwhelming anxiety. Anxiety is no good anytime, but especially before singing in front of a hundred or so people. Especially today, considering one of the few things I do remember before my tequila induced nap on Chase's lap is that he said he was coming tonight. And despite my weak attempt to rationalize the flutters in my stomach as part of a hangover, I know the quickly multiplying butterflies have nothing to do with alcohol consumption, but everything to do with where I am about to have breakfast and who will be at my gig later this evening.

It's not like this is the first time I'm meeting Chase's family. Hell, Mischa Merrimack is more of a mother to me than my own is. Despite not having stepped foot in her home in just about a year, I got a birthday text bright and early and got tagged in a super sweet Facebook post made by Mischa yesterday. Of course, there wasn't a peep from Linda, the woman not so affectionately known as the egg donor.

Not that I honestly expected anything though. Linda, my mother, was the woman who abandoned her husband and two fifteen-year-old children while they were at work and school. The only reason we knew it was done purposely was the signed divorce papers left on the kitchen table. The last any of us had heard, Linda was in California somewhere, fresh off her fourth divorce…and that was a year ago, so who knows where she is now.

Not only did she abandon her children and her marriage, but the rest of her family as well. My Gramma, Grampa, and my Aunt Grace—who I was named after—all still live in Abbott Hills and have never stopped being a part of our lives. My dad made sure of it, inviting them to every birthday and school event growing up…and they never missed one. Over time, they became just as much a part of the Capparelli family as me or anyone else. While my grandparents didn't often make Sunday dinners, my Aunt Grace was there every week. There wasn't a Christmas or Thanksgiving without a place set for my grandparents too.

The guilt of making a choice to step back from Chase and our friendship that coincided with a trickle down to Mischa, Tucker, and Lola makes the butterflies in my stomach do a set of pissed off back-flips. Mischa was under no obligation to continuously have open arms when it comes to me. I wasn't her daughter or one of her boys' girlfriends. I was just the sassy, smart-mouthed girl that had spent summers in her pool and played football with the all the boys on her street.

After hearing that Chase, Tucker, and Mischa were planning on spending their first Thanksgiving back in Abbott Hills home alone, I took it upon myself to invite them to Nonna and

Nonno's for dinner. Mischa had argued with me at first, not wanting to inconvenience anyone, but after my grandmother made a point to stop by her house and invite her personally, Mischa couldn't say no. The three, now four, Merrimacks have come to every holiday and family event since, because that's what they became…family.

All it took was a bottle, or three, of red wine for Mischa, my Zia Kat, and my Aunt Grace to become insta-bff's. Chase knew my Uncle Leo from football, but my dad took him and Tucker under their wings that day too. And then when Lola Grace Merrimack was born five years ago, she became the first "great grandchild" of the Cappa-O'Brien-Mack family. I would have been Auntie Hollis regardless—Tucker is the little brother I never had—but when both my Gramma O'Brien and Nonna "adopted" her as their own, it lead my Grampa O'Brien and Nonno, and everyone else to follow suit.

The baby shower we threw could have given some celebrities a run for their money. Tucker and Mila wanted for nothing, we made sure of that. And when Mila "pulled a Linda" and took off right after Lola was born, it was Mischa and my family that pulled together to figure out schedules, ensuring that Tucker didn't have to stop going to school and work. And that Lola didn't end up in daycare as a newborn.

For the first four years of her life, Lola spent alternating mornings with my Nonna and my Gramma O'Brien until I picked her up after my shift at the radio station. Afternoons were spent with me until Mischa or Tucker picked her up at night. I think that the day she started pre-school a year ago was just as hard on Nonna, Gramma, and I as it was on Tuck.

I saw Tucker often in passing because he works for my father, but if we weren't at Capparelli & Co. or Nonna's house for Sunday dinner, a holiday, or someone's birthday, I didn't see him or Lola. I made sure to have an Easter basket and I, of course, went nuts for her birthday and Christmas, but I was officially the worst God-mother, ever.

I needed to make it up to her…to all of them. It seems I'll be doing a lot of that, making things up to people. I need to make last night up to Davis. My brother kicked an entire house full of people out to come make sure I was okay. I need to make up for two years of being a shitty best friend to Chase. And, I need to make sure my pseudo-Mom, little brother, and niece don't think I forgot about them.

I'd take breakfast today to figure out what Lola was into these days and I'd go from there. But first, I needed to figure out what I'm wearing. Grabbing my phone, I check the weather app. Sunny with a high of 62 degrees today. After three weeks straight of ninety plus temperatures, this random cool mid-September day feels like a real New England Fall day – my favorite kind of weather.

Taking Chase's black Adidas athletic shorts, gray Abbott Hills Football hoodie, and his signature black snapback into consideration, I choose a pair of solid black leggings and a ribbed black cotton tank-top. After toying with a few sweatshirt choices, I settle on an oversized slouchy, maroon one that says "Hogwarts Alumni," fully anticipating getting teased immediately.

Giving my face a quick once over in the vanity, I take a seat. There's no way I'm showing up looking like Casper the Freckled and Hungover Ghost. The combination of a late night and dehydration left some hefty bags under my eyes as evidence. Not wanting to make it blatantly obvious that I am trying, I use concealer, but skip the contouring step, applying only a light layer of mineral foundation. A swipe of black mascara on my lashes and a once over with lip balm and I think I'm ready to go. Or, well, as ready as I'll ever be.

Any additional make-up I could possibly need for tonight goes into my black make-up bag. Bending down to grab the leather guitar case sitting in the corner of the room, I use my free hand to pick up the bag I put together just in case I don't get back here tonight before it was time to head to the restaurant.

With one last, final inspection in the mirror before I leave my room, I head back up to the first floor where Chase opted to wait. Just as I'm about to step foot into the kitchen, I hear him say "Hey, it's Chase." Knowing that is not how he would greet my dad if he came home stops me in my place. He must be on the phone. To give him his space—and partially because I'm nosy—I hang back, allowing him to finish his phone conversation without me in the room with him.

"So, something came up and uh, I'm not going to be able to meet up with you for dinner tonight. With school and football, I just don't know when I'll have free time in the next few months. I'm sorry, Amanda. I just didn't want to blow you off and, yeah. Well, this is awkward now, so, I'm going to hang up now. Bye."

Covering my mouth to stifle the laughter, I stay put until I gain my composure. I have no clue who "Amanda" is, but I'm assuming they had a dinner date. The last thing, whoever she is, is probably expecting on a Saturday morning is to wake up to that voicemail. A tinge of guilt hits me when I realize the reason he called off his plans is because he said he would come to my gig tonight. Maybe I should tell him I don't really expect him to come tonight. And I don't. Expect him to be there, that is. I just really want him to be.

Deciding that admitting I was eavesdropping probably isn't the best way to start rebuilding our friendship, I stroll into the kitchen as casually as possible. Chase turns from washing his coffee cup in the sink as I come into the room. I swear, the two of us got a weak ass version of Spiderman's senses. Instead of badass web-slinging and being able to sense danger, we can just feel each other's presence and have an odd sense of intuition when there is something going on with the other one.

"So, um, is this outfit okay for breakfast with the Merrimacks?" I ask, pointing over my outfit.

"Hol, I'd think you were beautiful in a potato sack," he laughs. "But yes, you look fine. Ready for blueberry pancakes? Mom's already texted me three times to make sure you were still coming."

I don't answer him right away though because I'm slightly stuck on the fact he just called me "beautiful." I can't even remember the last time someone told me I was beautiful. I couldn't tell you the last time Noah complimented my looks, and despite the space between us, Chase still made comments about me being his "pretty best friend" on just about every picture of me posted on social media. But this just felt, I don't know...different.

"I grabbed everything I would need for tonight, just in case we end up over there for a while and I don't have time to come back here before five," I tell him, feeling the need to explain the bag and my guitar, though he didn't even ask.

"Alright. Do you want to drive over there together? Since I'm going tonight, we can head to Cap & Co after? I mean, if you really wanted you could even crash at my house again tonight..."

He watches me cautiously, like he's trying to see if he crossed a line suggesting I spend the night at his house again. I know that by my own doing he doesn't understand, that even with work and family, how lonely the last year or so has been. I'm going to soak up any time that he's willing to give me.

If anything, the last day has shown me that I was going to be just fine without Noah and that I had missed Chase...so fucking much.

CHAPTER NINE

CHASE

THE STRONG, unmistakable combination of bacon and my mom's famous blueberry pancakes hits me the moment we step into my childhood home. Hollis hadn't said a single word or even so much as looked over at me on the ten-minute drive over to my mother's house. At first, I thought it might be the aftermath of yesterday finally hitting her. It wasn't until she let out a reluctant sigh and gave me a sad, fake reassuring smile when I came around and opened her door in the driveway did I realize what it really was.

She was nervous. A year ago, she would have gone barreling right in without me, not giving it a second thought. But today, she stops in the small square tiled entryway that allows you to go straight up the stairs to the second floor or to the right into the living room. Resisting the urge to wrap her in my arms and reassure her this will always be her home as much as it will be mine, I offer my arm instead.

Obvious relief washes over her as she allows me to lead us right into the living room. Instead of walking us straight into the kitchen, I let her take it all in. As her eyes dart from wall to wall, it's as if she's savoring the moment. Slowly capturing the newly filled walls that house photographs of my family she's probably only seen on Facebook.

The longer we stay put, the more relaxed she becomes as the tension slowly leaves her body. Purposely I stop, pausing longer than necessary at the distressed blue credenza that sits under the flat screen TV on the wall. A studio picture of me and Hollis from our high school senior prom sits next to a photograph of me, her, and Lola from Lola's first birthday party. Hollis may not have been in this house physically in the last year, but she's always been here.

"I asked my mom to put it away," I tell her honestly. "But she wasn't having it. Stop beating yourself up, Hollis. You've always had a place here, you always will."

"Yeah, what he said," chimes a voice in the empty door frame that separates this room from the kitchen. We can't take another step before Hollis is pulled from my arm and into a bear hug by my younger brother. Though there's a year difference between us, Tuck and I could easily pass as twins. We look more alike than Davis and Hollis do, that's for damn sure. We even have the same heart shaped birthmark on our right shoulder blades.

"Chase told us not to bring it up, but I'm glad you figured out that Noah is an A-S-S H-O-L-E," Tucker lowers his voice as he spells out "asshole". "You are way better than him and we missed you."

Of course, he did exactly what I very specifically asked him not to do. Hollis wasn't talking about it. She hadn't mentioned Noah once since the ride over to my house last night, and I wasn't going to push the topic either. She would when she was ready. Knowing that she would start to shut everyone out if everyone was in her face about it is exactly why I asked Tuck and my mom not to say anything. The entire reason we avoided her family's restaurant last night was because she wasn't ready to talk about it, and there's Tucker opening his big mouth.

Opening my mouth to call him out on being a dick, I only stop myself when I hear the pitter patter of little feet running down the staircase behind us. Tucker lets go of Hollis, anticipating the arrival of the littlest love of all our lives. And just as expected, right into Hollis's arms goes the four-foot wonder known to the rest of the world as Lola Grace Merrimack.

Her squeals of excitement fill the room when Hollis spins around with her. My heart starts to race, and I feel myself melting as Hollis adoringly tells my niece — our God-child — that her purple and gold polka-dotted dress is the prettiest dress she's ever seen before gently putting her back onto the carpet.

"What am I? Chopped liver?" I ask, scrunching down to get on Lola's level. "Lola Grace with the pretty face, get over here and give your Uncle Chase some of that!"

Winking at Hollis, her shoulders relax and the first smile that isn't forced spreads across her glossy lips. Any remaining anxiousness leaves her body when I use the same endearment Hollis's own uncle and God-father, Leo, uses with her.

Tucker and his ex, Mila, had chosen to keep Lola's name a secret while Mila was pregnant. So much so that not even my mom knew, and Tucker told my mom everything. As soon as Mila went into active labor, the waiting room of The Birth Place at Abbott Hills Catholic Medical Center was full of Hollis's family anxiously awaiting the arrival of the first great-grandchild. We were, we are, lucky to have Hollis and her family. My mom is an angel. An actual saint, but my dad? Well, he was good for saying he'd be there and then never showing up. He missed birthdays, graduations, every single football game I played in high school and college. It wasn't until I was drafted into the NFL did he seem to give a shit about me and Tuck. And then, once I retired, he went back to Washington and I haven't heard from him since.

It didn't matter that Tucker wasn't their grandchild by

blood. When a Capparelli and O'Brien woman loves you, they love you wholeheartedly. Hollis was the perfect combination of both of her grandmothers' hearts. She, with her Nonna and Gramma O'Brien, made sure that Tucker needed absolutely nothing for his baby girl…going as far as making Tucker a "dad bag" for the hospital.

Mila, Lola's biological mother, had no one the entire pregnancy. Her family had all but disowned her when she told them she was pregnant. The only daughter of Texas oil tycoons, Lorna and Buck Rogers, Mila and Tucker met while Mila and her family were in New Hampshire for summer vacation.

Their story is pretty cliché. Girl meets boy in a bar. Girl lies to boy about being on birth control, thinking "it can't happen to me." Girl gets pregnant. Girl's rich, snotty family doesn't accept the fact she got knocked up by a blue-collared guy from New Hampshire. To this day, we're still not sure why Mila came back to tell Tucker she was pregnant…or why she begged Tucker to let her stay with him, feeding him the sob story that her family told her she could either have an abortion or she would get cut off from her family's money. She showed up on Tucker's doorstep with ultrasound pictures and that was all it took.

Despite some serious reservations the rest of us held about the paternity of the baby, Tucker asked us to accept that the baby was his, so we did. And not just me and my mom, but Hollis and her entire family, too. Tucker is the least sentimental human being I know, and even he had water pooled in his eyes when Nonna cried at the news of her first "great grandbaby."

And, when Mila was asked about her family, the brutal honesty of the situation baffled every one of Hollis's family members. Each of them promising Mila that the baby would want for nothing. The Capparellis may not be oil tycoons from Texas, but for as long as I've known them, they've basically owned Abbott Hills, New Hampshire.

Hollis's Nonno and Nonna, Giuseppe and Camilla

Capparelli, opened the first and to this day, only Italian restaurant this town ever saw in 1977—ten years after they came to America with their three young children. Hollis's Uncle Leo is the oldest. Choosing to follow in his parents' footsteps, he's been the general manager of Capparelli & Co for as long as I've been in Abbott Hills. He was also the high school football coach and the reason I got to chase my dream of playing professionally.

He ran his football team like the restaurant, with high expectations. His wife Emily started off as a server as she was putting herself through college. Now they work hand in hand. Emily handling most of the behind the scenes things, like the books, and Leo handling all the day-to-day things inside the restaurant. Their son, Leo Jr. or LJ, is the front of the house manager, handling all the servers and bartenders on the floor.

Hollis and Davis's dad, Lorenzo, is in the middle. He owns the largest carpentry business in Abbott Hills. If you needed anything fixed or built, from coffee tables to home renovations, Lorenzo is the one you wanted to call. He's always booked out months in advance. Even with three crews—Tucker being the lead of one of them—they're never out of work.

Hollis's aunt, "Zia Kat", is the baby of the three. Katerina took the money her parents gave her for college and went to cosmetology school. At twenty, she opened Capparelli Cuts & Curls, a two-floor hair salon on Main Street, a block away from her parents' restaurant. Her last name is now Lindsey because she's married to Martin Lindsey, Lorenzo's best friend and the third project manager of Capparelli Construction & Carpentry. Ellis and Travis are their twins, who, by sheer luck are just two weeks younger than Davis and Hollis. Their daughter Elisabeth is seven years younger than the twins. Kat's also my mom's best friend and boss. Though, if you knew them, you'd say the term "boss" should be used lightly. Co-conspirators is more like it.

As a teenager, I was secretly a little jealous of the Capparelli kids. The six of them have been as thick as thieves the entire time I've known them and when we were younger, they wanted for nothing. From the outside, they look like spoiled, rich kids. It didn't take me long to realize they had the world handed to them on shiny silver platters because their grandparents and parents work their asses off for those platters and made damn sure the kids knew the value of hard work too.

And the Capparelli work ethic crossed down into the next generation. As soon as they turned sixteen, they were expected to help with one of the family businesses. Hollis, Ellis, LJ, and Ellis' little sister, Elisabeth all worked and still work at Capparelli & Co. Hell, even Tucker and I worked there as table bussers and dishwashers during the summer as kids.

LJ is the only one there full-time today. Elisabeth hosts on Thursdays, Fridays, and Saturdays while going to college full-time. Ellis bartends on Friday and Saturday nights, and works full-time at the salon. Hollis serves at Cap & Co. on Friday nights and does the music gig on Saturdays if it doesn't interfere with her radio schedule. Travis and Davis opted to work for Lorenzo until they joined the Marines right out of high school. When they both came home for good, they studied for six months, took the test, and both became Abbott Hills police officers.

And as hard as they all work, they love harder. Every single one of them would give the shirt off their back, without hesitation, if you needed it. That sneaky bitch Tucker got pregnant caught on to that real quick. Mila played every single one of them. Pretending to get close to Hollis, Ellis, and Elisabeth. She had my mom wrapped around her finger. Everyone was bending over backwards for a girl they barely knew because she was carrying Tucker's baby.

Until seven months into the pregnancy, when she tried to convince Tucker to put the baby up for adoption. At this point, my brother had seen the ultra-sounds, heard her heartbeat, and he wanted no part of giving her away. But Mila had decided she wanted no part of being a mother. Somehow, Camilla Capparelli worked her magic and convinced Mila to stay in New Hampshire until the baby was born. She denies it, but I don't doubt there was money involved.

When Lola was born, Mila wouldn't even look at her. She wanted no part in naming her and she refused to hold her. Even requesting that Tucker be moved to a different room with the baby immediately following delivery so she didn't have to see her. She arranged to have a lawyer come to the hospital and signed over her parental rights less than twenty-four hours after her daughter entered the world. And as soon as she was cleared to leave the hospital, she got into a taxi and we presume went back to Texas. None of us have heard from her since.

But those aren't the moments I remember about the first few days my niece came into the world. I remember my mom coming out of the room, with happy tears streaming down her face to let Hollis and I know Tucker wanted to see us first. I remember Hollis grabbing my hand and squeezing it so tightly that it hurt. And when I stuck my head into the hospital room, still filled with doctors and nurses, I remember seeing my little brother, sitting in a chair in the corner, filled with a pride and a love like I've never seen before. I remember my heart bursting when Hollis started crying as Tucker reluctantly handed Lola over and the way my heart skipped a beat when it was my turn to hold her.

But what stands out for me the most is when Hollis finally passed Lola to me for the first time and asked, "So, what is this beautiful little girl's name, Tuck?"

When my brother said, "Lola Grace, after the best big sister I could have asked for and hopefully, Lola's God-mother." Hollis clutched her heart, and then cried in my brother's arms as he asked me to be Lola's God-father.

It was a moment I will never forget for as long as I live. So,

right now, as Hollis clutches her heart and lets her bottom lip
out as Lola leaps into my arms, the memory of the very first day
Lola came into our lives plays back in my head. God, I've
shared so much of my life with Hollis. Come to think of it, every
moment that's mattered since she came into my life, she's been
there.

"Gram made boo berry pancakes because they're Zia's
favwit," Lola tells me, snapping me out of my thoughts and
bringing me back to the living room.

"They *are* my favorite," Hollis pipes in from behind us as my
mom walks into the room. "But you didn't have to make
anything special for me, Misch."

"Did you really think I would let a birthday weekend go by
without making my first favorite girl some blueberry pancakes?"
she shushes Hollis as she opens her arms and envelops Hollis
similar to the way her granddaughter did just a few minutes ago.
"Why don't you ladies go take a seat at table? Lola, you can
show Zia your beautiful drawings! Chase, you get that birthday
girl a coffee, and Tuck, come give me a hand with the eggs."

Knowing my mother is not one to argue with, I carry Lola
into the kitchen, placing her down at the round pine table in the
kitchen.

"Oh! I learneded a new song at school estaday," Lola
exclaims, when I put her down. "Wanna hear it?"

"You better believe it," I tell her, as she climbs onto one of
the four curved double seater benches that sit around the table.
For a long time, it was just Tucker, me, and my mom. She hated
the thought of a square or rectangular table, because, we "were
a team." There was no head. Like King Arthur and his knights,
we all had an equal spot at the table. No one was better than the
other.

The fourth bench sat empty most nights, until Hollis came
along. Then it became her spot. And when Lola was big enough

to sit out of her high chair, it was hers too. Today the two of them would share it and I can't tell who is happier about it, Hollis or Lola.

The smile on Hollis's face as she slides onto the bench with Lola is genuine, her eyes full of pure adoration. Any sadness or anguish she felt before walking into the kitchen has left her and that makes me more content than it probably should. With her attention captivated by the blonde haired, blue-eyed little lady to the right of her, I take the moment to soak her in. She's so fucking beautiful. It never ceases to amaze me how easily she manages to take my breath away. Even in leggings and a sweatshirt, there's something about Hollis that puts her above everyone else.

A sharp jab to my ribs from my brother tells me I've been caught staring. Shrugging, I don't take my eyes off her. Fixated completely as she offers my niece a spoon and shows her how to use it as a microphone. Clearing her throat, Lola begins belting a very off-key, but adorable rendition of the Star Spangled Banner. When she seems to lose the lyrics halfway, Hollis doesn't hesitate to help guide her along. When they're finished, they get a loud round of applause from me, Tucker, and my mom.

"You know," Mom starts as she drops a cup of chocolate milk in front of Lola. "Your Zia is a singer. That's her job, LoLo! She even sang the National Anthem when your Uncle Chase played for The Patriots!"

"I want to be singer when I grow up," Lola tells Hollis, matter of factly.

"Hmmm…"

I can practically see the wheels spinning in Hollis's head as she plays out something in her mind. Just as I'm about to ask her what's going through her head, she looks at Tucker and says, "So, I start my set at 6PM tonight. You should bring the little lady down. You should all come. It's family friendly till about nine."

"That sounds like a great idea," Mom answers for everyone. "And when it's time to go, LoLo can just come home and have a sleepover at Gram's, so her daddy can spend some time with his friends."

"Ma," Tucker begins to argue, "You already do so much. You don't need to –"

"You need time just to be Tucker," Mom cuts him off. "I'm old. I won't last past nine anyway. Lola can sleep over and you can have a night out."

"And drinks are on me, little brother," I tell him, knowing he's internally rationalizing being able to spend money on himself when there are all of the day-to-day expenses that come with being a single parent.

"And I'm buying dinner," Hollis pipes in, sneaking me a slight smile as if she understands exactly why I offered to take care of Tuck's drinks tonight. "Oh! Also! If you're okay with it, I can pull a few strings and get this little lady up on stage with me."

"You would do that?" Tucker asks, joining me in complete in awe of the woman sitting next to his daughter.

As if she's baffled by the question, Hollis brushes it off like it's no big deal. Her heart is so big for being kept inside all five-foot nothing of her little body. She has no idea what she's doing right now, the impact she's making on Tuck and Lola. To most people, it'll just be a song a little girl is singing with Hollis, but to Lola, it'll mean everything. Which means it'll mean everything to Tucker, too.

It's going to be a good night. I can feel it. Running with that thought, I pull out my phone and send out a group text to Davis, Travis, Ellis, Kinley, Hollis's dad, and her aunts, Kat and Grace.

Hol doesn't know I'm doing this, so, shhh. I know we'll all do the fam birthday thing tomorrow, but Tuck, Mom, Lo, and I will be at Cap & Co. for her gig tonight. She could use the love, can everyone come through?

Ellis is the first to text back, almost instantly, saying that she'll be there because she's bartending. Kinley comes back right after saying she and Davis are in and that she'll go by early and decorate. Followed by everyone else confirming that they would be there. Tonight, Hollis Capparelli is going to remember what it feels like when people show up and make you a priority.

CHAPTER TEN

HOLLIS

"YOU KNOW, after getting ready in that bathroom of yours, I may come over to get ready for work every Saturday."

Looking up from his phone Chase lets out a long breath, his eyes wide as I walk toward the couch. "I knew you looked good from your Instagram post, but damn, Hol. I'm going to get in so many fights tonight."

After spending most of the morning and a good portion of the early afternoon at their mom's, Tucker, Chase and I had said our goodbyes around two. Tucker had gone home to change and pack a bag to give to Mischa, who insisted Lola was fine at her house until it was time to go to Capparelli & Co.

Chase asked me no less than ten times if I was sure I wanted to spend the night again. When I said "yes" all ten times, he drove us back to his house to get ready for the night. Normally, I just keep it simple on Saturday nights with my standard ripped jeans, a band tee, a pair of Chucks and if my hair isn't up by the time I leave the house, it's tossed in a messy bun right before my set. Maybe it was because I needed the extra self-confidence boost after the break-up, or now knowing Lola was coming and expected to see a rock star, but tonight, "normal" just wasn't enough.

When we had stopped at my house this morning, I went to the back of the closet and grabbed the black cocktail dress I had originally planned on wearing to dinner with Noah last night. The low scoop neck of the sleeveless dress is covered by a lace bodice to the waist which leads to the short, flared skirt. Paired with nude wedges, it would have made the perfect date night outfit. But since it's not date night, I switched the wedges for knee high black boots. The few inches of my legs exposed in between the dress and my boots are covered by the black nylons I fought with for fifteen minutes. Feeling a bit like a little girl in tights, I wasn't sure if I would make it out of the house with them on, but given Chase's reaction, they might stay.

My favorite black lace choker and a fitted leather jacket finish off the rock star ensemble.

I even took the time to do my hair. Blonde, loose, bouncy curls fall right below my shoulders. A smoky eye, heavy winged black eyeliner, a metric shit ton of mascara, bright red lipstick, and a spritz of my perfume tie the whole comeback edition of myself together.

Before coming down, I had dropped my bag with my dirty clothes and make-up in the spare room I had spent the night in last night, assuming it would be my digs for tonight as well. Noticing the oval, full-length standing mirror in the corner of the room, I did something I never thought I'd do. After taking a few mirror shots of my outfit, I posted them in a collage on the radio station's, Capparelli & Co's, and all my social media accounts. Backspacing and rewriting it three times before adding the caption,

We gonna party like it's my birthday!

Come on down to Capparelli & Co. to celebrate my

28th birthday weekend! I'll be playing 6-9PM and then sticking around for @karaokewithcole after. @theelliscamilla is the mixologist on duty tonight! Come sip & sing with us!

Chase had not only liked the post on my Instagram mere seconds after I hit share, but left a comment with three fire emojis followed by a "my best friend is so damn hot" comment underneath. Which, funny enough, is the exact same thing I'm thinking right now with *my* best friend in front of me.

There's something to be said about a man in a crisp, clean white t-shirt and faded blue jeans. It's a classic, and easily my favorite look on a guy. And it just so happens to be what Chase is wearing right now. His facial hair is freshly trimmed down and shaped, and his signature black "snapback" hat is nowhere to found. His hair, faded from the bottom to the inch or so of hair on the top of his head, is styled with product. Something I can't even remember the last time I've seen.

"You're going to get into a fight?! Pfffft." I scoff, while making it incredibly obvious that I am looking him up and down. "I'm going to be on the clock tonight. I'm going to have to put Ellis on Chase Watch. Come karaoke time, the Cap & Co. Cougars are going to be all over you."

When he gets over to where I'm standing, he offers his arm to me and says, "I'll just let 'em know, I'm already taking a girl home tonight," he winks. "Shall we, Ms. Capparelli?"

With the lump in my throat, all I can do is nod. Linking my arm in his, I lean into him, using his body to steady my shaking legs.

I'm in trouble. So much fucking trouble.

———

CAPPARELLI & Co. is always busiest on Saturday nights, so it doesn't surprise me to see a packed parking lot. Chase pulls around the back of the building to the employee parking, stopping to let me out at curb, before driving all the way to the back of the lot. There's no question in my mind I'm the last one in tonight. The downstairs restaurant area is on a wait and the pub upstairs is standing room only.

Grabbing Chase's hand once he makes his way up to the sidewalk, we get a few funny looks as I pull him past the group of people waiting to be sat at a table. Coasting past the host stand, I wave to my cousin Elisabeth, who is taking a name for a call-ahead on the phone. The smell of roasted tomatoes lingers in the air as we make our way up the stairs that lead to the lounge.

Stepping over the threshold into the lounge is almost like going into a completely different restaurant. While the main seating area on the first floor is bright and cozy—very much like my Nonna's home kitchen— the lounge area is swanky and dark. The lounge is full of high top tables and a full bar with sixteen available spots. On Saturday nights, like tonight, there is a bartender, a bar back, and two lounge servers until nine. When the restaurant below closes at ten, a bouncer stands at the door to come into the restaurant and you are only allowed to come up to the lounge if you are over eighteen. Anyone over 21 gets a wristband that changes in color every weekend.

"Hey, El," I shout to the blue haired bartender, who is also my cousin, as I pass by with Chase still closely behind me.

"Oh! Hol…and Chase! You're here! There's a table up front reserved for you," she winks, waving back before turning to the cooler behind her, grabbing a bottle of water for me. "Heads up!"

Pulling her hand back, she tosses it to me, but before it reaches me, it's intercepted by someone sitting at the high-top table full of men in business suits in front of us. My stomach flips when I see Noah fucking McDougal reaching out to me, the plastic bottle of water gripped tightly within his hand. Snatching it from him, I walk past the table without a word, knowing full well after last night that if I don't get Chase away from him, Noah will intentionally say something to rile him up.

If Ellis, Elisabeth, or LJ here knew he was here, I would have gotten a text or a call as a warning. He hasn't been here since the charity event, the very first night I met him. What the fuck is he doing here?

Walking over to a table, full of black balloons and hot pink plates, I see a setting with my name on it. A classy, simple silver tiara sits above the plate. Leaning my guitar case on the ground next to us, Chase bends down to take the tiara and carefully places it on my head.

"You just look right here, Birthday Princess Hurricane," he says pointing up to his own eyes. "I got you, okay? He's not going to ruin this night for you."

"Okay," I nod, thankful he's being calm and collective. The alternative would be so much worse. The only thing keeping me calm is knowing that right now, Noah is on my turf. This is my element. These are my people.

"I need to go find LJ," I tell Chase. "Let them know I'm here and that he's here, too. Just in case."

Rolling my eyes, I turn for only a moment to put my guitar on the stage, whipping around at the sound of my brother's voice behind me. When I turned only a few seconds ago, it had been Chase and I, but now the rectangular table was surrounded by my brother, my cousin Travis, Kinley, my brother's best friend Kenny, Tucker, Mischa, and Lola. All of them holding gift bags, flowers, or more balloons.

"What is all this?" I ask, scooping down to pick up Lola, forgetting I was on a mission to find LJ.

"Well, you said it was a birthday celebration on your Instagram," Kinley shrugged, handing me a pink and black striped gift bag with her right hand. Her left hand is shoved into the pocket of the jean jacket she's wearing over a knee-length navy blue, sunflower-covered sundress.

"Yeah, okay, I posted that ten minutes before we left Chase's house," I laugh awkwardly, feeling uncomfortable with all the attention suddenly being placed on me. I know, it makes no sense, even to me. I spend hours every weekday with thousands of people listening to my voice and I'm about to sing in front of a hundred or so, but the seven sets of eyes intently staring at me makes me jittery.

"Well, Chase may have gotten the ball rolling early this morning," my Aunt Grace adds, joining our group.

Chase's expression turns to worry immediately, like he's nervous I'm going to get mad at him for setting this up. With Lola still in my arms I stand on my tiptoes, placing a quick kiss on his cheek.

"You know you're kind of incredible, Chase Matthew," I whisper, taken back a bit by my now racing heart thanks to the lack of space between us.

Quickly pulling back, I place the gift bag Kinley handed to me on the table, telling everyone that I am so excited to see them, but that I still need to find LJ. Lola and I weave in and out of the groups of people beginning to fill the lounge. It isn't until I get to the stairs to go back to the first floor that I don't feel Chase's connection to me anymore.

Making sure to wave or smile at all the Saturday night regulars as we go, I find my cousin and, I guess, boss, downstairs by the host stand. Growing up, Capparelli & Co. was run mainly my grandparents and my uncle. I loved that it was our family's, but my dad never worked there growing up. It wasn't until I was sixteen and I started working as a host did I truly begin to appreciate everything that goes into Capparelli & Co. daily.

Everything is made fresh and from scratch, including the pasta. My grandfather, at eighty-five years old, still grows the tomatoes used for the sauce in his garden at his home. Now that I'm older, I appreciate how much of a family affair it is, especially on Saturday nights now that Ellis, Elisabeth, and LJ work here too. Even though they've long since "retired," Nonna and Nonno still spend every Saturday here, visiting with the guests, running food, or helping in the kitchen. My Uncle Leo is now the general manager and can't be found in the same place twice all night. His son, LJ, is the front of house manager and is all over the floor talking to guests and helping the servers until he comes up to the lounge when the restaurant closes.

Even though he's technically the manager of both floors during a shift, it's rare to see him up in the lounge before nine while Ellis is working. Even though she's technically a Lindsey, to say that Ellis is the loudest and bluntest out of all Capparelli cousins would be the understatement of the century.

As if on cue, the lounge will slowly start to fill as the restaurant empties out for the night. But right now, and for the next hour or so, it's the busiest down on the main floor. Family dinners, date nights…people will wait for hours to get a table at Capparelli & Co. When I spot LJ right away at the host stand, I find myself letting out a breath of relief. That was easier than I thought it would be.

In black trousers and a deep red button-down dress shirt, LJ stands out from all the other employees in all black. Hanging back for a minute, Lola and I stop, as he breezes right through the guests queued up to get their name on the wait list. A big, genuine smile sits on his face as he greets every single person that steps foot into the waiting area.

Lola's eyes are big with fascination as she simultaneously watches him take names in between sending the other hostess to seat guests as tables pop up as open and clean on the point of service computer on the wall next to them, while my other cousin Elisabeth answers the non-stop ringing of the phone. When there's finally a pause in guests coming through the door, he places his pen in the breast pocket of his shirt, then lets Elisabeth and the other hostess know he'll be right back.

"Well, well, well," he says making a beeline to the spot Lola and I have been hanging back, waiting. "No one told me the prettiest five-year-old in all of Abbott Hills would be gracing us with her presence tonight!"

Lola unwraps her arms from around my neck and jump leaps into LJ's arms. She has every one of the Capparelli men completely wrapped around her little finger. Earlier, I had offered to pay for Tucker and Lola's dinner, but it was more likely that my uncle and grandfather would get wind Lola was here and the table upstairs would slowly fill with all her favorite foods.

"Rumor has it, she's going to sing a song or two with me tonight, too," I wink, before walking back to the staircase that leads to the lounge.

"Oh, Ellis will have to call down before that happens," he calls ahead to me as we take the steps back to the second floor. "I'm sure Elisabeth, Dad, Nonna, and Nonno want to see too. You think Tuck would care if we go live on Facebook?"

"I don't know," I shrug. "Ask him. The whole gang's here tonight."

Pointing toward the table in the front, I'm surprised to see that my Zia Kat and Uncle Martin, my dad, and a woman I've never met are now sitting at the table with everyone else.

"Holy shh," LJ starts when we get to the table, before remembering who is in his arms. "uuugar cookies. You got your dad to come out?"

"I had nothing to do with it," I shrug, pointing to Chase, who half waves in response. "This is all Chase."

Smiling appreciatively, my older cousin nods to Chase before leaning down to me, "I know it's too soon, but I can't wait till *that* happens."

"Hey, LJ," Kinley stands up, sliding into the one-armed side hug, before getting right to the point. "I'm sure Hol didn't say anything, but Noah's here."

Scanning the room, my cousin finds the table—now covered in pilsner glasses of beer and food—that Noah and three other men, also in business suits, are sitting at. Pulling the small, black walkie talkie clipped to the pocket of his slacks to his mouth, he gives Harold, the head of security, a heads up.

Right now, Harold is probably downstairs eating dinner, before it gets busy up here. Within the next hour, he'd be up here keeping an eye on things until nine and then making sure no one under twenty-one came in after ten thirty when we reopened the doors after dinner.

After relaying a quick physical description of Noah and confirming the table he is sitting at over the walkie-talkie, LJ exchanges a glance and a nod with Davis and Travis. None of them have to say a damn thing out loud for it to be obvious to everyone around us exactly what just happened. LJ just gave them permission to "handle it," if necessary. Not that Noah stands a chance of even getting close to me with Chase watching me like a hawk. He might be giving me space physically, but I can't move throughout the lounge without feeling Chase's eyes following me.

I don't know what Noah thinks he's going to accomplish by coming here tonight, and honestly, I really don't care to find out, I just want him to leave. The sooner he leaves, the sooner everyone else stops stressing about him being here. All I want, other than Noah to leave, is to sing and have a good night with my friends and family. We spend every Sunday all together, but it's been a long time since my dad or my brother have come out to see me play.

I purposely avoided coming here last night, because I didn't want to be baby-sat. By now, everyone knows about Noah and I breaking up. So all eyes are on me, waiting for my reaction to him being here, ready for me to break down believing that I'm more emotionally invested at this point than I am. To explain that I'm not would end up with me having to tell everyone how the last few months have sucked, and then comes the need to know every little minor detail that led up to last night. I love my family, and I know it's all out of love and concern, but I'm fine.

Eager to get away from the silent pity party for Hollis, I nod and follow when Kinley asks me if I want to go with her to the bathroom. As soon as I close the outer door of the three-stalled ladies' room, she looks down as if she's checking to see that we're alone and frantically turns to me blurting out, "I didn't need to pee. I need to talk to you."

"What's up? Are you okay?" I ask, instantly being the worried, concerned one out of the two of us.

"Yes, no, yes," she rambles nervously, slowly pulling her left hand out of her pocket, the glimmer of a diamond on her ring finger catches my eye. "I know it's the worst timing ever. And I don't want you to think we're being insensitive. But, I didn't have food poisoning last night. I've been getting sick a lot lately. And, my period's late. So, I took a test and…"

"Oh my God," I squeal excitedly, with wide eyes. "Are you?"

"I am," she nods, a forced grin spreading across her face as she looks at me anticipating my reaction. "We're not really telling anyone until I'm three months, just to be safe. But my mom and dad know, Cole knows, your dad knows, and now, you. I wanted to especially tell you because this all happened because I started freaking out about my mother and being pregnant without being married, because you know we need to handle all that now. I mean, look at all we had to do to spin Cole dropping out of the pre-law program so the press didn't think she was flunking out or a just giving up…"

Kinley's mom, Helen, has only been worried about keeping up appearances in the last few years. After being the Mayor of Abbott Hills for five years, she got heavily involved in the

Obama presidential campaigns. In 2016, she ran for Senate in New Hampshire and won. Helen is a good mom, and she loves her daughters, but now they all think about what other people will say when they make decisions. All it takes is one asshole reporter to spin the truth, and they're suddenly tabloid material.

"Yeah, I get that, but I'm confused," I tell her. "And don't get me wrong, I'm so excited and glad I know. But why are you making such a big deal out of me knowing before everyone else?"

"I am so excited too. Like, so excited. But last night I started stressing out about telling my mom. Davis told me that it's not how he planned it, but he's been waiting to do it for a little while…and then he got a jewelry box out of the top shelf of the linen closet, got on one knee and well, you know, proposed. And of course I said yes, but I don't want you to think after yesterday that we're being insensitive. I don't want you to be mad at your brother. I need you to know the why."

"Oh my God. Breathe, Kin," I laugh when I realize exactly why she was just making a big deal out of my birthday. "That's why you made a big deal out of celebrating my birthday tonight, isn't it? I don't doubt Chase got everyone together, but the table, the balloons, the gifts…that has you written all over it."

"I mean…"

"Kinley," I put my hands around each of her upper arms. "I would be happy for you and Davis any day, every day. No matter what is going on with me, Davis is my brother and you've been one of my closest friends, foreveeeeer. It's okay. It's more than okay. Come on, let's go tell everybody you're getting married."

Wrapping me in a hug, she whispers a thank you before letting go and making her way back out the door. She pauses with a hand on the door handle to turn to me and say, "Oh, and don't think I haven't noticed Chase with his eyes glued to you since I got here."

No one can argue her commitment. The girl is newly pregnant and engaged and she's still here, reaching for the idea of Chase and I being together.

"It's because Noah's here," I shrug, brushing it off. After last night, Chase isn't going to let Noah get anywhere near me.

"You're as safe as you're ever going to be here tonight. Chase could leave right now and know nothing will happen to you with your dad, your cousins, your uncles, your brother, Tucker, and Kenny here," she shakes her head, smiling. "No. This isn't about Noah. This is about the fact that you look like a dang smoke show right now, Hol. I guarantee if we go out there right now and I ask him, Chase will tell you himself."

"You will do no such thing," I demand as my stomach flips at the thought of her calling out Chase in front of our friends and my family like that.

I don't doubt he would handle it just fine. He'd make a crack about how he has the prettiest best friend in the world. But the reality of it all is that Chase isn't looking at me in any way other than a "best friend" looking out for me because my ex is here.

And I kind of hate myself a little for being disappointed that it's not more.

CHAPTER ELEVEN

CHASE

HOW LONG DOES it take two women to go to the bathroom?

Never mind the fact that I've never understood why women need to flock together to go pee, Hollis and Kinley have been in that damn bathroom for over ten minutes. I know because I've been watching the door of the ladies' room since they went in, ready to jump up and handle it if Noah decides to try to catch her attention on the way back.

The unease as soon as she saw him was enough to tell me she wants nothing to do with him. I'll be damned if he gets even a minute of her time. He had his chance, for two entire years. That ship has sailed, and sunk, never to be seen again. And it was his own damn doing.

Ellis had been over once already to take down our drink orders. Despite the fact Harpoon Octoberfest was on tap, I had asked for a Cherry Coke. I won't be drinking until I know that bastard is gone. Mixing alcohol with the way Hollis looks and McDouchegal being present would not end pretty.

A combination of relief and panic washes over me when the wooden door of the bathroom begins to slowly open. Kinley steps out laughing mischievously, like she's got something up her sleeve. Right behind her, in her short black dress, comes Hollis, shaking her head at whatever scheme Kinley has cooked up. Moving just enough so Hollis is now completely in my view, Kinley smirks at me. Shit. Looks like someone's on to me.

After hugs and a few minutes of pestering from Kinley, Hollis opens the presents from everyone. After the final gift is opened and everyone is individually thanked with hugs and quick pecks on the cheek, she turns her attention to her dad and introduces herself to his date.

Erica, the middle-aged redhead, looks uneasy as Hollis begins rapid-firing questions about how they met, what she does for a living, where she lives, if she has any kids...All it takes is finding out she works at an animal shelter in the next town over for Erica to gain the warm, kind Hollis I love.

You know, in the best friend, I respect her kind of love. Strictly platonic. Which is why I'm "platonically" checking out her ass while she's bending over to talk to Lorenzo and Erica.

After a few minutes of small talk, she stands up straight and nods to her brother. Doing the Capparelli telepathy twin thing, they say whatever they need to say without needing to speak a single word.

"I guess that's my cue," Davis chuckles, standing up, clearly understanding his sister. Pushing his chair in, he follows Hollis to the small wooden stage that their grandfather built by hand when he found out that Hollis's Saturday night performance would become a regular one.

Loud cheers and a "Free Bird!" come from somewhere in the back, making Hollis laugh as soon as she steps foot onto the stage. It's no secret that people come on Saturday nights just to see her sing and have Ellis serve them drinks. Despite having spent a good chunk of last night telling her that it was okay she stepped back from our friendship when she was with Noah, the fact that I didn't do my part as her friend and hadn't been to see her yet is sitting heavy right now. This isn't just her job or some side hobby for her. Music is like air to Hollis. She needs it to breathe.

Despite not having a clue what they're saying, the lighthearted banter between Hollis and Davis is hilarious to watch. They go back and forth, laughing as Hollis takes her guitar out of the case. After giving her brother a playful shove, she hands him her guitar and hops up onto the red cushioned stool that sits in the middle of the stage.

Resting the bottom of her black boots on the metal bar, she moves the microphone stand up and down until it gets to a position she's happy with. While she does that, Davis plugs her guitar into a special acoustic amp to the left of her.

"Davis is up there, she's okay," Kinley leans in, from the left of me, nodding up toward the stage. "Chase, she's fine."

"Oh, no, I know," I answer, quickly - too quickly, so I add, "It's not that at all."

Good one, Merrimack. Because that should help the situation. Kinley might think she's sneaky about it, but she's not very good at hiding that she's been pushing for me and Hollis to get together since high school. She's never said anything directly to me, or even so much as hinted about it until tonight, but I've heard a few comments that have been made when the girls think I'm out of earshot. "Soul mates" seem to be the words that get thrown around quite often.

"Yeah, that's what I thought."

Kinley smiles smugly to herself a bit, before turning her attention back to the stage. Sighing, knowing that arguing with Kinley is pointless, I turn my attention back to the stage too... but mostly to Hollis, who is completely oblivious to the fact that every eye in this lounge is now fixated on her. Nodding to Davis, he hands her the oak colored guitar and slides the microphone out of the plastic clips that keep it in place on the stand.

"Check, one, two," Davis's voice fills the room, "Alright, I know normally LJ introduces this little lady, but lucky for me, I get the privilege of doing so tonight. Without further ado, here to serenade you all for a couple hours is one of the most talented women I know. Please join me in welcoming the baddest of all bad asses, my twin sister, Hollis Capparelli!"

After placing the microphone back in its spot, Davis and Hollis exchange the Capparelli cheek to cheek kisses and he steps off the stage. Applause and cheers fill the lounge and a few exclamations of "I love you, Hollis" come from our table.

Once the room quiets down, I use my opportunity to make sure I'm heard by yelling out, "Rock me like a hurricane, Hollis!" It's cheesy as fuck, but every person sitting at our table laughs, especially when Hollis's cheeks turn a rosy shade of pink.

"Well, then…that being said, how's everyone doing tonight?" she opens with, running her fingers over the guitar strings, strumming a little as she messes with the little knobs at the top. Our table takes the bait and starts cheering again, this time, gaining a few hollers from Ellis at the bar too.

"My fan club, everyone," she grins, pointing to all of us, winking at Lola. "Well, hi! I see a lot of familiar faces in the crowd tonight, but just in case you're new, like my brother said, I'm Hollis Capparelli and I'll be singing you a song or twelve tonight. The first hour I kind of wing it, let you all eat your dinner, drink some beers, but hour two, is when the fun starts. That's when I start taking requests."

Her stage presence is so commanding. From the moment she steps on the stage, she's demanding everyone's complete attention. As she warmly smiles at a few tables next to ours, I know Noah isn't the only guy I'm going to have to watch out for tonight. It baffles me that she has no idea just how captivating she is.

As if she needed any help having multiple men fall in love

with her tonight, she continues by saying, "So, as of last night, I am newly single for the first time in two years…"

With that, comes whistles, an "I can change that" from a guy at the bar, and a whole chorus of cheers. Groaning to myself, Tucker looks over and sighs. I know he's thinking exactly what I'm thinking —if we stick around after Hollis's set is done, there will be a slew of guys to keep an eye on.

"We're going to keep this PG, since it is a family restaurant and there are children present tonight, but long story short…"

She starts to sing the opening line of "I Will Survive" by Gloria Gaynor and silence fills the room just as quickly as the cheers did. For most of the first verse her eyes wander, but always linger a little longer when she reaches me. It isn't until the chorus that her eyes are transfixed behind us. Although I have a good idea, my suspicion is confirmed when I follow her gaze landing directly on Noah McDougal.

I don't think I've ever been prouder of her than right now in this moment. She's telling him to fuck off in the best way possible, in front of the best audience possible. And he takes note by flagging down the petite, blonde server walking around the lounge. As soon as she pulls a bill out of the black book in her hands, Noah hands her a small handful of cash before standing up and walking out of the lounge. The three men he's with all look confused by the abrupt walk-out, but follow him out to the exit.

Once I know Noah has left the room, I let out a breath and turn my attention back to Hollis, who is looking directly at me, as if she was waiting for me to turn around. So proud of herself, she's smiling ear-to-ear like a cat that caught a mouse.

With a final dramatic strum, she wraps up the first song and the room booms with a mixture of applause and cheering, especially from our table. Everyone knows why she picked that song, and who she was singing to. At this point, everyone also knows he walked out as he realized she was letting him know that she would be just fine without him. Once the applause lessens, she thanks everyone while she tweaks the knobs up at the top of the guitar again, tuning it to get the sound she wants.

"Before I get too far into this set, I want to bring up a guest-"

Hollis doesn't finish before Lola puts down the mozzarella stick she's eating and hops off Tucker's lap, skipping up to the stage. When she gets up to Hollis, she stands patiently as Hollis adjusts the microphone stand, lowering it in anticipation of the smaller person that is about to take her spot. Standing up with her guitar strapped over her shoulder, she helps Lola up onto the stool. Everyone at our table, including me, pulls out their phones, wanting to capture this forever. Leaning in to Lola, Hollis says something resulting in Lola quickly shaking her head side to side. Pondering for only a second, Hollis leans back in, this time getting two thumbs up and a big smile in response.

"My Zia and I would like to desdacate this next song to Uncle Chase."

I'm certain that her mispronunciation of "dedicate," pulls on every heartstring I have. That is, until Hollis and Lola begin to sing "Can't Help Falling In Love With You" a capella. Like in the movies, everyone pauses in place and freezes. As adorable as my niece is, I know it's the woman standing back behind her, easily belting out the song that I jokingly told her "would be our wedding song one day" when we were at a wedding of a mutual friend together a few years back.

Letting Lola have the microphone doesn't take away from the raw, breathtaking talent coming from Hol. There isn't a person in this room that isn't completely enamored with her. It is a moment that Hollis made for me in a memory that Lola would get to treasure for the rest of her life. Having every intention of recording the two of them, I still have my phone in my hand, but looking around, I see that plenty of people will capture it and decide to put it on the table instead. Soak it all in.

With Hollis guiding her, Lola starts the second verse of the song she's heard a thousand times over her lifetime. The strings of Hollis's guitar stay untouched until the third verse. Tucker gives me a hearty pat on the back from the chair next to me, his eyes glossy from the tears he's trying not to let slide down his cheeks right now. My mom and Hollis's aunts, on the other hand, make no effort to hide theirs, as tears stream down their faces faster than they can wipe them.

Only allowing myself a few seconds with my attention somewhere else, I look back just in time for them to get to the line in the song about being meant to be. When Hollis locks eyes with mine, any resolve I thought I had goes right out the fucking window. I've pushed them aside for years knowing I had lost my chance, but there's no way to ignore these feelings now.

It might not be tonight. Or tomorrow. Or the day after that. But I've never felt so certain that there would come a day Hollis Capparelli would be mine.

CHAPTER TWELVE

HOLLIS

IF YOU ASK me next week, I won't be able to tell you all the songs I sang tonight. But I will remember this night for the rest of my life. Being up on stage with my God-daughter, seeing the way her eyes lit up when I picked her up and put her on my stool will be forever embedded into my head and heart. And then, of course, there was the way Chase looked at me while I was singing. Everyone else in the room was watching Lola, but Chase's eyes never left me. It took everything in me not to walk off the stage and go kiss his stupid face after spending three whole minutes of him staring at me like I was Aphrodite in the flesh.

Originally, I had asked Lola if she wanted to sing a song from Moana, the newest Disney movie she is obsessed with. After spending most of the time I was getting ready at Chase's house listening to the soundtrack, I was sure that's what she would want to sing. Figuring it was a given that she would say yes, I was a little stumped when she shot it down. All it took was looking over at Chase, with those bright green eyes staring at me like I hung the moon, to know what song to sing.

But now that we're done, and Lola is back down at the table

sitting on Tucker's lap, I have no idea how I'm going to follow this up. Catching on to the fact my whole family came up to see Lola and is still sitting or standing around the table with Kinley and Davis, I have a brilliant, "light bulb above the head" idea.

"While all my family is up here, Davis and Kinley, will you please join me on the stage?"

Immediately, Kinley's cheeks turn a rosy red and Davis grins ear to ear, both presumably knowing *exactly* why I'm calling them up to the stage. Kinley had told me in the bathroom that she didn't want everyone to know that she was pregnant until she was three months along, but the only reason she wasn't telling anyone they were engaged was because everything happened between me and Noah just last night. While Chase and I were at his mom's house this morning, Kinley and Davis were at Kinley's parents' house, telling them and Kinley's sister Cole. This was followed by a visit to my dad's house to break the news to him.

Respecting her wishes and never wanting to take away their moment, I wouldn't announce the pregnancy, but I didn't want Kinley to feel like she had to sit with her left hand in her jacket pocket, torn between wanting to be excited for herself and Davis, and not hurting my feelings. Standing up first, Davis offers his hand to Kinley who doesn't hesitate to take it. Joining me on stage, Kinley leans in, and asks me if I'm sure. I answer her by waving my hand to the crowd. Taking a seat on the stool, I readjust the mic stand as I run through the possible songs I could play to commemorate their announcement.

"So," Davis starts, looking down and shuffling his feet before turning his attention back to the woman by his side. "I asked Kinley a question last…"

"We're getting married!" Kinley squeals excitedly, cutting him off while holding up her left hand.

Chuckling, Davis nods while the stage is immediately infiltrated by members of our family. The lounge is, once again, loud with applause and cheers. By now most of the crowd is Saturday night regulars. People who are here every Saturday, faithfully. People who know me and my family, at least at face value.

"This one's for my brother and my soon-to-be sister," I say into the microphone before I start a cover of "I'm Yours" by Jason Mraz, their song.

Bright bursts of light come rapidly as flashes from everyone's cameras take pictures. Watching everyone in front of me celebrating leaves me torn. Pushing a small ping of jealousy back down, I smile and find myself looking for Chase in the crowd. It's not that they're getting married. Anyone can get married. Fuck, I was planning to, and look at how Noah and I were together. It's what they have together. I'm jealous of their love. The closest thing I've ever had to something like that is what I have with Chase.

As much as I would love to envision the fairytale, happily ever after, I know I would never get that with him. It's been twelve years since he saved me, for the first time, in gym class. If something was going to happen between us, it would have by now. I just wish he would stop looking at me like I'm the only girl in the room. False hope is a dangerous thing.

Somehow, I manage to make it through the next few songs before I start taking requests. Fifty minutes and a dozen songs later, I announce that it's going to be "my last song and they better make it a good one." The lounge chatters for a minute, and then it all just stops when Chase stands up from the table full of our friends and family, beer in hand and says, "To Be With You."

Sneaky bastard. Choosing a song about waiting and wanting to be with someone. The song I used to sing to him all the time in high school when the crazy girls he used to mess around with were being, well, crazy, in the hopes that he'd take a hint. As I start singing the song made famous by Mr. Big, I realize just how dangerous false hope is.

I need to put the distance between us until my heart calms the fuck down. After being closed off for so long, my heart wasn't used to being used to feel things. If Noah and I had been happy and head over heels in love, and we just broke up unexpectedly, I would mark these down to rebound emotions. But Noah and I were over long before yesterday. It's as if my entire relationship was a dam, built by time and memories, keeping any feelings for Chase pushed way back. But now, that dam had been destroyed, and there was nothing stopping them from naturally flowing freely.

Accepting my feelings for him means learning how to deal with the fact that we will never be together, that he will never be mine. I did it once when we were kids and our friendship became better because of it. I don't know if I could do it again, and have our friendship survive this time.

Avoiding his eye contact, I look straight ahead to the back of the room. For the first time all night, my voice shakes, I stumble on a few notes, and I forget the lyrics to a song I've sung a thousand times. The last strum of my guitar doesn't come fast enough, and I find myself having to fight back the overwhelming tears trying their damnedest to break through when I say goodbye for the night.

"Thank you for joining me and my family in a few memorable moments tonight," I say, holding my water up for cheers as I force a smile, making sure to make eye contact with everyone but Chase. "If you are, or have someone with you under 18, it's time to cash out with your server and as always, I will be back to serenade you all next Saturday night. Cheers!"

Standing up, I turn the amp off and unplug my guitar. Dropping the cords into my guitar case, I remember I need to be lady-like in this dang dress. Bending at the knees, I place my guitar into the case, snapping it shut.

"I can't believe I forgot how amazing it is to be in a room when you sing."

"You're biased, best friend," I laugh nervously, shaking it off, hoping he can't read my thoughts and that he stays where he is.

"No. You're amazing," he says, repeating his sentiment, pointing to my guitar case. "Let me take that for you. I have strict instructions from Ellis to tell you that you need to go see her. I guess there's no one under 21 tonight, so she has something for you."

Capparelli & Co. has always closed at nine the six days a week it's open for as long as I can remember. Monday through Friday the doors open at four and close at nine. Saturdays are the busy days. Servers start coming in at eleven and we unlock the doors for guests at noon; it's the only day of the week the restaurant is open for lunch. And Sundays, unless we have a private event, the restaurant is always closed. My grandparents have always thought it was important for their employees to have at least one day off.

Even though at one point in the week we all tend to cross paths, Sundays are for our family. Everyone—including the Merrimacks—head to Nonna's around noon and we spend all day eating, drinking, and watching whatever sports game is on. It wasn't until LJ, Ellis, and I started working here and collectively came up with the idea to stay open later and turn the lounge into an "after hours" spot.

Abbott Hills isn't a big town. In fact, Capparelli and Co. is only one of three places open past ten at night in town. Between nine and ten, the restaurant closes its doors to allow the servers below to finish their shift and have any guest that isn't over twenty-one leave the second-floor lounge. It's normally an easy transition. Most of the locals understand, but sometimes there's one or two that don't think they should have to leave. When my uncle made his agreement with the town to keep the lounge open for bar hours, the deal was no one under eighteen after ten. After the first few times of Ellis having to deal with a few high school-aged douchebags, my uncle hired a security team to come on board after nine. They help with the nine o'clock transition, watching the door and making sure no one gets too crazy.

Usually on Saturday nights, I'm leaving with everyone under eighteen. Not that I ever have anything exciting to do, but I've never stayed for karaoke. Come to think of it, the last time I did karaoke was my 21st birthday...with Chase.

Thinking about the memory makes me smile. I was a broke college student, living two hours away from home in Rhode Island. My sorority sisters tried all day to convince me to go to a frat party, but I was in no mood to deal with a bunch of drunk, horny boys. It was a Saturday night. I could have gone home. My dad and Nonna all but begged me, but it wasn't the same without Davis. As an enlisted Marine, Davis didn't get the option of getting to come home for his birthday. So, despite being incredibly homesick, I felt guilty going home to be with our family when he couldn't. So I had stayed at school.

While the girls in the house were getting ready to go out, Chase texted me to wish me happy birthday with a follow up asking what I was up to. As soon as he found out I wasn't doing anything, he called me and told me he was on his way. Just like that. Going to Boston College on a full football scholarship, Chase was only about an hour from me in Providence. He rented a hotel room ten minutes from my sorority house for himself and showed up just a few minutes after the house emptied out.

I remember being slightly surprised he didn't ask me if I wanted to change out of the leggings, oversized Dropkick Murphys t-shirt, and flip-flops I was wearing before leaving. Luke, my on and off again, whatever he was at the time, would have never would have been okay with me leaving dressed like that or with a make-up free face, which I also had at the time.

"You never know who you may run into," he would say. Looking back, Luke and Noah probably could have given each other a run for their money with their pretentious asshole tendencies.

But Chase never said anything about my outfit, my hairstyle, or the lack of make-up on my face. Wanting to avoid anyone from my school, we went to this little hole-in-the-wall Chinese food restaurant the next town over. The drinks were strong and there just happened to be a karaoke contest that night. After splitting a Scorpion Bowl and drinking three Blue Hawaiians myself, Chase convinced me to enter. "To Be With You" won me a $100 gift card to the restaurant and $100 cash.

Chase had refused to take the gift card or the prize money at the end of the night for our tab, which was ninety-nine percent my drinks, because after splitting the Scorpion Bowl, Chase had switched over to ginger ale, straight up.

"What's got you all smiley, Cousin?"

Before I can answer, Ellis hands me a glass full of the same bright blue mixed drink I drank on my 21st birthday. The irony of the memory and this moment coinciding isn't lost on me as I reach for the pineapple and coconut infused rum drink.

"Before you even try to pay for it," she holds her hand up, stopping me as I reach for the cash I had shoved into the pocket of my jacket before leaving Chase's. "Uncle Leo said to tell you happy birthday and that drinks for the crew are on the house tonight."

In the entire time I've known my uncle, I've never known him to give anything away for free, even to family. He lives and breathes doing what is best for this restaurant. Which means no freebies for anyone—even for us. The confused look on my face must convey what I'm thinking because my cousin bursts out in a fit of laughter.

"Yeah, I know," she agrees. "I pretty much thought the same thing you do. But I'm not going to argue with him. Apparently, he brought a bunch of pizza up to the table too. I think it's the birthday-engagement combination."

"Uncle Leo's getting soft in his old age," I smirk, shrugging and pulling out money regardless of what she said, dropping a twenty on the bar. "Toss this in the tip bucket."

With my drink in hand, I make my way back to the decorated table in the front where my brother and our friends are sitting, eating pizza. The guys talk mostly about sports while Kinley and I talk about our plans for the annual Capparelli and Co. Halloween charity event that happens next month.

Sometime in that hour in between when my set ends and ten, Nicole "Cole" Christian comes strolling up the stairs, yelling a request for "strong, able-bodied men who want a round of drinks on her."

I don't know what the response is usually like for her, but this week, she lucked out. Chase, Tucker, Davis, Travis, and Kenny all jump up as soon as she steps foot over the threshold. Handing her keys to Kenny, she takes a seat next to Kinley.

"Normally there's only one or two guys willing to step up and it takes them twenty minutes to bring all my shit up. I could get used to this," she laughs, grabbing a slice of pizza while the fellas head down to bring up her equipment.

Cole's dad and Kinley's mom met while they were both going to a support group for people who have lost their spouses to cancer. Cole and Kinley were just toddlers and they don't remember life without each other. And although while growing up most of the drama in our little circle was started between the two of them, now they're inseparable. And if you ask them, they're not step-sisters, just sisters.

Before I took over Saturday nights, my uncle was working tirelessly to book bands to play live every weekend. I had suggested that Cole—who had just dropped out of law school on a whim and was starting out her karaoke business—and I take the night in shifts and it caught on quickly. Some people came just for my acoustic set, some people came just for karaoke, and others stayed the whole night.

When Chase and Tucker come back into the lounge, each holding one end of a folding table, Cole salutes us and hops up on the stage to direct them. After taking a small sip of my drink, I blindly reach for another slice of pizza. Startling me, Kinley bursts out laughing from her spot directly across from me. We're the only two sitting at the table right now, so I assume she got a text or something, because I know I didn't do anything funny.

"You two are ridiculous," she holds up her hand as I open my mouth to defend myself when I realize she's talking about Chase. "Save it. Chase can't move without you gawking at him like he's that pizza you're about to eat."

———

THE SMELL of coffee and maple bacon simultaneously infiltrate the barefoot beach dream nuptials of me and Chase, pulling me back to the real world. It's now Sunday morning. I sang, we drank, and I slept over at Chase's last night. Tucker had been so drunk that he ended up leaving his car at Capparelli & Co. and crashing in Chase's guest room, leaving me in a slight panic. Once Tucker started stumbling, Chase had pulled me aside, asking if I wanted to stay longer or if I would be okay with leaving earlier than planned.

Worrying about his brother, instead of taking Tucker home, he brought him to his house instead. I had every intention of asking him to bring me home after he dropped off Tuck, but Chase offered to make cheese fries and I don't have enough willpower to say no to cheese fries. After we split a heaping pile of fries, he offered to sleep on the couch, but I had shrugged it off. There was no reason we both couldn't sleep, fully-clothed, in the same bed.

Bracing myself for the oncoming heart palpitations, I roll over to face Chase only to find his half of the bed empty. The grumbles in my stomach motivate me to move toward the smell of breakfast. My plan to hijack the platter of bacon Chase is adding to is thwarted when I step into the threshold of the kitchen. The open concept of the kitchen and dining room allows me to see the dining room is full of brown and yellow balloons.

An enormous vase holding at least two dozen sunflowers sits in the middle of the table, a small silver box sits next to the flowers. I try to search for words, any words, but fall short. Luckily, it only takes Chase a second to notice me standing there, like a complete idiot, unable to speak.

"Well, good morning," Chase laughs, turning his back to me, adding in, "How'd you sleep?"

"Chase, what is all this?" I ask, ignoring his question.

When he turns back around, with a huge chocolate muffin that holds one lit candle, my legs begin to wobble, and I lose any will to demand an explanation. Blaming a non-existent hangover, I brace myself in the doorway, shifting all my bodyweight to the side closest to the archway.

"Make a wish, Hurricane," he leans in, his voice low as he holds the muffin close enough for me to blow out the candle.

My first instinct is to wish that this perfect weekend never had to end. It's funny how life happens just the way you need it to sometimes. If someone told me forty-eight hours ago when I was driving home from Boston that I would be ending the weekend feeling genuinely happy, in Chase's kitchen nevertheless, I would have laughed in their face.

"You know," Chase starts, chuckling to himself while he pours a cup of coffee. "I'm starting to think our friendship might be based on breakfast perks."

"One, I didn't know you were doing all of this," I wave my hands around the kitchen and dining room theatrically. "And that's rich, coming from the guy who notoriously says, given the chance, his last meal would be my chicken parm."

Hopping up onto one of the two cedar bar stools behind the breakfast bar that divides the open space between his kitchen and the dining room, I add, "It's your own fault you know. You invited me to your mom's. And here you are, cooking for me. All it would take is one bad batch of pancakes or some runny eggs, and I promise, I'll never come back."

He pauses, only for a second, before handing me a solid black mug. His bright green eyes lock with mine as I take it into my hands, smiling as the smell of my favorite blueberry coffee hits me. It seems he really thought of everything. His eyes don't leave me as he takes two spoons full of sugar from the white milk glass bowl next to the coffee maker and adds to his own mug, or when he twists the cap off and pours a splash of milk into his coffee, or when he stirs it all together, tapping the spoon gently on the edge of the mug before blindly tossing it into the sink to the left of him.

There's so much left hanging in the empty space between us, but I refuse to be the one that crosses that line. That stupid metaphorical line that has been drawn between us since we were teenagers. Moments like this make me wish I could read minds. As if my thoughts about wanting to know his were said aloud, a mischievous grin slowly spreads across Chase's face.

"I'll make you well-done eggs every Sunday morning, for the rest of my life, if that means I get to see you sitting up at my breakfast bar every week."

Winking before turning his attention back to the pan of sizzling bacon, Chase knows that this time, I have no rebuttal. There is no witty comeback, no sarcasm...I've got nothing. And it seems to go without saying, we both know I'll be right here at his breakfast bar, next Sunday too.

CHAPTER THIRTEEN

CHASE

MOST DAYS I head to the teachers' lounge for lunch, instead of sitting at tiny desk in my tiny office off the boys' locker room. But today, I just wasn't in the mood to deal with Bethany Callahan. The new sophomore English teacher didn't seem to get the hint that I wasn't interested. I wasn't even being subtle anymore. But no how many times I declined drinks after work, she just wasn't letting up.

Bethany Callahan is instantly forgotten about when I see a voice memo from "Hurricane" pop up. Pressing play in the message, I hear, "Hey Mack Daddy. Ew. I know I text it all the time. But, um…Gross. Why did you ever call yourself that, you fucking dork? Also, I hope there were people around to hear that you used to call yourself that. For those of you in the back, Chase Merrimack used to refer to himself as The Mack Daddy."

A girlish giggle comes from the phone for a good thirty seconds before she continues,

"ANYWAY. Um, fuck, what was I going to say? Oh! I'm driving right now so this is just easier. And I can't come for cheeseburgers. I switched my shifts at Cap & Co., so I'm bartending tonight. But I mean, if you'd be down for midnight snacks, count me in."

God, I'm so glad there isn't anyone around me. One, because I'd never live down the Mack Daddy thing, and two, because everyone would see how this woman affects me. A simple one-minute voice memo and her little giggle has me grinning…and thinking of the best midnight snack for her to come home to.

Holding the gray microphone down next to the text area, I say, "One, that nickname was legit as fuck. And your brother is the one that started calling me it, *actually*. Two, so cheeseburgers are a no go, but I can make a stop at Kaighan's Creamery for a pint of Cookie Monster ice cream?"

"So that's why you won't go out for drinks?" a disgusted, bitter tone comes from the doorway of my office. "You could have just told me you have a girlfriend."

Standing there with her arms crossed, Bethany—the apparently batshit crazy English teacher that can't take a hint—taps her heels on the concrete floor of my office demanding a response. If this was last year, I would have been all over it, all over her. She looks like Teacher Barbie come to life. Her platinum blonde hair falls right below her shoulders, styled every day.

Her perfect tan, her perfect make-up, her bright red, perfectly trimmed nails just seem fake. Even her bright yellow, preppy sweater vest, white collared shirt, and dark denim pants come off as calculated. Hollis's freckled face, ripped jeans, messy buns, oversized black glasses, and band tees flash through my head as Bat Shit Crazy Barbie continues to tap her heels on the floor. Instead of denying the fact that Hollis is my girlfriend, which I probably should have, I look Bethany right in the eyes and shrug.

"I just didn't want to go out for drinks with you, Bethany," I say, trying to sound remorseful, but coming up a bit short. "I'm sorry. I didn't want to be a dick, because we work together, but really, I'm just all set."

"You are such an asshole," she glares before dramatically turning while shaking her head in disbelief, as if the thought of me turning her down was inconceivable.

Seriously?! What the fuck was that? I could understand if I gave her any indication I was interested, but I barely even looked at her when we were in the same room, never mind held a conversation about anything other than the weather, or when I repeatedly shot her down for drinks. And the guys wonder why I don't go on multiple dates, never mind try to settle down.

As if on cue, my phone dings letting me know I have a voice memo. Hollis. A happy, relieved sigh leaves my body as I tap 0 9 1 5 in, unlocking my phone. Bethany who?

———

OVER THE LAST FEW WEEKS, Hollis has spent more nights in my guest room than in her own bed. We're not dating. We're not even sleeping together. In any manner. I sleep in my bed and the guest room has unofficially become Hollis's room. Unless there's a thunderstorm, like two nights ago, when she climbed into bed with me.

We never discussed her staying over, it just kind of happened. And I would be completely lying if I said I was bothered by it. We weren't doing anything more than drinking coffee together in the morning and eating take-out and watching movies together at night. And laughing. A lot. God, she makes me laugh.

I'm going to miss waking up to her standing in my kitchen, in a pair of my old football sweats from college. The three pairs of pants that, up until recently, had been sitting at the very bottom of my last dresser drawer, had officially become her "sleepover sweats."

It started with her birthday weekend and then turned into an almost every night thing when Davis and Kinley's wedding needed to be planned in just shy of three weeks. Three fucking weeks. Now, I don't know much about planning weddings. I've never been engaged, and the last time I was in a wedding party, I was seventeen, so I don't even know what exactly goes into planning a wedding. What I do know is that people usually have a year, sometimes two, to plan this shit.

The day after their engagement announcement, Kinley came to Sunday dinner at Hollis's grandparents' completely frazzled, and Davis went right to the beer. Despite an original plan to keep the pregnancy quiet, Kinley started sobbing when Ellis offered to make her a martini. After a mug of tea and a whole slew of happy tears from Ellis, Elisabeth, Nonna, and Hollis's aunts, Kinley spilled that she had wanted to wait until she was three months to tell everyone but the more she thought about it, the more she genuinely wanted to get married before she had the baby. But she also didn't want to get married when she was the size of a blimp. (Her words, not mine!)

While everyone was gushing over the baby and trying to comfort Kinley, Nonna, like a 5-foot Italian ninja, snuck out of the room, and pulled Nonno away from the football game we were watching. Before anyone knew what was happening, Kinley's parents and sister Cole were knocking on the front door.

After an hour and a half of being closed off in the formal dining room, it was decided there would be a small, intimate wedding at the Capparelli's summer cabin in the White Mountains on the Saturday night of Columbus Day weekend. Later that same afternoon, Kinley asked Cole, Hollis, Ellis, and Elisabeth to be a part of her bridal party. Following suit, as expected, Davis asked Travis to be his best man and me, Kenny, and Tucker to be groomsmen.

When he pulled me aside and asked, Kinley watched like a

hawk and winked pointing to Hollis mouthing, "bridesmaid." The fact she still thought I had no idea she has been trying to push me and Hollis together for years is hilarious to me. I let her go along with it, because the thought of me and Hollis together wasn't exactly upsetting anymore. Not that it ever was, but I found myself welcoming the idea more and more every day.

While the wedding is going to be small by typical wedding standards, there was still so much that needed to be done in such a short time. In the days that followed, I would come home from football practice at five and without fail, Hollis's Jeep would already be parked in front of her brother's house next door.

It was about seven o'clock the Thursday after wedding planning started when there was a knock on my front door. Not expecting anyone, I opened the door in just the plaid flannel pajama pants I was wearing. Much to my surprise, a very stressed-looking Hollis pitifully looked up to me and all but begged for "any kind of alcoholic beverage." I poured her a glass of wine, we ordered pizza, and she fell asleep on my couch. When her brother knocked on my front door, looking for her around midnight, she was still sound asleep on my couch, the credits to Iron Man scrolling down the TV hanging on the wall. Davis moved her Jeep into my driveway and told me to leave a note for her saying she could skip their run in the morning before heading back next door to his place.

The next night, I knew she would be working the bar at Cap & Co., so for the first time in my life I went and sat at the bar, getting both dinner and drinks by myself. Which ended up being me spending most of the time internally talking shit to every guy that flirted with her or excessively tipped her. And when her shift was coming to an end, she made a comment about how she couldn't wait to go home and drink some hot cocoa. Like an idiot I said, "You know, I have hot cocoa and mini marshmallows at my house."

As soon as I said it, I had a new fear that she would laugh in my face and shut me down, like we weren't best friends for half our lives, but a girl I was genuinely trying to take home. Instead of laughing, she put together a box full of pastries and cookies from the restaurant downstairs and told me that if I didn't mind her using my shower, she was in. Then, wearing my old sweats she came with me to my mom's for breakfast again, and I went with her to her Saturday night set.

From there we just fell into an unintentional routine. After she finished helping Kinley, she would drive her Jeep into my driveway, we'd figure out dinner, and then do it again the next day. Friday nights after games, I would head to Cap & Co., and there would be a Captain and Coke waiting for me before I even got to the bar. I was even making a point to get up a bit earlier than I needed to during the week, so I could see her before her morning run and when she left for work.

The thought of starting my day with Hollis Capparelli had made it surprisingly easy to abandon the warm covers I always had to drag myself out of every morning. Before, I would stroll down the stairs with just enough time to spare to go through a drive-through and get a cup of scalding, burnt coffee. It had been too easy getting used to walking into my kitchen to see her pouring a cup and getting the same begrudged, evil eye I got every morning when she handed over that first cup to me.

Which is why now, I wait. I could go to bed. I could leave the door unlocked, text Hollis and tell her I'll see her in the morning. But, the truth was, I wanted to see her, to make sure she made it okay. It's crazy how easily you can become used to someone's presence and how empty a house, a person, can feel when that presence is gone—even if just for twenty-four hours, like Hollis had been.

She had to pick up her dress from the seamstress yesterday

and wanted to go home to pack and practice the song Davis and Kinley asked her to play for their first dance, so she'd spent the night at home. Her home, not mine. And I'd slept like shit. The house felt empty without her in it.

So I had tried to make dinner plans with her, in the hopes of getting her back here. And though dinner wasn't possible, as soon as she said that she would come over after her shift, my whole day got better. Pulling a carton of cookie dough ice cream from the freezer, I grab a spoon and just dig into the pint. In the late hour of the night, the silence of the empty house is deafening. Which is weird for me, the confirmed bachelor who up until recently, relished in the thought of having his own space. It wasn't until Hollis started spending more time here did I realize just how empty this big house feels when she's not here.

"You better have another spoon for me."

And just like that, everything feels right in the world again.

CHAPTER FOURTEEN

HOLLIS

THERE IS no feeling better than the sense of being home. As my feet hit the dirt below me, with Chase by side, that sense completely washes over me. Ahead of us is the summer cabin that has been in my family for as long as I can remember.

This is my safe place, my refuge when the world becomes too crazy and I need clarity. I've been all over the United States, to Italy, and England…and there is nowhere on this earth I love more than the Capparelli Cabin.

Over bowls of ice cream last night, Chase had suggested we head up early today just to make sure no last minute decorating was needed or cleaning needed to be done. Knowing that my grandmother hired a cleaner and the only decorations were the flowers and the arch my dad built, I still agreed. Not because I wanted to clean or decorate, but because selfishly, I wanted to come back to my favorite corner of the world before all the craziness of wedding weekend happened.

Not that the last few weeks hadn't been complete craziness. If I wasn't working, I was either with Kinley helping her with something wedding related or with Chase decompressing from helping Kinley with wedding related things. Three weeks.

That's how long they had in between Kinley's kitchen meltdown about being a fat bride and when the crews would come to winterize the cabin. And, Kinley was determined to make it happen.

My brother and my cousin Travis had to pull some serious strings to both be off this weekend, so most of the planning ended up falling on Kinley, which trickled down to Cole and me. So many little details needed to be figured out. Like dresses, the fellas' tuxes, food, an officiant, flowers, music…now I know why people take years to plan this shit. It wasn't even my wedding and I was ready for it to all be over, just so we could have some form of normalcy again.

Though I don't know what normalcy would mean for me and Chase. At this point, we were spending so much time together, it feels weird when we aren't. It has gotten to the point that my dad asked what was going on with us and if I was moving in with him. Weirdly enough, something that was never asked the entire two years I was with Noah. Pushing it off under the guise that it was just easier being right next door to Kinley when she needed me, I assured him after the wedding, I would be back home, bothering him all the time.

With Monday quickly approaching, I needed to deal with, and find answers for, the looming questions I had. It made no sense to stress over going back to my basement apartment at my dad's. I had a place to go. Chase's house wasn't mine. And it's not like there is anything between us that would keep me at his house more permanently. He was just being a good friend, giving me a place to crash right next door to where I needed to be most of the time that also happened to be closer to my work.

He's had plenty of opportunities to make a move, and he hasn't. Any silly hope I had imagined was just that, false hope. Once this weekend was over, we would go back to being the people that saw each other occasionally within our circle of friends and on Sundays at my grandparents for dinner. I needed to accept that.

"So, wanna be roommates tomorrow and, maybeeeee, Sunday?"

Unlocking the front door, I push it open, allowing Chase to walk past me, his arms full of the bags of groceries for dinner tonight. Since tomorrow was going to be crazy, tonight was going to be low-key, at least for the girls. Kinley, Davis, and the crew would all come up tonight after they all got out of work. After dinner, Davis, Chase, and the rest of the guys would leave and head into town to spend the night at a hotel.

She was giving up a lot having a smaller wedding, but the two things Kinley wasn't willing to compromise on was that Davis didn't get to see her before the wedding and that her dad walk her down the aisle.

Tomorrow after the "I Dos" and mini-reception, we planned on having one last official goodbye to summer weekend with everyone. There was no school on Monday because of Columbus Day, so I knew that Chase was in no rush to go home, but we hadn't talked about staying up here past Sunday.

"Sunday?" I ask, following him to the kitchen and immediately begin taking the food out of the bags. "And you sure you want to crash together? I called dibs on the yellow room, and that just has one bed."

"Yeah, I was thinking we could crash up here an extra night after everyone leaves," he starts, quickly adding, "if you want. I know how much you love it up here. And I figured you'd be in the yellow room."

When my grandparents decorated the cabin years ago, they had color coded each of the four bedrooms of the cabin. While the blankets and décor have changed throughout the years, the themes have remained the same. The blue room is the master bedroom. It goes without saying that Kinley and Davis get that all weekend. The yellow bedroom, which is my favorite, looks over the backyard. Like the master bedroom, it has a fire place, its own private bathroom, and it's also the only other room in the house that has a bed bigger than a single.

The pink room, where Ellis and Cole would more than likely end up, housed two full-size beds covered in baby pink comforters. And then there's the green room, the room my cousins and I spent most of our time in growing up. Two sets of wooden bunkbeds, handmade by my father sit on each side of the walls of the room—just enough beds for Travis, Tucker, Kenny, and Chase…which, I assumed would be what happened.

"You don't want to crash in the green room with the guys?" I ask while pulling up the music app on my phone. Putting on my cooking playlist, I decide to focus on the prep for the chicken tacos I'm making for dinner tonight. Not wanting to seem too eager about the thought of sharing not just a room, but a bed with Chase for two nights, I pretend to be distracted by Frank Sinatra and the need to find a crock-pot.

"Stop," Chase says, grabbing my hand as I reach for the cabinet in front of me. "Just for a minute."

"Fly Me To The Moon" shuffles into "Sway" by Dean Martin as he guides me back and places his other hand on my hip.

"Dance with me."

It's not a question, or a request. The stubborn side of me wants to tell him that he doesn't get to tell me what to do, but the words "you're not the boss of me" never leave my lips. Wrapping my fingers in his, I'm like putty in his hands as I let him lead me around the kitchen. My hips move to the music as if they've been hypnotized.

His silky basketball shorts and my thin yoga pants are a dangerous combination. With every spin we make, I become more aware of the very little fabric separating us.

Alabama. Alaska. Arizona. Arkansas. California. Colorado.

Connecticut. Delaware…Fuck, even the Sunshine State can't distract me from the closeness we share right now. Holy shit. Who knew Dean Martin could be so damn sexy?

As the song comes to an end, Chase lifts the arm of the hand holding mine, twirling me like a princess. With a little too much gusto, he pulls me back to him. Slamming into his chest instantly sends me into a fit of giggles.

"What's so funny, Hurricane?" he asks. The playful tone of his voice doesn't match the intensity of his stare though.

False hope, Hollis. Don't allow yourself to go there. Once this weekend is over, you're back home. Chase will never be anything more than your best friend.

"Nothing. It's nothing. Forget it." I ramble nervously, playfully pushing him. "All is good in the hood."

"*It's* obviously something," he says before pushing me back with the same lightness. Instead of answering him, I just push back, this time a little harder. With the same lightness as before he pushes back, but this time I lose my footing and stumble backwards. Just as I'm sure I'm about to fall back on my ass, Chase wraps his arms around my waist and pulls me back up to him.

I fully intend on pushing myself off him with some smart-ass comment, but the second I look up to him, any will I have to speak or move is lost. Instead, those annoying stomach knots come back and my heart starts rapidly beating. Letting go of the hold he has on my waist, I assume he's going to step back, so I try to think of the next thing to say.

Instead though, one hand slides behind my head into the back of my hair and he uses the other to tip my chin up, leaving me no choice but to face him.

My eyes meet his and I'm done. Gone. Any resolve I had about pushing those feelings away have flown out the fucking window, never to return. My knees buckle beneath me and I find myself grabbing the back of Chase's shirt to steady myself.

Before I can make my excuse of needing air, Chase's fingers pull on the hair at the back of my neck and his lips crash on mine.

I didn't know that it was possible for the world to completely stop and spin faster, simultaneously, until right now. The reality of Chase's lips on mine hits me like a bolt of lightning and stills me like the sound of waves crashing all at once.

This is Chase. My best friend since I was fifteen. The boy I swore to let go of ten years ago. With his lips on mine. I mean, it's not our first kiss, but holy fuck, this is happening. Right now. Jesus, Hollis, get your shit together. Kiss the man back.

Letting go of the grip my hands have on the back of his shirt, my hands slide up to Chase's neck. Pressing my fingers into the back of his neck and pulling him to me is all the affirmation he needs to keep going. With each second his lips linger on mine, my breaths become shallow and I feel myself melt into him completely. His tongue slides over mine, so tenderly. Each kiss long, slow, and calculated like he's reveling in it and cherishing each one I'm giving up to him.

When he pulls his lips off mine, my eyes fly open. His bright, green eyes lock with mine quickly before they make their way to my lips and back up again. Together, the hand that's been holding my chin up to face him and the one in my hair, slide down my neck, slowly and meticulously trailing the outline of my body. Every part of me becoming hypersensitive with his touch. Each breath I take comes faster and heavier than the last one before it.

He finally stops at my waist, wrapping both arms around me, tugging me closer, closing the small gap that was left between us. A cocky smirk of acknowledgment spreads across his lips when I gasp. Leaning back down, he lets his lips hover right above mine, asking me to meet him halfway.

Just as I'm about to oblige, I hear, "Fucking finally!" from the doorway behind us. Like a snap waking me up from hypnosis, I move back, fear and panic searing through me.

"I, I," I stutter as I pull away, stepping back from Chase. "I need some air."

Grabbing the sweatshirt I'd dropped on the counter when Chase and I first got to the cabin, I pull it over my head and all but run for the door. Taking the cobblestone path that leads to the backyard, I make my way to my favorite wooden outdoor swing by the firepit. There are stacks of wood ready for the weekend. Bags of charcoal sit next to the three grills.

"It's the air in these mountains. I can't catch my breath and my heart feels like it's going to beat out of my damn chest," I explain as Kinley takes a seat on the swing next to me.

"Oh, okay," she laughs. "I didn't realize we were referring to Chase as 'the mountain air' now."

In an attempt to deny it, to her and myself, I shake my head, "No. It's not Chase."

"It's always been Chase," she argues, knowingly.

Without warning, a flood of all the emotions I've been trying to push away hits me like a tidal wave. She's right. From the very first day he walked into the gymnasium our sophomore year of high school, it's been him. That's why even in the two years I was with Noah, I would drop anything if Chase called me. It's why every time something happened, good or bad, I want him to be the first to know. It's no coincidence. It's just Chase.

It's always been Chase. And maybe it was time I stopped fighting the universal pull that kept bringing us back to each other.

Seeing the worried, terrified expression on my face, Kinley reaches for me, "Oh, Hollis."

"This is your weekend," I tell her, trying to come up with an excuse to push this off. It was just a moment, it meant more to me than him. If he felt the same, he would have come after me. It would be him on the swings with me, not Kinley.

"Yeah, you're right," she agrees. "And I want you to march your little butt back into that house and go talk to Chase. Because it's my weekend and I say so. You're not getting out of this one, Hol."

Standing up, she offers her hand to me, "Come on, Hurricane," she teases by calling me by Chase's nickname. "Let's go make sure your brother hasn't killed Chase for kissing you and then you can go tell him that you looooove him."

"You're a real pain in my ass, preggers," I laugh, standing up. She shrugs, and we walk around to the front of the house. As we're about to go through the front door, the sound of tires on gravel comes from behind us. Tucker's red Silverado pulls up and parks behind Chase's truck. Right behind him a smaller black truck pulls up followed by a small black sedan.

His truck isn't parked for more than fifteen seconds before Tucker hops out of the driver's seat and jogs over to us. Pulling Kinley and I both into his infamous bear hug as Kenny and Travis come walking up the driveway together. Davis and Travis have been best friends with Kenny since he moved into the house next to us in kindergarten. When Chase and Tucker moved to Abbott Hills, the only way Chase could hang out with them at first was if he brought Tucker with him. The three of them would get so annoyed when Misha insisted Chase let Tucker tag along.

Being as smooth as his brother, it didn't take Tucker long to make friends of his own. For a while, we didn't see much of Tuck, but after high school every time the guys got together, it was the five of them. I couldn't imagine anyone else standing next to my brother on the day of his wedding. Right behind Kenny and Travis, with their arms full of bags, are Cole and Ellis.

"Hand 'em over," Travis chuckles, as Cole struggles with her suitcase and duffle bag.

"You're a lifesaver," she sighs with relief, as she hands the bags over to my cousin.

As Travis is taking Cole's things, Tucker weaves in and out of the small group of us to help Ellis with her things. The whole group of them—including Chase and my brother—may be sarcastic smartasses, but their mamas raised them right. There would never be a moment any of us girls would struggle if one of the fellas were around.

"Coming up here never gets old," Cole smiles, as she one-arm hugs Kinley and me.

"You guys definitely picked a good time of the year to do this," Tucker agrees as he looks around, pointing to the bright yellow and red leaves of the maple trees all around us.

"You couldn't have asked for better weather this weekend, Kin," Ellis adds in. "Sunny and 70 tomorrow. Perfect."

As everyone continues to go back and forth about the trees and weather, the sound of Davis and Chase's loud laughter from the kitchen catches my attention. So my brother hasn't killed him, and they're laughing. That's a good sign.

While everyone else went to bring Cole and Ellis's bags in their room, I try to sneak into the kitchen. Hip-hop blasting from the phone catches my attention first, followed promptly by Chase dicing up tomatoes while my brother shreds lettuce. The crock-pot I had been looking for is on the counter, the green light indicating that it's been turned on is lit up, and the lingering smell of salsa and powdered ranch dressing in the air means Chase started the chicken for the tacos I had planned on making tonight. His Hollis senses must be tingling, because Chase turns around from the counter and flashes me a concerned and puzzled look.

"How'd you geniuses get into my phone?" I ask, before

Chase can go through with asking if I'm okay like I know he wants to.

"One One Zero Seven," Davis deadpans. "Come on, Hol."

I want to wipe the cocky grin off Chase's face, but I don't say anything. This one time I'll let him bask in it. What else could I do? 1107. November 7th. Chase's birthday. There's nothing I could say that would give me any other valid excuse for using those numbers as my lock code.

"Alright Chase," Kinley says, putting her hand out. "Give me that knife. One of us can take it from here. Hollis has some official bridesmaid and groomsman things she needs to go over with you. Alone."

If looks could kill, I would have just murdered her. Everyone has made their way to the kitchen and all of them are now looking back and forth between me and Chase, knowing full well it's complete bullshit. If there was wedding stuff to talk about, we would all be talking about it. Not just me and Chase, alone nevertheless. My cheeks are burning by the time she shoos him away from the counter. Davis doesn't say anything, but nods once, giving me his silent approval.

Knowing this won't end until Chase and I at least leave the room together, I roll my eyes and shoot one last side-eye glance over to Kinley. Closing the door behind him once we get to the yellow room I'll be staying in tonight, Chase turns to me, his face full of confusion.

"What's going on Hollis?" he questions. "Everything okay?"

"No," I tell him, panicking. "Yes. No. Why did you have to go and do that?"

"What? What are you talking about?" he asks, his voice laced with concern. "What the hell did I do?"

"Nothing," I blurt out before dropping my shoulders and adding, "Everything."

"Hollis."

The way he says my name with such authority sends chills

up my spine. Whoa. Chase Merrimack with the smolder appeal. Fuck. And here I was thinking I could weasel my way out of this conversation. Tucker's voice on the other side of the door letting Chase know they're all getting ready to head out saves me from having to explain myself. Seeing my opportunity, I open the door and tell him to "have a great night with the fellas." Reluctantly, he sighs, following his brother to the front door where Kenny, Davis and Travis are waiting.

Once I get to the kitchen where the girls are gathered, I pick up my phone to find something more appropriate for girls' night. Two seconds into me searching through playlists, a text pops up from Chase.

"Just so you know, our conversation from the bedroom is far from over. See you in the morning, beautiful."

CHAPTER FIFTEEN

CHASE

I HATE when things are left unfinished.

Which seems to be the ongoing theme of Hollis's and my friendship, or whatever it is we have. Just as Hollis was going to let down her guard, my brother came knocking on the door, letting me know it was time to go. She used it as her excuse to avoid the conversation we desperately needed to have, practically pushing me out the door with the rest of the guys.

And it's not that I minded time with the fellas. I couldn't remember the last time the five of us were able to just sit around drinking beers, eating pizza. Right now, I would just rather be at the cabin, figuring out what the hell was going on with me and Hol though. No matter what she said, there was no way it was "nothing." That kiss was so far from nothing.

Respecting her space and the time she needed to move on from Noah had been a priority, but maybe it was time let her know how much I wanted more. More than the back and forth, more than mixed signals, more than the jealousy or the worry when she's with someone else. Just more.

"So, Mack," Davis starts, calling me out specifically. "What's the deal with you and Hol?"

"Is this a trick question?" I ask, grabbing another slice of pepperoni pizza from the tray in the middle of the table. As soon as we left the cabin, I knew it was only a matter of time until one of them asked me. To be honest, I was surprised it had even taken this long.

We left four hours ago, wrapping up our night of "bachelor party" fun now. After confirming the ladies' plans for the night didn't collide with ours, Davis's groomsmen split the cost of renting out Frankie's Funway. If someone had told me when I was sixteen that the park I spent many nights terrorizing with the guys would be where I spent the night before one of them got married, I would have laughed in their face. But Davis had made it very clear that the strip club was the very last place he wanted to be tonight, so when Travis brought up the idea of reliving our youth at Frankie's, we'd been all for it.

Nothing and everything had changed since the last time I had been there. A lot of the park was the same, but we were all older and some of us, wiser. But you put five guys, no matter how old, in any competitive situation and shit was going to go down. After playing the most competitive game of mini golf ever, we headed over to the batting cages, then laser tag, and then finally wrapped up the night with a lap around the go-kart track.

Most friends would have let Davis win, knowing it was his night, but we're more the kind of friends that want to make sure you stay grounded. Up until now, we had only heckled each other while playing. Even the short walk down the street to the pizza place had been spent giving each other a hard time and bragging about our personal wins.

"Hey, man," my brother adds from across the table. "Davis asked what we're all thinking."

"Do we need to give you the Cappa boys speech?" Travis questions, jokingly puffing out his chest and nodding to Davis before we all burst out laughing.

"Honestly," I start when the laughter subsides. "I don't know. I'm kind of leaving the ball in Hol's court."

"Well, you'd be an improvement over the last guy," Davis nods before taking a sip of his beer. Without so many words, I just got his blessing. Hollis never required her brother's approval to do anything, but I know it matters to her. Which means, tomorrow after all the wedding craziness, it was time Hollis and I had a chat.

———

AFTER MEETING in the hotel restaurant for breakfast, the five of us all head back up to Davis's hotel suite. Sports Center is playing on the TV in the background, but for probably the first time in our lives, none of us are paying attention to stats and sports news, as the suite slowly begins to fill.

Over the next hour, Davis's family trickles in slowly. Once everyone is accounted for, he opens the sliding door of the hotel closet. A dozen suits hang in the closet, each one with a name tag written in Hollis's big, bubbly handwriting. The first five suits are navy blue, followed by six gray ones. Davis's is the first suit, his white vest and white bowtie separating him from the rest of us.

As I fiddle with the navy-blue bowtie that matches the rest of the groomsmen, Lorenzo Capparelli leaves Davis's side and makes his way over to me. I've never feared Hollis's dad, because I've always been the good guy. But there's something intimidating and terrifying about him coming at me with intent right now.

"So, Hollis says that she'll be back home after this weekend," Lorenzo starts, as he adjusts my tie. "I just want you to know, I'll be okay if she isn't. When she came home from college, I told her that the house was empty without kids in it, but I knew the only way she would accept my help would be if I made it about me. So if she doesn't come back home, I'll be okay. No matter what she tries to tell you."

Just like his son last night, in not so many words, I just got his blessing to move forward with Hollis if I want to. To so many people, this might seem old-fashioned and out of date, but the Capparellis are as close as they come. Their old school family values don't stop at Sunday dinners. When they say, "family first," they really, legitimately mean it.

That's why today, every single member of Davis's family would be in attendance. Kinley's mom is a US Senator, the combination creating a laughable idea that this would be a "small" wedding.

"Make sure you fellas turn your phones off," Davis reminds us as we begin to make our way down to the lobby. "Lord help any of you if you ruin a pregnant woman's wedding with a ringing cell phone."

Kinley and Davis couldn't have asked for a better day. After listening to Hollis stress as she stalked the weather channel for the last week, even I had been relieved when Mother Nature decided to play nice today. The combination of sunshine and anything above fifty degrees in October is a rare thing in New Hampshire, but the sun was shining, and my weather app said it would be in the low sixties all day today.

It only takes ten minutes for us to get to the cabin, the longest stretch of the drive the worn, dirt driveway leading to the cabin itself. Stepping out of the limo, we are greeted by my mom and Davis's aunt, Zia Kat. As soon as I step out, my mom's eyes begin to water. With Tucker and Davis following behind me, she sighs happily, pulling each of us, one by one, into hugs.

"My boys," her voice wavering as she looks all of us over. "Wait till you see Lola, Tuck. And, wait till you see Hollis. I mean, don't get me wrong, Kinley looks beautiful, but Hol, is just…well, you'll see," she says, turning her attention back to me. I had no doubt Hollis would look beautiful, but the way my mom left it made me wonder if there something more she was trying to tell me.

"Oh!" Kat exclaims as we make our way toward the backyard where the ceremony and reception would be. "The whole reason we were sent out here was to tell you that if any of you fellas need to use the bathroom, make your way inside now. The ladies are behind closed doors."

None of us need to go, so while my mom and Hollis's aunt dip back into the house with Hollis's dad, the rest of us continue to the backyard. Straight ahead, a large white tent sits, the doors open, allowing us to look in.

Next to the tent is the chatter of excited guests anticipating our arrival. Slow classical music comes through the speakers set up next to the rows of white folding chairs that lead to the arch handmade by Lorenzo Capparelli. Davis says hello to members of Kinley's family as he makes his way toward the front with Travis. The rest of us wait for our instructions. Kinley had been convinced that since it was a small wedding, they didn't need a rehearsal dinner, but as I stand here with my hand in my pockets, it would have been nice to know what I was supposed to be doing right now.

As if he was reading my mind, Hollis's Grampa O'Brien walks up to us and motions for us to follow him, making our way back to the front of the cabin.

"Wait till you see Hollis," he whispers to me as we walk together.

Everyone is either trying to push us together or we've done a horrible job of hiding the fact that there's something going on between us the last few weeks. As soon as we make the corner, Kinley is the first person I see. Nervously waving to us with one hand, she clings to her dad's arm with the other. Her mom, understandably, already wiping tears from her eyes. My mom wasn't lying when she said that Kinley looked beautiful. A wreath of white flowers sits on top of the waves of blonde hair and the light, white fabric of the lace-sleeved dress is fitted at the top but leads to a flowing skirt. The specific style would never leave you to think that Kinley is almost three months pregnant.

"Hot damn," Tucker whispers under his breath next to me when Ellis steps out of the front door. My mother and Hollis's aunts follow behind them, and I stare at the door, anxiously anticipating Hollis's arrival. Beads of sweat begin to pool in the palm of my hand as I wait for her, and I can only imagine how nervous Davis must be waiting for his bride. Or how nervous I'll be when my own wedding day comes. Shaking any crazy ideas out of my head, I chuckle as Hollis's grandmothers come out and immediately begin fussing over me, Tuck, and Kenny.

"Hollis will be out in a minute," Nonna smiles slyly when she embraces me with her signature hug and cheek kisses.

And that's when it happens. That's when the whole world stops. There's no background noise. If there is, I don't hear it. All I hear, all I see, is the laughter of the girl I've loved since she threw a fit about me cheating in gym class.

Walking arm-in-arm with her dad, her eyes lock with mine the second she steps down onto the grass. As much as I try to will myself to move, I'm frozen. Stuck in a trance. Sliding her arm out from being linked with her dad's, she pats his arm as he nods in my direction.

With each step she takes, I feel my heart beating faster. Wiping my hand on the inside of my pockets, I suck in the pooling saliva in my mouth. There have been hundreds, if not thousands, of times I've seen Hollis in the years of us being friends, but I've never seen her looking as beautiful as she does right now.

Her hair is dark, and it's cut into the sleek, stacked bob that had been "her" hairstyle from about six months after I moved back to New Hampshire up until Noah and his ignorance came into her life. The flower wreath on her head is full of dark red flowers pulling together the color of her dress. Hollis had shown me a picture of the dress from the store's website, but the model's picture did it no justice.

The long, burgundy dress leaves just enough exposed skin at the top of the dress to be sassy and sexy while still being classy. A thin ribbon defines her waist and leads to the bottom half of her dress...and the slit that goes all the way up to her midthigh.

As everyone gushes over my niece who just came running out, I can't pull myself away from Hollis to even look at Lola. Like a snake charmer, she has me hypnotized. Nothing and no one else but her exist right now.

"Well look at you," she whistles when she stands in front of me. "You clean up nice, sir."

Before I can say anything to her, a new song begins to play from the speakers.

"Ave Maria," Hollis says. That's our cue."

Hollis's aunts and uncles rush to their seats before both sets of her grandparents link arms and begin the processional toward the tent in the backyard. After Kinley's grandparents walk down, Kenny escorts Kinley's mom, followed by Hollis's dad and my mom.

One day, my mom would have the chance to do all the things that mothers do with their sons on their wedding days with me and Tucker, but today, she would get to do those things with Davis. When he pulled both me and Tuck aside and asked us if it would be okay to ask our mom to do everything a mother does with a son on their wedding day, including a mother-son dance, without hesitation, we both said yes. And so did she when he asked her.

Ellis offers her arm to Tucker, who whispers something in her ear, getting himself playfully whacked before Ellis shakes her head and slinks her arm into the crook of his. The ladies seem to know a lot more about what's going on than the guys do and that becomes even more clear when Hollis extends her free hand to me, implying that we're next. Before sliding her arm in mine, she turns and blows Kinley a quick kiss.

Leaving only Cole, Lola, and Kinley with her dad behind us, we slowly make our way down the aisle. Hypersensitive to Hollis's body next to mine, I lean over and finally whisper, "You are beautiful."

Reluctantly, I let her pull away and make my way over to the side of the arch that Hollis's brother, cousin, and my brother stand on. I'm smirking when I see Davis fidgeting, rocking in place at the front of the church.

I get it, man. I get it.

CHAPTER SIXTEEN

HOLLIS

FOR THE FIRST time in a long time, I feel completely like myself. My hair is once again cut short, the longest pieces of my hair falling right below my chin — something Ellis convinced me to do last night after a few glasses of wine. As soon as I said yes, she ran to her room and came back with shears and a spray bottle. Over a foot of hair is gone, and I feel lighter. Not even just on my head, but my soul too.

Ray LaMontagne comes through the speakers as I sway back in forth in Chase's arms, surrounded by my family and our closest friends. Everything just feels right. After Davis and Kinley made everyone cry with the most beautiful wedding vows, we took what felt like a hundred pictures and made our entrance back into the reception.

Once again arm-in-arm, Chase and I had been introduced together and we've been close to each other ever since. The two of us feeding off each other's energy, trying to keep the party going without making it too obvious that Kinley was sitting under a fan, sipping on ginger ale, and popping Tums like they were mints. My family knows she is pregnant, and so do her parents and sister, but no one else knows and that's how it needs to stay. At least for a few more weeks, according to Kinley's mom.

The press was ruthless when it came to political scandals. It didn't matter that Davis and Kinley had been together since high school, if the local newspapers found out she was pregnant before she was married, there would be something said. Especially once they found out a Capparelli was tied to the mix. Sometimes being famous in a small town had its perks, but this wasn't one of them.

Once I see Kinley move to a table full of older women I don't recognize, I take full advantage of the fact "Jump In The Line" by Harry Belafonte is now playing. Grabbing Ellis and Tucker, who had been suspiciously closer than normal tonight, I whisper yell, "Help us start a conga line!"

Within minutes, I am leading a twenty-person conga line. Instead of resting his hands on my shoulders, in typical conga line fashion, Chase's hands are on my hips, guiding me as I shake to the rhythm of the song. As we make our way around the tent, "Conga" by Gloria Estefan starts up, and I raise my Blue Hawaiian to the DJ.

The wedding bartender, JoAnna, is the Monday and Tuesday night bartender at Capparelli and Co. and had "accidentally" poured too much rum into my drink. With only two down, I am already starting to feel a slight buzz. Which easily explains my tingly lips and the warm fuzzies I feel.

Once the conga line begins to disperse, I decide now, right now, this very second, would be a good time to turn, stand on my tippy toes and kiss Chase. Chase, who looks hot as fuck in his blue suit pants, his vest, and an unbuttoned white dress shirt with the sleeves rolled and pushed up. Chase with his perfectly styled hair and his cleanly shaped, trimmed beard.

The beard is so soft today. Hesitant in his response, it takes Chase a second to kiss back and once he does, I melt. Like an ooey, gooey ice cream cone on a hot day. Placing my hands on his chest, I steady myself on the satin navy vest.

With a low chuckle and a smirk in response, Chase rests his hand on the small of my back, closing the space left between us. As another slow song begins, he kisses the top of my head and steps back just enough to offer me the hand that isn't still placed right above my ass. It doesn't take long for us to find our rhythm together.

"I've wanted to do that for hours," I admit, as we sway together.

"I would have kissed you hours ago," he whispers into my ear before letting go to twirl me, pulling me back possessively. "All you had to do was say something."

"So, what you're saying," I whisper back, suddenly feeling brave, "is that if I want something, all I have to do is say something?"

"Well, I mean..."

"Spend the night with me."

As the song comes to an end, he uses the opportunity to dip me, pulling me away and locking eyes with me, as he brings me back up. "I'm pretty sure I already asked you to do that yesterday."

Smiling, I quickly peck him on the cheek before walking back to the bar to get a refill on my drink. Not that I wanted to be drunk, but if I was going to get naked in front of Chase, I was going to need a bit more liquid courage beyond warm fuzzies. Tipsy sounded like a good place to be. Stopping at the wedding party table, I grab my clutch and then squeeze myself into an open spot between Tucker and Travis, placing my empty glass on the bar.

"It's about fucking time," Travis laughs, nudging me in the side with his elbow.

"I don't know what you're talking about," I say, trying to

feign innocence, knowing damn well he's talking about me and Chase.

"Yeah, okay," the sarcasm oozing from Tucker's words on the other side of me. "Even a blind man could see that you and big broski finally are doing the thing."

"The thing?" I ask. "What the fuck is 'the thing?'"

Before Tucker can answer, JoAnna comes over and takes our drink orders and this time I add a shot of rum to my order. Taking the shot before walking away, I leave the empty shot glass on the bar and throw a few dollars into the tip bucket. Dropping my clutch on the table, I scan the crowd for Chase. When I find him with my dad and uncles, the anger written all over his face sends me into emergency mode. If my dad and uncles are giving him some version of the "don't you try anything with Hollis" talk that my brother and cousin used on the guys we grew up with, I will be putting my foot down. I am twenty-eight years old. They have no right to get involved in my love life.

Or well, life. They have no right to stick their noses in my life. Because I don't love Chase. Yeah…I can't even convince myself of that in my own head. Preparing to stand my ground, I begin to think of all the things I'm going to tell my crazy, overprotective relatives. Just as I'm about to open with the solid argument I've built in my head, I stop myself when I hear Chase say, "I'm gone for twenty-four hours and the whole team falls to shit. I don't even know how to fix this."

My Uncle Leo—who was the football coach for years while Chase was on the team–turns and tells him that the best thing to do is to send an email and make sure to acknowledge the situation, but not let it ruin his night. "Leave it in Abbott Hills" and "deal with it" when he gets home.

As soon as they bee me, my dad and uncles excuse themselves, as if I'm the one person who can solve whatever Chase's problem is.

"Come take a walk with me, Coach," I say. Leaving my drink on the first open table I see on the way out of the tent, I take Chase's hand in mine, leading him away from the reception.

"I'm gone for one fucking game, Hol," his voice is laced with frustration. "One game and they lose to Alvirne by 24 points..."

As we walk down the dirt driveway, I squeeze his hand slightly, knowing he hasn't gotten to the real issue yet.

"I knew about the loss right after the game last night," he explains. "But, I didn't think anything of it. You know, you win some, you lose some. I figured I would give them the weekend, and we would come back and figure out what happened on Tuesday. Well, while you were getting a drink, I decided to check my phone and found 18 missed texts from players. Every single one of them pissed off because of bad coaching calls. My starting quarterback was benched in the first quarter because he made the call to execute a play he and I went over in practice instead of repeating the same play that was getting them nowhere on the field. It ended up being their only scoring drive. My players deserve better than that."

The guilt he feels for being here is written all over his face as he pulls out his phone and begins reading me some of the texts from his players.

"It's not the loss that pisses me off," he continues. "They're kids. What pisses me off is that Aaron walked into the locker room after the game, punched a locker, and told them all to 'get out of his face, Coach NFL will deal with you little shits on Tuesday.' Like, who the fuck is he? One, to be flipping out on my players, and two, to talk shit about me behind my back?"

Aaron Hanover Sr., the assistant coach's father, is the superintendent of the school district, so when Aaron Jr. got dishonorably discharged from the military and had no other plan, his father pulled some strings and got him the job as the assistant to the offensive coordinator. Chase's final year on the high school team was Aaron's first year coaching. While Chase was setting records in college, being drafted into the NFL, and winning Super Bowl rings, Aaron Jr. was on the Abbott Hills sidelines yelling at high schoolers.

During the 2015 Super Bowl, Chase not only broke franchise records, but tore his patellar tendon in the fourth quarter. I had never felt as helpless as I did when I watched him drop to the ground from the stands. After the Patriots secured a 28-24 win, Chase refused to have surgery in Arizona. After getting pain medicine from the team doctor, Tucker, Misha, and I flew back with him on the redeye. I spent more time between doctor's offices and physical therapists in the few months that followed than I had combined my entire life before he was hurt.

After that season, the Patriots chose not to extend his contract due to complications with his recovery. His agent got a few calls when he became a free agent up for grabs, but Chase took it as a sign and chose to hang up his cleats, calling it the end of his career as a professional football player. That summer he sold his house in Massachusetts and moved back home to Abbott Hills. One of his first stops was to the high school to visit his old coach, my uncle Leo.

Following my grandfather retiring from Capparelli & Co., my uncle formally announced his retirement as the football coach, knowing he would have to spend more time at the restaurant. Instead of Aaron getting the head coaching job when the position opened, Chase did. Though my uncle never took the position within the school, having Capparelli & Co. too, the head coaching position is the only coaching position that allows the option to also be a full-time gym teacher, getting your own office in the athletics department.

Every other position is only seasonal and part time, which means no benefits and no office. Aaron's issue with Chase comes right down to jealousy. And somehow in the small world craziness that is my life, Aaron and Noah's, as in my exdoucheroo, mothers are best friends. They were raised the same way, by the same conniving type of women and workaholic fathers. So that's pretty much all you need to know about Aaron's character.

"I'm sure going away with me for the weekend doesn't help matters," I start, holding my hand up to Chase as he begins to defend me and our friendship or whatever this is. "Wait. Stop. Let me finish. How about we still leave Sunday night like we originally planned, and you have the team over to that big house of yours for a pizza party? Like, a morale boost before you guys meet back up for practice on Tuesday. Before we go back to the reception, reply to that group text, tell the boys that you hear them and that you want them to come over on Monday. Send all the parents an email saying that you know what happened, you're out of town at a family wedding, but it will be dealt with, with urgency. Mention the pizza party in the email, so they know too. And then you deal with Aaron on Tuesday."

For the first time since I walked over to him standing with my dad and uncles, the anger dissipates from his eyes. The world does that stop and move faster thing again when he stops us in place, takes my face into his hands, pulls me to him, and leaves a slow, soft, and very deliberate kiss on my lips.

"Oh, and I'm coming over for pizza too," I shrug. "I'll talk to Uncle Leo about doing a catering order from Cap & Co. when we get back. If there's nothing already going on, I can place the order tonight."

"What would I do without you, Hurricane?"

"Live a very miserable, very boring life," I suggest, taking his hand again as we make our way back to the reception.

"Don't I know it."

CHAPTER SEVENTEEN

STILL HOLLIS

NOT LONG AFTER we rejoined the reception, the temperature started to drop slowly, and then all at once, everyone left the cabin. Even though our group of friends had planned on staying the night tonight, Kinley and Davis chose to go back to the hotel in town and everyone except me, Chase, Tucker, and Ellis went back to Abbott Hills after the festivities.

Tucker and Ellis pretended to still be sleeping in different rooms, and who knows, maybe they still are. What I do know is that right now, while they are definitely not sleeping, they are, in fact, in the same room. The only reason I know is because I just finished creeping down into the kitchen to grab the bottle of tequila and the limes I know were left from the guacamole I made last night.

Any buzz I had from the reception is long worn off and if I am going to make the first move with Chase, I need some liquid courage. Hearing my cousin moan Tucker's name followed by a whole bunch of "shhhhhh's" and laughter wasn't part of the plan. But that made banging on the door and yelling, "keep it down you damn hooligans," before running back to my room for the night that much funnier.

Chase was outside, supervising the caterer and DJ packing up their equipment, something I had been doing with him until he noticed me shiver and sent me inside to warm up. After lighting a fire in the room, I decide to take a bath and wash the day off. Getting dressed up and having a face full of make-up is fun occasionally, but the truth is, I'm much more of a 'let my freckles show, band tees, and ripped jeans' kind of girl.

After a half hour of warming up and relaxing in the Jacuzzi tub, I drain the water and step into the walk-in shower to wash off the bath salts I had been soaking in. The water pressure from the shower is so relaxing that I find myself fighting the urge to close my eyes. When all the salt is rinsed from my body, I turn the water off and wrap myself in one of the oversized fluffy white towels hanging on the wall.

During the last month that I had spent sleeping at Chase's house, I never thought to wear anything other than a big t-shirt and flannel pajama pants. He has seen me stumbling to the coffee maker, braless, hair all over the place more mornings than not over the last thirty days. Hoping this weekend would change things for us, I had stopped at the mall after work earlier in the week. Why I felt I needed to spend almost $100 on a black bralette and matching shorts that barely cover my ass is still beyond me. But I did.

And now they're sitting next to a plastic storage container of cut-up limes, the salt shaker from the kitchen table, and a bottle of tequila staring back at me from the counter I left them on. I had packed flannel pants and an oversized t-shirt just in case I chickened out. But those aren't what I took from my suitcase. And now my options are to go back out there wearing the bridesmaid's dress I had worn all day, go out in this towel, or... suck it up, be brave, and go out in the bralette and booty shorts.

Stalling, I reach for the pump bottle of lavender lotion off the counter. After lathering my legs, I drop the towel and slide the bottoms over my legs. I never, ever wear underwear to bed, but maybe I should have grabbed something. Hooking the bralette, I stare at myself in the full length mirror hanging behind the door.

What if he isn't on the same page as I am? But then, why would he have kissed me? If I wear this out there, it's going to sends a message…the kind that says, "I want to do more things in that bed than just sleep next to you, Chase Merrimack." Am I ready for that?

Opening the container holding the limes first, I brace myself for the burn that's coming. Turning the top of the salt shaker, I grind sea salt onto a lime wedge and then pull the round cork topper off the bottle of tequila. Tipping the bottle back, I shudder as the burn of the clear liquid slides down my throat, then suck on the salted lime as soon as I've put the bottle down. Deciding one wasn't enough, I take one more shot before putting the top back on the bottle.

Ready as I'll ever be, I put the lid back on the remaining limes, leaving them on the counter with the tequila for now. Sucking in a breath, I slowly open the door. Like a magnet, my eyes find Chase. Black, red, and white plaid cotton pajama pants hang just below his waist leaving that stupid V muscle showing like a damn beacon. His hair is wet and tousled, like he had taken a shower. He must have used the guest bathroom down the hall. And of course, somehow, the mess makes him even more attractive.

"I was just about to check on you," he says, not taking his eyes off his phone. "The players seem excited about the pizza party. You're a lifesaver, Hurricane."

Instead of answering him, I focus my attention on the TV above the fireplace. Harry Potter. It only takes a few seconds for me to recognize that it's the first movie. As Hermione fixes Harry's glasses on the train, I find myself wishing I had a wand and could pull the flannel pants and t-shirt I had packed from my suitcase without drawing attention to myself. Accio Dignity.

"Whoa," Chase says, looking up, and locking eyes with me for just a second before I turn away, focusing on the movie again.

"I'm going to change," I stumble over my words, trying to find the ones that don't make me sound as pathetic as I feel. "I brought other pajamas, should have grabbed the other ones. I'm sorry."

Oh. My. God. What the fuck was I thinking?

Just as I bend down to reach for the suitcase, Chase's hands are on mine, pulling them back, the rest of me along with them. I didn't even see him get off the bed or hear him walk across the room, stopping behind me. Stealthy mother fucker.

"Hey, wait." His voice is low as he brushes the hair that has fallen in front of my face. It's the shortest and the darkest it's been in a long time. When Ellis convinced me to chop my hair off last night, she also convinced me to cover all the blonde highlights with a deep, dark brown. Right now, it's as close as it's been in years to my natural hair color.

"This was dumb," I manage to stutter out, refusing to look at him. "I feel so dumb. I don't do shit like this."

As he pulls me back to being upright, I feel more exposed than I've ever been in my whole life. I'm no prude, I wouldn't say I'm as experienced as most of the girls Chase has been with, but fuck.

This is just different, on every level. Aware of everything happening right now, I'm pulled in so many different directions. The crackling of the fire as it snaps, the movie playing on the TV. The smell of open air and the mountain. The fresh air is permeating my lungs and despite being up here for a day, it's making it harder for me to breathe. The same lie I weakly attempted to use to convince Kinley yesterday. I should probably just accept that it's Chase.

As his arms slide around my waist, finding their spot in the small of my back, he leans down and answers my tangent by shutting me up with a long kiss. When he pulls back, he takes my bottom lip into his, sucking the lingering taste of the salted lime off me.

"That's lime and tequila," he nods with certainty as he slides his tongue across his lip, tasting the transfer from our kiss. "You plan on getting wild tonight, Hol?"

A girl enters one white t-shirt contest on Cinco de Mayo after taking a few shots of tequila and she never hears the end of it. Nobody ever mentions that it was for charity, ever. Of course not.

"Shut up. It was just one shot," I defend myself while holding up one finger. "Okay, two. I'm kind of terrified over here."

"So, talk to me." The sweet, gentle patience in his voice reminds me of the hundreds of phone calls in high school where I called him freaking out about whatever melodramatic teenage catastrophe I was facing at the time.

"I feel like I did when we were younger," I say before I can stop myself, the words pouring out. "Except you know, with less clothes on. You're my best friend, Chase, and I'm nervous to be around you. Nervous. You finally notice me as not just your nerdy best friend and I'm a complete mess…again. I'm tripping over my words, I'm worried about saying the wrong thing, doing the wrong thing. I don't do this girlie, having butterflies, catching feelings shit, Chase. I don't like it."

"You think I didn't notice you?" he scoffs as if the thought absolutely baffles him. "I wasn't in a good place when we first moved back, Hol. I was pissed off at the world. I didn't want to be here. My life was back in Washington. I didn't give a shit about the girls I fucked with back then. You deserved more than that. You were, and still are, the coolest chick I've ever met."

"That didn't stop you from kissing me on my sixteenth birthday," I remind him. Letting go of me, he walks back to the side of the bed he was lying on, reaching down to grab something I can't see. When he comes back to me, he places his snapback on my head, backwards just like he wears it. His hands linger on the brim of the hat before sliding down my back, this time taking a firm handful of my ass with each hand.

"I'm still not even sure how we pulled that off," he chuckles, referring to how we convinced my dad and his mom to let me spend the entire weekend at his house without Davis. "I remember the first night was easy. I had football the next morning and you fell asleep on the couch. But the next morning, after football, I walk in the door to see you in little fucking shorts and my hat on backwards, just like this, baking and singing in the kitchen with my mom. I went to shower and came down and you were playing video games with Tuck."

"I woke up to blueberry pancakes with birthday candles on them that morning," I smile as the memories of that weekend come back to me. "Your mom made me feel so damn special that weekend."

As I talk, Chase slowly backs up to the bed. There's no way to cover up the loud gasp that escapes when he picks me up and guides me down so I'm now straddling him on the bed. The thin fabric of our pajamas leave very little left to the imagination.

"It was kind of like this," he laughs, his fingers trail my back, causing more goose bumps with every motion. "Except, if I remember correctly, your crazy ass jump tackled me."

"You called me a wee leprechaun!" I practically shout, defending the actions of my younger self.

"Yeah, that does sound like something I would say," he laughs. "I grabbed you from falling off the bed, you froze and got the same look you still get in your eyes when you want me to kiss you…"

As his voice trails, so do his fingers. Shivers run up and down my body when he traces the inside edge of my shorts. For the first time, his fingers slide up underneath.

"No one else knows how many times since then I've wanted to see that look again. My hat on your head. Short little shorts on my lap," he groans after starting our back and forth game, realizing there's nothing but me underneath the shorts.

"No one else knows that's the best, and my favorite, kiss I've ever had," I admit, trying my damnedest not to lose my composure right now. "And then, you proceeded to avoid me like the plague for weeks."

"Says the girl that chased me out of her house and would only answer her phone just to hang up on me after we kissed again in her room, a few months later," he scoffs. "And wait, hold that thought. Best kiss you've ever had? Like, out of all the kisses? Every single one of them?"

"So, who's going to be the awkward one after this weekend?" I wonder out loud, choosing not to feed his ego with telling him our first kiss was the kiss I compared every single kiss after to.

"What if I just keep kissing you after this weekend?" he suggests as he places a slow, long kiss on my collarbone. Another one follows on my neck, my jawline, right next to my lips…

"I guess, I'd just have to keep kissing you back," I shrug, before pursing my lips in a dramatic kissy face.

Taking my cue, without hesitation, his lips are on mine. Short and sweet pecks, every one of them lasting a bit longer than that last. If this was someone else and they were telling me about how they were feeling right in this moment, I would have some solid "Get your shit together, be in the moment. It's just a guy," advice for them.

But it's not just any guy. It's Chase. Am I building it up to being more than it is? Probably. I've never been the girl to put a dude on a pedestal—even Noah. The love was there, especially in the beginning, but there were never internal fireworks, room spinning, world stopping moments like there is with Chase.

HOLY. SHIT. Focus, Hollis. Hyperventilating is not attractive, girlfrand.

His lips linger on mine before he pulls back. When I realize he isn't coming back for another kiss, my eyes flutter open. As I look at him, with that stupid, cocky grin spread across his face, I can't help but hope it's not completely obvious I was just losing my damn mind.

"Spill it, Hol" he laughs. "I can see the smoke coming from your head."

Mind reading bastard.

After a few seconds of contemplating pushing it off, I know Chase would see through it if I try to bullshit him.

Instead, I manage to whisper, "I just told you, I'm scared."

"Of me?" he asks, concern replaces the cockiness on his face instantly. "Oh, Hollis. At any point, you tell me you need to stop, and it stops, you hear me? We're not doing anything you don't want to."

"Of change. If we do this, whatever this is, I'll be done for," the raw honesty, spills from me once again. "And there will be no going back, Chase. I spent years pushing any feelings I had for you away. Years of pretending we were just friends and eventually I was cool with it. But, if we do this, I don't know if I'll be able to push it back again. I don't think I could do this casually or just go back to being besties if this is going where I think it might be. Are you sure you want to deal with all that?"

"Abso-fucking-lutely."

CHAPTER EIGHTEEN

CHASE

"NO ONE ELSE KNOWS I'VE wanted this since the day you walked into gym class."

As soon as she had the reassurance I was ready for this, the shy, vulnerable woman that had appeared out of nowhere disappeared and she, once again, became the calm, collected, one-step-ahead-of-the-rest, Hollis Capparelli I've known half my life.

Using my own game against me, Hollis whispers confessions against my skin with each kiss she leaves. With each new secret, I feel my willpower slowly strip away, piece by piece. Letting her guide what happens gives me the reassurance that this is something she wants, but when she tells me that "no one else knows she got herself off in the shower thinking about me" this fucking morning, I'm done. Any resolve I had to let her take control of the situation is long gone. I flip us over, so I'm now hovering over her.

"My turn," I whisper into her ear, before placing my lips on her jawline, letting them linger before I start giving her my own confessions. "No one else knows I still hate Luke Whats-His-Face from college because he got a piece of you I'll never have."

Leaving a trail of long, slow kisses from her neck down to her collarbone, I purposely pause at the hemline of the black bra she's wearing.

"No one else knows I wanted to kiss you on your birthday, but knew you weren't ready for it."

As if this night couldn't get any better, I notice the clasp for her bra is in the front, between the cups. With a muttered confession of no importance, I unsnap the two little clasps holding her bra together.

"We've spent the last ten years dancing around this, Chase," she says against my mouth. "I don't want to wait anymore. We have all the time in the world to come back and do everything else and right now, I want you, I need you."

I hadn't considered we would do anything in bed besides sleep, so I'm completely unprepared for this. Remembering that I don't have any kind of protection with me, I feel my heart sinking. Fuck. I didn't plan on having sex with anyone from the wedding, this weekend had been about soaking up every second I could with Hollis. So grabbing the condoms sitting in my top drawer in my bedroom hadn't even crossed my mind.

"I didn't think we would be, and yeah, I didn't bring any…"

"I've been on birth control since before college, Chase," she cuts me off. "I'm okay with it, if you are."

Needing no more convincing, I answer her by taking her lips in mine. Our tongues dance together, each kiss becoming more feverish with anticipation. Positioning myself between her legs, I slowly slide inside her. Every intention of going slow and savoring every second of being with her went out the window the second she moaned my name and arched her back, gripping at the sheets below us with one hand, digging her nails and leaving her mark all over my back with her other.

"I appreciate what you're trying to do here, Chase," her breath is heavy, as she chews at her bottom lip, her eyes begging me for more. "But I need you to stop trying to be romantic about this."

"Then tell me," I whisper in her ear, as I purposely slide out of her slowly, drawing it out. "Tell me what you want."

Slamming into her, over and over, any chance of keeping this "romantic" is gone.

"Jesus Christ, Jesus Christ, Je-" she mutters over and over, as her eyes roll back in her head and she covers her mouth, stifling what I imagine would be the sexiest fucking moan.

"Jesus Christ has nothing to do with this, sweetheart," I chuckle, as I pull her legs up, hold them up for a second, before taking the hand she's gripping the sheets with and place it right above where my dick is inside of her. "Two fingers, move them back and forth like this while I fuck you, and keep your eyes right here or I stop."

"You're so mean," she pouts, as she begins to rub her fingers across her pussy.

Taking my cue, I slide up as deep as I can go, and just like I knew it would, it only takes a few seconds to feel her tighten up around me, her body shaking as she lets go and reaches for something, anything, I think. My own release coming right after Hollis getting her own.

Falling onto each other, both of us are emotionally and physically spent. Tonight wasn't like anything I've felt before. After laying in the torn apart bed for a few minutes, I lean over, kissing her on the forehead, getting the sweetest little sleepy smile as her eyes flutter.

"I would do anything to be the reason you smile like that again," I admit. "But before you fall asleep, baby, let's get you in the shower. I'm sure you don't want to sleep all sweaty and the sheets need to be fixed…"

"Say that again," she sleepily asks, as she reaches for me.

"Before you fall asleep, let's get you in the shower?" I repeat, gently pulling her up and off the bed.

"No, no, no," she shakes her head, taking my hand, following me to the bathroom. Watching me with adoring eyes as I start the shower, I pull her in with me once the temperature is just right. "The part where you called me baby."

Taking the bottle of body wash she had left in here from her shower earlier, I squeeze a few drops onto the spongey bath thing she has hanging from the handle controlling the water temperature. As she leans into me, I wash her back, her whole body lifting as she sighs contentedly. Stepping back, I turn her around, letting her fall back onto me. Her head leans back onto my chest as I wash her shoulders and then begin to make my way down. Once I get to her stomach, I turn her back around, and kneel, the water from the shower dripping all over me. Washing her thighs and her legs, I push her legs apart gently, taking the sponge to her, letting my fingers brush against her warm, swollen clit. A caveman-like pride fills me, knowing I did that. That I left my mark on her. Branded for the night, she's mine.

"Chase," she warns, as if my fingers down there are doing more than clean.

"What baby?" I ask, feigning innocence, knowing damn well exactly what I'm doing.

"You need to stop," she smiles, coyly, as I pull my fingers back.

"Do you really want me to? Because I will…" I kiss the top of her nose, letting her know the ball is completely in her court. I don't want her to feel pressured into doing anything she doesn't want to do.

"You need to stop if you don't intend on following through," she finishes, as her hands find their way into my hair, giving it a little tug.

Sliding one finger in, and then another, I work her clit until I can feel the contractions of her tightening around me. As she begs me for her release, lifting her left leg, settling it on the small shelf meant for holding bottles of shampoo and conditioner. Kissing her thigh, and moving closer with each kiss, her grip on my hair gets tighter with each kiss.

With my fingers still working inside of her, I suck gently, getting a string of "fucks" from Hollis in response. Sliding my tongue across her pussy, I move it in the same motion as my fingers and it isn't more than a minute before she's trying to brace herself on the shower walls, calling to me as I pull my fingers out, selfishly wanting the taste of her all on my lips.

"No one else knows you're the only guy that's gotten me off with his tongue."

She bends down, outside of the shower, reaching for the sponge I dropped when I decided to follow through. As the water runs cold behind us, I tell her I'll be out in a minute and as much as I would kill for what I think she had planned, she just nods and steps out of the shower without a word, covering herself with a towel.

Quickly washing myself off, I grab the other towel, drying myself off before wrapping it around my waist. In the five minutes I had been in the bathroom without her, Hollis had stripped the bed and remade it, leaving a ball of yellow linens on the floor.

"What side do you want?" she asks, looking at the bed from the side closest to the door.

"That one," I point to the side she's standing on.

We cross paths halfway and it takes all my willpower not to grab her and start something again. Her heavy eyes and quiet, sleepy voice stop me though. Choosing to climb into the bed, I extend my arm as an invitation for her to come lay with me instead.

Ten minutes of me running my fingers through her now short black hair and rubbing her scalp, her breathing gets heavy and consistent. Kissing the top of her head, I lean my own into hers.

My heart stopping when I hear a very sleepy, almost incoherent, "I love you, Chase Matthew."

"I love you too, Hollis Grace," I whisper back, not sure if she hears it or not. Our breaths follow a similar pattern, and before long I drift off, feeling the most content I've ever felt in my entire life.

———

I'M NOT sure what time it is, but I've been staring at Hollis peacefully sleeping next to me for a while now. God, she's so fucking perfect. Which is why I can feel my heart breaking knowing what I'm about to do.

Leaving this bed, this room...leaving her is going to be the hardest thing I've ever done. But, I have to. For my heart. For hers. Nothing good can come from the way the world will completely implode underneath us if we let this get too far. I thought I could do this. I thought that we could cross that line and move forward together, because that's all I've ever wanted since the day she, quite literally, stumbled into my life.

She said over and over last night that she wouldn't be able to go back to the way things were if we crossed the line we did, but what happens when we keep this going and everything falls apart? What the fuck do I know about forever? After watching my parents' marriage crumble, I purposely avoided any serious commitment, assuming if the day ever came, Hollis would be the only exception. What happens when she realizes that if we're together, there's no one to save her from *me*? I'm the one that swoops in and saves the day and I can't be "that guy" if we're together.

And I can't expect her to give up everything and everyone else she loves for me. I can't and I won't.

Things are going to change. But I cannot live a life without Hollis Capparelli. We'll get past this weekend. She's going to be angry for a while, but once she has time and I get the chance to explain to her that I walked away for the sake of our friendship, she'll understand. We've gotten through so much. We can get through this too.

I just know I can't lose her forever. Even if that means letting her go for now.

CHAPTER NINETEEN

HOLLIS

THE LOUD CRINKLE of plastic pulls me from a sound sleep. Panic jolts through me like lightning when I see Chase walking with his covered groomsman suit, and haphazardly fold it and stuff it into the gray overnight bag he brought with him. The tightness of his lips and the solemn sadness in his eyes cause me to pull myself up from the warmth of the yellow comforter I lie under.

"What are you doing?" I ask, rubbing my eyes. "What time is it?"

The room is still dark, with no sun peeking through the curtains. The birds haven't replaced the chirp of the crickets. When I had gone down to the kitchen to get us waters, the clock hanging on the wall had read quarter after one. Shortly after I crawled back into bed, I had fallen asleep to Chase's fingers weaving in and out of the short, tendrils of my hair.

"Uh, it's a little after five. I'm going to head home," Chase says, refusing to look up from his now closed overnight bag. "Get ready for the pizza party with the boys. There's a ton of shit I need to do back in Abbott Hills."

"Um, okay. Give me a few minutes, I'll get my stuff together," I tell him. "You could have woken me up instead of creeping around in the dark like a weirdo."

My legs feel tight as I stretch them out across the bed. I'll need to not only rehydrate, but repair my vocal chords after a weekend of eating and drinking like crap—something Chase has been teasing me about since we were kids. No greasy foods, no dairy, and minimal alcohol before I need to sing. Which means like after the night of my birthday, I would spend the next week cleansing my system and loading up on tea. My rambles about grabbing green tea, lemons, and Pedialyte get cut short when Chase interrupts me.

"That's the thing," he adds, still avoiding eye contact. "Do you think Ellis would mind giving you a ride back? I can ask Tuck, too. I think it would be best if I went back by myself, did the party by myself. It's what's best for the team."

"What's best for the team? Or what's best for you?" I shoot back, not buying a single thing that just came out of his mouth. Being friends with someone for half your life, you tend to know when they're lying or trying to bullshit their way out of something. Both of which Chase was doing right now. "What aren't you telling me, Chase?"

"I just want to fucking go home, okay?" he yells, lowering his voice when he sees me jump. But that doesn't stop him from spitting out a venomous, "Damn it, Hollis. Not everything is about you."

He doesn't say goodbye or look back once as he storms out of the room. Before I can stop them, a burst of tears spring from my eyes. I should have known. Letting my guard down, letting him in just that little bit more. Sixteen years of friendship, gone. I said too much last night. There's no turning back now. It's out there. I can't take it back.

He just chose to leave. No matter what he says, I will never believe it was about the football team or a fucking pizza party, which was my idea in the first place. He left because it was too much for him. What I felt was too much. He left because I told him there would be no going back if we did what we did last night, and now that he's not caught up in the heat of the moment, he remembered this is not what he wants. I'm not what he wants.

The Hollis that always runs after him after a fight, never letting him get the last word, is nowhere to be found this morning. Even after he's left me standing there, I can't find words to yell back to him. Instead, I just stand there, baffled, as the warm salty tears continue to fall.

Ripping open my suitcase, I pull my trusty over-sized t-shirt and flannel pajama pants out. I should have just put these on last night.

There's a light knock on the door and a, "Hey, Hol, you okay?"

Tucker and Ellis both peek their heads in, Tucker pushing the door open all the way and wrapping me in bear hug as soon as he sees me crying. Ellis rubs her eyes sleepily before leaving the room without a word. This is probably the earliest she's been up in years, and I'm sure the slamming front door was not the wake-up call they imagined.

"I don't even know what I did," I begin to try to explain. "He just left using the bullshit excuse of the pizza party before he so sweetly let me know that not everything is about me."

"Well, you *can* ride back with me," Tuck offers. "I wanted to stop by your Dad's anyway to talk to him about work stuff."

"I'm actually going to call him," I tell him, the idea coming to me as I say it. "My dad, I mean. See if he and Uncle Leo wouldn't mind running my Jeep up tonight after dinner. Go hiking today, spend another night."

"Or, I could stay," Ellis suggests, handing me a cup of coffee as she rejoins us and sits on the bed. "And we can ride home together tomorrow. I'll give you your space. I'm sure as fuck not hiking or running, but while you're gone, I'll go into town, get some stuff for dinner, a bottle of wine, and just be near if you need me."

"Deal."

With that, Ellis practically forces a breakfast of strawberries and granola down my throat before allowing me to change into the pair of black nylon athletic pants, pink racerback tank top, and the running shoes I had packed just in case I could squeeze in a walk or run through the trails before going home this weekend. I didn't think that I would have a whole day to aimlessly wander around the woods, but if that's the only good that comes from this day, I guess I'll take it.

Grabbing a sweatshirt and a few bottles of water, I toss them in an old hiking backpack that's left in the closet by the front door for this exact reason. Well, it's there for hiking the trails behind the cabin, not necessarily avoiding reality like I'm trying to do, but that's neither here nor there.

Just as I'm about to walk out the door, I hear Tucker call my name from the other side of the house. Stopping, I expect him to ask me not to say anything about him and Ellis.

"Don't worry," I reassure him. "Your secret is safe with me."

Puzzled, he just looks at me, my comment obviously lost on him. "Ooooh! Ellis!" he laughs. "Yeah, I appreciate that. But, that's not what I was coming to talk to you about."

"Alright, now you've got my attention," I admit, having no clue what Tucker could need to talk to me about so urgently that he chased me down.

"Listen, I don't know what went on with you and Chase -"

"Tuck," I stop him, warning that I don't want to get into it with him.

"Just don't give up on him, okay?" he starts. "If I know anything about my brother when it comes to you, it's that he doesn't do anything if he doesn't think it will be what's best for you. Just, don't shut him out, Hol."

"He made it very clear that not everything is about me this morning," I shrug. "I get that he's your brother and I would never ask you to be in a place that puts you in between us because you have to pick Chase. And I know that."

"But, I love you too, sis," he says, offering me a small, sad smile. "Don't forget that."

"I won't," I assure him. "I love you too, little brother."

There isn't an ounce of blood or a single strand of genetics that makes him my little brother, but he was just as much a part of my heart as any of the Capparelli fellas. And he earned that space. Not by his last name or the family ties that bind us together, but by his own love and his loyalty. No matter what happened or didn't happen between Chase and I at this point, I would make sure Mischa, Lola, and Tucker never questioned my love for them. This would not be another repeat of what happened when I was with Noah.

Giving him a quick hug, I ask him to text me during the week to set up a "Auntie Hol & Lola" dinner date and begin to make my way down the long dirt driveway. As I walk toward the bottom, I scroll through my texts until I find the last one from Mischa and send her a quick, "Coffee this week?"

Without waiting for her response, I tuck my phone into the side pocket of the bag on my back. It only takes me fifteen minutes to walk to the entrance of the state park that holds the lake and the small mountain on which I plan on spending most of my day. The Broken Brook Trail is something I could go through in my sleep. The familiar feel of the ground underneath me gives me more comfort than I anticipated. The three miles to the peak is an easy climb, and despite the warmer fall weather, the trails are empty. The entire hike up, I didn't see a single person. It's like the universe figured it would do me a solid, knowing the shit show that was my morning.

Taking in the bright red and yellow leaves that cover the trees on the ground below me, I pause for water and to take a picture of the scenery around me. Uploading the photo with the caption, *"My Only True, Forever Loves – Music & the Mountains."* Ending the post with a black heart emoji, I tap on share.

The truth was, the silent still of this mountain was my source for strength and inspiration…until Chase. I'd spent most of my adult life saying I would never leave this place, or well, New England and all it took last night was for Chase to say he would build me a wraparound porch for me to agree to move to Louisiana if he got the coaching job he applied for at LSU. As we laid there together, I promised I would do all the cooking and he promised to keep me safe from alligators.

I would have followed him to the frozen tundra of Alaska and lived in a fucking igloo if he asked me to. But he didn't. He left. He knew what last night meant to me, to my heart, and he chose to leave anyway. He chose to leave me and everything we promised each other behind.

I told him over and over, there was no coming back from this. There isn't a chance in Hell we can go back to being friends after this. I can't. I won't. I pushed a teenage crush away, but there is no way I can look him in the face and pretend I'm okay right now, or ever. How do you look at the person you know is your soulmate and know they chose not to be with you? I'll be civil when we cross paths again, because I would never expect my family to give up on him. He'll still be at every family event. He'll be at Sunday dinners and holidays.

Right now, I can't take any more of the gut-wrenching twists in my stomach, so I pull out my phone and open the music app. Some people drink, others eat a pint of chocolate ice cream or binge shop, but the only thing I've ever needed is music. Loud music in my ears, that's all it takes to tune out the craziness of the world around me. Going back down the mountain is easy. The Dropkick Murphys' live album playing loudly in my ears made it an effortless descent, reaching the bottom in half the time it took me to get to the peak.

What I wouldn't give for it to be March and Dropkick Murphys to be playing in Boston tonight. Davis, Travis, and I have been going to their St. Patrick's Day show since we were old enough to take the train into the city by ourselves. My brother and my cousin spent their fair share of time in the pit when we were younger, but I stuck to crowd surfing and squeezing my way up to the front to get on the stage at the end. Tonight, five foot nothing or not, tonight, I would have made my way into the pit.

Just as I was about to take the dirt trail exit leading back to the main road to the cabin, I stepped to the left and Flogging Molly, Blood or Whiskey, The Mahones, and The Pogues fill the earbuds for the next two hours as I run the paved running trail that loops around the lake.

"Forever" by Dropkick Murphys begins to play and I stop in my tracks. My feet suddenly feel heavy. Deciding to take a small break, I take a seat on the edge of the water. Before I know it and can stop it, I'm holding my knees with my face down onto my thighs, trying to hide the tears flowing. From who, I don't even know. There's no one around, there hasn't been for hours. This place made up so much of who I am is now just an empty space for my thoughts to scream.

———

"ONE, TWO, THREE, FOUR, FIVE."

"Uno, due, tre, quattro, cinque."

"Uno, dos, tres, quatro, cinco."

Shit. I don't know any other languages.

After a night of watching classic Adam Sandler movies and avoiding talking about Chase and Tucker, Ellis and I said goodnight and made our way to each of our bedrooms. It had been nice to lie on the couch, eat junk food, and drink wine with my cousin. There are few and far between instances we get to spend any time just the two of us, and though there wasn't much conversation tonight, I think it was a night we both needed.

Sliding into bed, I cover myself with the comforter, resting my head on the pillow Chase laid on for only a second before tossing it off the bed. He's not even here and he's still taunting me with the traces that he left behind. As I watch the blades of the ceiling fan spin around, I try to do everything, anything, I can do to not think about Chase. He left. He chose not to stay here with me. He hasn't called. He hasn't texted. He was active on Facebook an hour ago, so I know he's not dead in a ditch somewhere. Not that I would ever admit out loud to checking Facebook Messenger just to see when he was last active…

I'm not too sure why I thought staying in this massive cabin would be a brilliant idea. Even with Ellis just down the hall, and the music blasting in my headphones, the quiet stillness is a loud reminder of who isn't here. There's nowhere I love more than this cabin, more than this mountain. This is my safe place. This has always been my refuge from the craziness of the world.

When my mom left, I came up here…with Chase and our friends. When I didn't get accepted to Berkley, I came up here…with Chase. When I found out that Davis was being deployed to Iraq, I came up here…and Chase knew exactly where to find me. Everywhere I turn, there's a memory with him. The newest ones of his lips on mine and our bodies colliding in these sheets replay over and over in my head.

God, how could I have been so stupid? How could I have even tangled with the thought of letting it become more than what it was? How could he kiss me? How could he keep kissing me after I told him that it would change everything? That I couldn't go back to the way it was after that? How did I let myself fall for the unattainable Chase Merrimack? I knew better than anyone that his heart was untouchable. Chase didn't love. Chase didn't do relationships or commitment.

For the first time since my mom left, I sob until there's absolutely nothing left in me. I cry for the love lost, the love that could have been, and the love that never had a chance.

CHAPTER TWENTY

CHASE

MY LIVING ROOM IS FULL. Twenty teenage boys have taken over the first floor of my house and are now screaming at the football game on the TV. But somehow, the whole house feels empty. I feel so empty. There is no time for self-pity though. I knew what I was doing. I knew who and what I was leaving behind at that cabin yesterday, and now I need to deal with it. On my own time.

Right now there are boys watching me, counting on me to be the hero, depending on me to stand strong and defend them. When the game was over, I would hand out the permission slips they would need to bring to school tomorrow. Pulling every string I had, I managed to get the team a sit in during a Patriots practice, followed by a tour of the facility. A few hours on the phone between yesterday and today with the principal, the superintendent of schools, and multiple people at Gillette Stadium, I managed to pull off the best apology I could think of for these boys.

Nothing was left to be figured out by the school. The Patriots' bus would pick them up after homeroom, and we would be back before the bell rang at the end of the day. And

Aaron was put on paid leave until a full investigation was made into him threatening my players. I would have preferred his ass fired, but I'll take what I can get for now. Which is why I invited Tuck over today, too. He was watching the game with the Capparellis, something I couldn't do even if I wanted to. After the game, he and Lola were going to come over for dinner. Though knowing where they were leaving to come here, I knew there was a good chance they would come with full bellies. The Capparelli women used any excuse to make the day into a festive event.

With Aaron gone, I would need the extra help on the field. Knowing that Tuck had asked to change his crew's shift so that he had time to pick up Lola from kindergarten meant he would be out of work by the time practice started. Covering my bases, I had already called my mom and asked her if Lola could come to the salon on bad weather days or if she didn't want to hang out at the field. Not only had she eagerly agreed to help with Lola if Tuck said yes, she, completely oblivious to the events of the day before, made sure to let me know how excited she was to have coffee with Hollis on Thursday.

Luckily, the doorbell rang, and I had an excuse to get off the phone with her before she called me out on my awkward silence. When I opened the door, Kandi, the Capparelli & Co. catering coordinator, handed me a stack of pizzas and then went to her car and grabbed a heaping stack of her own, too. Twelve extra-large pizzas - "six cheese and six pepperonis," she told me, as I brought them to the breakfast bar. Reaching in my pocket for the cash to pay for them, she waved it off, handing me a blank receipt with handwriting I recognized right away.

Good luck, Chase.
-H

So impersonal, so unlike her. I don't know what hurt worse,

her cordial demeanor or knowing that even with everything that happened, she made sure the boys of my team were taken care of. It was like a slap in the face and a knife to my heart at the same time. For the first time in my life, I couldn't concentrate on the game in front of me. All I could think about was her. I worried if she was okay, wondered if she was hurting like I was. Despite knowing that what I did was for the best in the long run, it didn't make it any easier right now.

The next hour rolls together like big snowball of events. The eruption of cheers when New England wins the football game is minimal compared to the roar when I tell my team how I planned on making up their Friday game. Handing out the permissions slips, I reiterate to them half a dozen times before they leave that they must have the forms filled out to go tomorrow. As the last kid is being picked up, Tucker and Lola walk through the front door. The bright, excited smile of my sweet niece makes my heart forget how much self-inflicted hurt it was feeling.

"Hiiiiiiii, Uncle Chase!" she squeals as she jumps into my arms. "Guess what?"

"What's that, Lola Grace?" I ask, genuinely smiling for the first time since I left the cabin.

"Auntie Hollis is takin' me to see Taylor Swift tomorrow! *THE* Taylor Swift. And, Uncle Chase," she exclaims, her words rolling into each other as she jumps up and down. "She said I can meet her."

"Whoa. You are gonna have so much fun!"

"I know!!!" She giggles and spies the boxes of pizza from Capparelli & Co. still sitting on the breakfast bar. "Is that Nonno's pizza?"

"It is," I tell her. "I was going to see if you guys wanted to order something else. There's plenty left if that's what you want though."

"I'm good with Cap & Co. pizza," Tucker interjects. "Just

beer me, set Lo up with Disney on the big TV, and then you can kiss my a-s-s while I pretend not to know you need my help with the team."

Mom. I should have known she would give him a heads up. No doubt begging him to help me out.

"And don't worry," he continues as he takes a piece of cheese pizza out of the box for Lola, popping it in the microwave, and grabbing a bottle of water for her before making his way to the living room. "I didn't tell her about Hollis."

"What about Hollis?" I question, following him into the next room, wanting to know what he knows, or what he thinks he knows. Hollis's Instagram post a few hours after I left said that she was in the mountains, but it didn't look like anyone was with her. If he had something going on with Ellis, it wouldn't surprise me if Ellis told him anything Hollis said. I know that Hollis trusted her cousin, but Ellis wasn't exactly known for being the most discreet or trustworthy when it came to keeping people's secrets.

He doesn't answer me as I set up the TV for Lola, putting on Disney Junior for her. As soon as she sees Mickey Mouse come onto the TV, Tucker and I are invisible to her. Once he's sure she's content, without a word, Tucker heads back into the kitchen, and helps himself to a beer in my fridge before taking his own slice of pizza.

"I don't know man," he says, popping the cap off his beer and taking a big sip. "All I know is that you guys were all over each other at the wedding, you stormed off the next morning, and I walked in to see Hollis crying like I've never seen anyone cry in my life. I mean, I'm talking I was reminding her to breathe, Chase. And then she disappeared into the woods for hours. She wouldn't talk to me about it. She wouldn't talk to Ellis later after I left…and I'm not here to point fingers, because I love you both, but before she left, I asked her not to give up on your stubborn ass and she looked me in the eyes and told me that you gave up on her…"

Opening my mouth to form a rebuttal, I find myself at a loss for words. When I left, I had no idea it would have that kind of effect on Hollis. I knew she'd be pissed, but sobbing so hard she couldn't breathe? If that's not throwing salt on an open wound, I don't know what is.

"Yeah, exactly," Tucker agrees to my non-vocal response, as if he can read my mind. "And then she makes plans with mom, outside of the house. She gives me suite tickets to the Bruins game and asks me if she can bring Lola to see Taylor Swift. Like, she's trying to tell us that no matter what happens between you guys, she's not leaving this time."

As my brother grabs another slice of pizza, I inhale and then exhale a big breath.

"Hollis and I," I sigh, then continue, "Crossed a line we shouldn't have this weekend. We said a lot of stuff in the heat of the moment. And I wanted it, man. It's no fucking secret I've loved that girl since we were kids. I thought it was finally fucking happening. But man, it's only been a month since she broke up with Noah. What if this was just some rebound thing? And even if it's not. Man, what the fuck do I have to offer a girl like her? She wants the real thing. What the fuck do I know about being in a committed relationship? I don't do the girlfriend thing. So, what happens when she realizes I am not boyfriend material? We lose years of friendship and we're right back to where we started, except then, we don't even have a friendship."

"You are a fucking idiot," my little brother shakes his head in disbelief when I take a break from my mini tangent. "Hollis Capparelli would move Heaven and Earth for you, ya dumbass. You don't think she's loved you just as long? Fuck, we all knew you guys would end up together, eventually. Who fucking cares about Noah. He's a douche and according to Ellis, it was over looooong before they broke up. I cannot fucking believe you walked away from her. I love you, big bro, but man, you are so dumb."

"Even if I wanted to try and fix this, it's too late, Tuck," I sigh. "By now, Hollis has her mind made up and I can promise you, she'll want nothing to do with me."

"Then you better think of something pretty fucking epic to win her back."

With that, I know he's right. Sending Ellis and Kinley texts, I get the ball rolling. This is going to take some work, and I'm going to need some help.

CHAPTER TWENTY-ONE

HOLLIS

AUTO-PILOT. That's what I've been on all week. No matter where I go, I can't escape Chase. When I went over Ellis and Cole's apartment for our weekly dinner on Tuesday, they had ordered from La Mesa. Hoping to avoid a margarita-fueled meltdown, I passed when Cole offered me one. Which quickly led to being interrogated by Kinley, and me having a completely sober meltdown at the kitchen table.

He's in the songs I play on the radio in the morning...when I have to pretend that everything is okay, and my life isn't fucking falling apart behind the airwaves. And then came coffee with Mischa. I put on a brave face and a fake smile, but like the good mom that she is, she saw right through my act, and eventually, she broke me. Just when I thought I couldn't feel any worse, there I was, sobbing like a fucking idiot in the middle of Starbucks.

I tried so hard to act like I was just angry, that I could just push him and my hurt aside and move on. But I was broken. Completely shattered. At night, he was the ghost haunting my dreams. Every morning, I would wake up with stupid false hope only to be crushed down by the reality of the situation I had found myself in. In the morning on the air, on the drive home, at the three concerts I co-hosted during the week, I felt like a fucking zombie.

I had my bartending shift covered on Friday night, Cole covered for me on Saturday doing a double set of karaoke, but there was no way I could escape tonight.

Tonight, my favorite day of the year, and I am an empty shell of a person, dreading what lies ahead of me.

"Does your sour puss have anything to do with the fact that you'll be seeing Chase tonight? Because I saw him today, Hollis Grace with the sad face. He's doing no better than you."

Tonight is the one Sunday of the year there is no dinner at Nonna and Nonno's house, because tonight is the 20th annual Capparelli & Co. Halloween Gala. Twenty years ago, my Nonna and Gramma O'Brien put together the first Gala after my Gramma O'Brien—a high school math teacher—had gone to my Nonna when the high school's girls' basketball team desperately needed a sponsor or they wouldn't have the funds to play their winter season. My Nonna not only sponsored the team that year, but decided that the one season wasn't enough. With just a few weeks to spare before Halloween, she and my Gramma worked together to put together a big party with all the proceeds going to the high school's athletic department. Every year it gets bigger and better.

When I started working at The Ranch, I invited a few people to the event and before I knew it, the radio station was involved too. Just like the last couple years, I would MC the first half of the event during the live performances and then Troy, The Ranch's night time DJ, would go live on the air and DJ the event for the rest of the night. Normally I live for this night. Every year I try to top the previous year's costume and this year, I had been able to pull some strings at the radio station. Managing to get a few bigger names to come perform, it drew in a larger crowd than normal. Devin Dawson, an up-

and-coming country artist, had even agreed to do a meet and greet, donating all proceeds to the Athletic Department as well.

Instead of telling my cousin that I want to do anything but go to the Halloween Gala tonight, I shrug it off, telling her I'm just tired. I don't want to put on my peppy morning show persona and yeah, I really don't want to see Chase.

Leaving me to get changed into my costume, Ellis tells me she's going to use the mirror in the bathroom and she'll be back in a few minutes. After about ten minutes, the door opens back up and my cousin lets out a "whoa" while motioning for me to turn around.

"Is that a good whoa or a bad whoa?" I ask nervously. After the hour it took to do my make-up and the pep talk I needed to give myself to pull the tags off the costume, I hope it isn't a bad "whoa."

"That is partially a 'whoa, Chase is going to lose it when he sees you' kind of whoa and an 'Uncle Lorenzo and Davis, who are both upstairs, are going to have heart attacks when they see you in this costume' kind of whoa," she laughs as she zips the back of my skirt for me.

Taking another look in the mirror, I suddenly feel thankful that I got my behind out of bed every morning for those runs with Davis. For months, I had planned on going as hipster Ariel from The Little Mermaid tonight. I figured a clamshell t-shirt, a pair of mermaid leggings, a red wig, and a pair of big black specs would do the trick. Then Tuesday after work, Ellis and Cole called to see if I wanted to go costume shopping with them after our weekly dinner. I already had everything I needed, but I didn't want to sit in my house stewing over the Chase situation any more than necessary.

The owner of the boutique is friends with my aunts and helped Cole and Ellis pick out the perfect, last minute costumes for this weekend. Despite me trying to convince them that I was content with my hipster Ariel costume, somehow I let them talk me into buying a whole new, very different mermaid costume.

The hot pink sequined sea shell cups with underwire fit looks like a sparkly push-up bra. A very fitted metallic green skirt with the scale pattern hugs every single one of my curves all the way down to the ruffled organza "tail." Ellis had spent an hour using fishnet stockings over my face, creating scales on my face and neck. Finishing off the costume is a huge, dramatic seashell crown. For a girl who spends most of her time in jeans and band tees, I feel completely out of my element right now.

I look around my room for anything I may be forgetting, put my lipstick in my clutch, and walk downstairs to see my dad and brother waiting at the bottom. It feels like a cliché movie scene except I'm not in a ball gown and there's no date waiting for me at the bottom the stairs. Coordinating their costumes this year, my dad and Davis are quite possibly the cutest thing I've seen in my entire life. They're both in faded jeans, white high-top sneakers, and have big black wireless headphones sitting around their necks. My dad's shirt is black with white letters that says, "The Original" on the front and "Poppa Cap" on the back. Davis's shirt says, "The Remix" on the front and "Big D" on the back.

"I wish you were sixteen, so I could go tell you to change your costume," my dad sighs before turning to my brother. "You look like a mermaid princess, but isn't there some law that says the sister of a police officer needs to completely covered, Davis?"

"Ha," my brother laughs. "I wish, Pop. I'm going to spend half the night reminding my co-workers my sister is off-limits."

"What about me?" Ellis pouts, causing a scoff from my dad. Her bright blue hair is pulled into a messy bun, tied with a black bandana at the top. A short bright orange jumpsuit cut just below her ass with "PRISONER" and a slew of random numbers painted on the back is halfway unbuttoned, exposing her lacy black bra. Everyone knows that at last year's Halloween event, she went home with Davis's superior. The year before that was Travis's partner…

"Your costume is, uh, appropriate," my brother starts. "But, you've already slept with half the department, so if you're trying to catch the attention of any of Abbott Hill's finest, I suggest you try the rookies."

"Four guys," shaking her head in disbelief as she corrects him. "And one of them was before he was a cop, Davis."

Before Davis can argue, we are interrupted by the doorbell. Shaking my head at the two of them, I make my way to the door, assuming it's Troy here to meet me before the Gala. When he texted me this morning, asking if I wanted to together, I didn't think anything of it before texting him back a quick "Sure! Sounds great!" I assumed it was just because we were both going to the same place tonight and it was my family's event.

Opening the door, I find Troy, just like I thought. He's in a sleeveless navy-blue shirt, both of his fully tattooed arms are on full display. The white collar of the shirt has red trim and a bow at the center. His shirt is tucked into the matching blue pants. Everything is tied together by the white shoes and white hat with an upturned brim on top of his head.

He's dressed as a sailor…and he's holding a bouquet of roses.

Shit. Shit. Shit. He thinks this is a date.

———

KEEPING WITH TRADITION, the entire O'Brien-Capparelli family make their entrance into the annual Gala together. Or well, I should say the three members of the O'Brien side of my family and the whole, crazy crew of Capparellis walk in together. Because of that, I had easily been able to come up with the excuse to brush Troy off, mentioning that I totally spaced the photographers and my Nonna and Gramma O'Brien's insistence that we all go in together.

My brother picked up on my hesitation to go with Troy right away, asking me if I was ready to go, leading the way and opening the passenger door to his car, without even needing me to imply I needed an escape route. Twin telepathy came through with no time to spare.

Guilt had filled me for a few minutes, hoping I hadn't given Troy the impression that this was anything more than the two of us working an event together. It quickly passed when I remembered in just a few more minutes I would be facing Chase for the first time since he left the cabin.

No matter what was going on between us, he knows what this night means not only to my grandmothers, but to my aunts and his mom, too. The Gala that started as a joint project for my Gramma O'Brien and Nonna has become something that my Aunt Grace, Zia Kat, and Mischa Merrimack have taken over together with Kinley planning the specific party details. Chase, Tucker, and Mischa have been walking in with us for the last ten years, too. There's no way he would miss it.

"I don't know what happened, but I'll bet he's just as nervous to see you too, Hol."

I could bullshit my way through a response with anyone else, acting like I'm fine, that I have no idea what they're talking about. Hell, I just did it with Ellis an hour before in my bedroom as we were getting ready, but my brother would call me out before the lie even left my lips. So instead, I let out a reluctant sigh. My brother doesn't need to know the details, especially not tonight, but I'm sure by now he's noticed that my Jeep hasn't been in his neighbor's driveway once since the weekend of the wedding.

Pulling into the hotel, an entire row of our family's cars is parked in the front of the lot. Chase's truck is nowhere in sight, giving me temporary relief, only to remember he could have driven in with Tucker, Travis, Kenny, or even his mom. Pushing through the revolving doors, I am greeted with faces of shock and awe. Looking behind me to see what everyone is gawking at, I feel my cheeks warm once I realize they're looking at me. The heat of my flushing cheeks continues to rise as I shrug, wince, and brace myself for the backlash of the most revealing costume I've ever worn to a Gala.

"Hot dang, Hollis!" my cousin Elisabeth squeals, making her way through the crowd of our family gathering in the lobby.

Dressed as a pink fairy—her little dress and wings matching her bubble gum pink hair—she appropriately all but flies over to me. Since this is the first Gala that has happened since she turned eighteen last December, tonight will be *her* first Gala, ever. Linking arms with me, together we make our way to the front of the group. My heart drops when I hear my aunt exclaim, "Alright, we're all here. Lead the way, ladies."

Ellis swoops in beside me, sliding her arm into my free arm to the left, and the three of us make our way down the black carpet leading into the ballroom. The local newspapers, TV reporters, and hired photographers from the high school photography program are set up like paparazzi standing behind two roped off areas to each side. Smiling brightly as a dozen flashes go off, we pause half way through, looking in both directions on cue.

The room doesn't open to anyone else for another hour, but it's tradition for our family to get there before everyone and make our entrance together. We take an overabundance of professional photos, get first dibs on bids for the silent auction, and my uncles get started at the bar...this year I think I might join them.

As we walk into the ballroom, Ellis, Elisabeth, and I all gasp simultaneously. While my aunts and Mischa Merrimack put in the time and effort securing the sponsors, setting up the silent auction, and working with the high school culinary program to create a menu for the night, Kinley and her company oversee decorating. Trying not to create an overly specific theme that would limit people's costume choices, for the last five years Kinley has created some of the most creative general Halloween themes for the Gala. I wasn't sure she would be able to top last year's Jack-o-Lantern theme, but I was happily proven wrong the moment we stepped foot into the ballroom.

Annie Lennox's "I Put A Spell On You" plays through the speakers as we make our way to our assigned table, passing the biggest candy bar I've ever seen on the way. Above us, purple and black paper lanterns fill the ceiling space. Our table is covered in a deep purple tablecloth and a large black rose kissing ball centerpiece sits in the middle of the table. Kinley and her crew managed to make spooky elegant and sexy.

When Kinley started her party planning business, the Halloween Gala was the first big event she hosted. After the first gala, it was like the floodgates opened for her. She's been booked non-stop ever since. This is the biggest event she plans every year. Even with the $150 ticket cost, all 500 tickets sell out every year. People come from all over New England to go to the Capparelli & Co. Halloween Gala.

Turning just in time, Kinley catches us as we're putting our clutches on the table. Her eyes light up as she gives us an excited wave from across the room, turning back to a group of five other women within seconds. All of them, including Kinley, are dressed in black leggings, all white sneakers, and referee shirts.

"Drinks?" Davis asks, coming up on the side of me with my cousin Travis.

Since it's just us, the gathering around the bar is still small. I won't be able to drink more than one cocktail before I have to start hosting, but I need something to settle these nerves. Any second now, I'll bump into Chase, and I don't know what's going to happen. Catching Ellis's eye, I point to the bar. A small smirk and a nod of acknowledgment is all I get before her eyes snap back to Tucker, who is by her side and dressed like a police officer. Now her costume choice makes perfect sense.

As we wait for the bartender to finish making drinks for my dad and uncles, I feel my stomach knot up. Chase is here, in the room, close to me. Come on bartender guy, small talk is cool and all, but I need alcohol, stat.

"Don't go home with him," his voice is a demanding growl so low in my ear it sends shivers down my spine.

"What the fuck are you talking about?" I turn to face Chase, feeling the unnecessary need to defend myself. "And even if I do go home with someone it's no concern of yours, Ch-"

I stop short when I see him. Saliva pools in my mouth instantly, causing me to gulp. Holy shit. He's dressed like a fucking pirate. The white dress shirt he has on is half unbuttoned, showing his defined pecs. When Ellis said she saw him earlier, I assumed it was at the store or something, but it must have been to do his make-up because his eyes are surrounded by black eyeliner, his eyelids are dark and covered in make-up too. His normally perfectly styled hair is covered by a wig of dreadlocks with random beads, a plain, worn red bandanna, and an aged brown leather pirate hat finish the look. He looks like Jack fucking Sparrow and I'm pretty sure I understand the term "the thirst is real" because holy fuck, I want some of that.

"Whatever this beautiful siren wants," Chase tells the bartender when he makes his way over to us, "Goes on my tab. Anything she drinks tonight, it's on me."

"Alright," the shaggy redhead shrugs. "What can I get for ya, love?"

"Um, the darkest rum you have on the top shelf and Coke," I tell him, breaking my lock on Chase when I turn to face him to add. "Please."

Every night before the cabin, I would have argued with Chase. But, what the hell. If he thinks buying my drinks tonight is some sort of white flag or apology, then more power to him. It's not going to change anything, and I'll get drunk, for free. If the only way I can hurt him back is through his wallet, then so be it.

CHAPTER TWENTY-TWO

CHASE

"SHE LOOKS FAKE."

"Yeah, if by "fake," you mean she looks like a perfectly crafted Barbie doll. Good for Chase."

"Oh, please. I try not to judge based on first impressions, but she was all but dry humping him. Come on...A horny chihuahua has more self-control."

"Alright, fine. She totally looks like Bimbo Barbie and I already want to punch her in her fake, orange face."

Rolling my eyes as I realize my best friend—the woman I am in love with—and her cousin are talking about me and Bethany, my crazy co-worker who had not only shown up after hearing I would be here, but then when she got here, promised me "just one dance and I'll leave you alone for the night." Expecting her to keep true to her word, I let her drag me to the dance floor and was mortified when she started to give me an upright lap dance. When she didn't take the hint after I told her my mother was here, I excused myself to the bar for some water. Truth be told, Hollis had just wrapped up her half of the night as MC and I wanted to get her attention before anyone else did.

"I usually refer to her as Bat Shit Crazy Barbie actually," I chuckle, leaning in between Ellis and Hollis who have inched their way up to the bar, and are waiting for their drinks. Huffing, Hollis forces a smile toward the bartender and tosses some money on the bar.

"I can and will pay for my own drinks tonight, thank you very much."

As she brushes past me, I notice her drink is a lot darker than her normal Blue Hawaiian she usually drinks at events like this. The fruity rum drink makes her a happy, lovey drunk, typically.

"What's the mermaid drinking?" I ask the bartender after ordering my beer.

"Jack & Diet with lime," he shouts as he pours my beer from the tap behind the bar. "What's the deal with you two anyway?"

Fuuuuuuck. Hollis is drinking Tennessee whiskey. Which only means one thing. She's pissed and I can guarantee it's with me, deservedly so. I've got my work cut out for me tonight, but I'm determined. If nothing else, she'll hear me out. She deserves that much, to know it wasn't her or the thought of us being together.

"Long story short," I answer taking the last beer I'll be drinking tonight from his hands, "She's amazing and I fucked up."

"I knew it!" Travis, dressed as lumberjack, pipes in from the side of me. "I knew something happened. My cousin isn't a very good liar."

Well, that's not the response I would have expected from any of the Capparelli fellas. My confusion must be written all over my face because he laughs before motioning for me to follow him, "Come on, man. We all know you've been avoiding us because you know you screwed up. You guys are gonna kiss and make up. You haaaave to. You're Hollis and Chase. If you guys don't work it out, the rest of us are fucked."

Deciding sitting is probably the best way to stay out of trouble, I pull out a chair next to Davis at the table we were assigned with Travis, Tucker, Kenny, and Hollis's cousin LJ. Which is right next to the table Hollis, Ellis, Cole, and Elisabeth are sitting at. If Ellis and Tucker are trying to hide that there's something going on between the two of them, they need to quit staring at each other.

"Oh, look who decided to join us," Davis nods to me as I sit down. "So, what's the plan?"

"The plan?" I ask, taking a long sip of my Long Trail Harvest. My favorite brown ale is only seasonal, especially from the tap. I mean, any beer that has Vermont maple syrups wins me, but if I didn't need to stay sober to make sure I'm good to drive at any given time, I would be drinking more than two beers tonight.

"The plan," he repeats. "You know you're gonna need help to get my sister to stop for two seconds to even talk to you, so what do you need from us?"

Before I answer him, I look around the table. My brother, Kenny, and Travis are all watching me, waiting, expecting my answer too. Man, I'm not one to get sentimental, but I am one lucky bastard. Davis and Travis have spent most of their lives chasing away any guys that just thought about attempting to date Hollis or Ellis. I can't count how many times I heard, "You come near my sister again, I will break your fucking legs" growing up. Though, in their defense, all the guys were douchebags. If a stand-up, good guy had come along, I don't think either one of them would have ever gotten involved.

Opening my mouth to tell them that I have no idea what I'm going to do yet, I stop and follow Hollis as she and Cole get up and make their way over to the dance floor. It only takes a few songs before some dickhead dressed like a gladiator gets her attention and leads her to the bar.

"A distraction," I answer, finally. "We need a distraction."

CHAPTER TWENTY-THREE

HOLLIS

AS EACH SONG fades into the next, I feel myself caring less and less about the fact that Chase is sitting off to the side, watching my every move. Cole's date had blown her off, so we decided early in the evening to implement the buddy system. Originally Ellis had been part of this deal, but she jumped ship the second Tucker asked her to dance. Traitor.

Tonight, I just wanted to be free, to drink and dance and for just one night, to not worry about the stupid tricks my heart and head are playing on me. But that wasn't about to stop me from letting the hot Gladiator dude and his friend, Captain America, from buying me and Cole shots. Oh, no. That would be rude and foolish. And I am neither rude nor foolish. Well, I might be considering what got me to the point of needing to leave my heart behind tonight, but that's beside the point right now.

As the four of us walk over to the bar, Captain America makes a horrible joke about crossing universal comic book lines by buying Wonder Woman a drink, sending Cole into hysterics. Great. There goes the buddy system. While we wait for our round of cinnamon toast crunch shots, Captain America and

Gladiator Dude introduce themselves. Captain America—a lawyer named Sam—and his cousin, Deacon—the hot gladiator—were sent here by Sam's dad and boss, a corporate sponsor of the gala. Sam's date blew him off last minute, so Deacon had been his last-minute ticket filler. Just like that, Cole becomes putty in his hands, explaining that she too, was blown off by her date.

"And you?" Hot Gladiator Deacon leans over and asks as the bartender drops the four shots on the bar. "Please tell me no one was stupid enough to blow you off tonight."

Taking a shot from Cole's hand as she passes them back to us, I hand the first one to him, "No, no one blew me off."

"So, where's your boyfriend?" he questions, a glimmer of hope sparks in his bright blue eyes as he anticipates my response.

"No boyfriend either," I answer, tipping the shot glass back between my lips.

Shuddering as the alcohol trickles down, a lingering trail of burning cinnamon slides down my throat. Before the bartender gets too far, Gladiator Deacon pulls out his credit card and orders another round for the four of us, another Jack and Diet Coke for me, and a Malibu and Sprite for Cole, despite Captain America telling him that he has a company card for their expenses tonight.

"Sometimes, you just want to be the one that buys a pretty girl a drink, Cousin," he winks at me as he hands me my drink.

The next shot goes down a little easier, burning a bit less than the last one, which means only one thing. I am well on my way to being drunk. Confirming that is my sudden decision that I don't need Chase Merrimack or his kisses and that if he wants to be with a fake blonde airhead, more power to him.

Because, you know what? I. Don't. Care. I don't care about him or his perfect smile, and his stupid laugh, and the way he can make anything better just by being in the same room as me.

The only problem being that, even in my almost drunken stubbornness, I know I'm lying just to convince myself, because I do care. So much. Too much.

In a poor attempt to stop myself from thinking about Chase and why I was stupid enough to fall in love with him, I pull Deacon—the hot Gladiator—to the dance floor with one hand, furiously sucking my cocktail through the straw the bartender kept replacing in my drink. Normally I wouldn't drink with a straw, but I had made a joke that I needed to get alcohol in me quickly when I ordered my first drink tonight and the brilliant bartender had thrown a pink bendy straw in before handing me the glass of whiskey and diet cola.

As much as I try not to look over at the table the guys are all sitting at, I can't help but notice as Kenny, Travis, Davis, Tucker, and Chase all make their way over to the DJ booth. My brother says something to Troy who nods and hands down his microphone before heading back to his set-up on the stage, giving the guys a thumbs-up.

Holding up his fingers, counting one, two, three, my brother holds the mic while he, Travis, Chase, Tucker, and Kenny all lean into the microphone and say, "This one's for Hurricane Hollis!"

The guitar and banjo intro to "Shipping Up to Boston" by the Dropkick Murphys fills the room. All five of them raise their glasses to me, but the smirk on Chase's face says more than enough. This was all him. Turning to Deacon, I thank him for the drink and excuse myself to give those fuckers a piece of my mind. They know it's coming too, because Davis laughs and pulls Travis in front of him like a human shield before I make my way over to them.

"Shiiiiiit," Travis laughs when I stand in front of the four of them, with arms crossed. "You didn't think this angry punk rock thing over very well, Merrimack. She's little, but damn it, she scares me."

As my favorite band blasts in the background, I remind them that I am twenty-eight years old and I do not need them trying to interfere every time I look in the general direction of anything with a penis. Two minutes go by and Troy cracks a joke about needing to slow things back down "after that one" from the stage. An Ed Sheeran song begins to fill the room as I turn to walk away. Though I had planned on tearing into Chase, the truth was I couldn't. I knew in my very core that if I got into it with him, even here in a room full of hundreds of people, I would end up crying. And that is not something I am about to let happen tonight.

I only get a few steps away before he grabs my hand, his touch causing me to freeze in place. As much as I would love to act like I'm this tough, give no fucks kind of girl with no feelings, the truth is, he's my weakness. Chase Merrimack is my kryptonite. Especially Chase Merrimack dressed like a freakin' pirate. He knew exactly what he was doing dressing like that tonight. He knows about my childhood dream, and how ridiculously obsessed with Jack Sparrow in Pirates of the Caribbean I am.

"Chase, please," I beg, knowing that the second I'm in his arms, I'm done for. "I can't do this."

"Just one song," he pleads. "Please. Dance with me, Hurricane."

As if I really had a choice. I wrap my fingers around his and let him lead me onto the dance floor. As I start to pull away, "Let It Be Me," the same Ray LaMontagne song that we danced to at Kinley and Davis's wedding begins to play, and I feel myself melt into him once again. As he sings the lyrics softly next to my head, goose bumps start from the tip of my fingers and creep up my arm. With that, as quickly as I was sucked into the moment with him, I snap back to reality. I can't believe I lost sight of the fact that he reassured me over and over that what we were doing meant more than just the sex we were having, and then, he left me. He left me with a shattered heart and then disappeared for days, with not so much as a phone call.

"Excuse me," I say, pulling my hand out of his, stepping back. "I suddenly would like to go home."

"What? If you think anyone in this room is going to let you leave with the amount you've drank tonight, you're out of your damn mind. I'll bring you home, if that's what you really want. But there is no way you're driving-," he pauses like he's waiting for me to respond, and finishes, "-or walking by yourself."

"Ooookay. Whatever you say, Merrimack. Can you please move now? I'll find my new friend Deacon, and I'll ask him to bring me home or maybe, I'll just spend the night with him. I don't think he'd mind having the company in bed tonight," I snap back, flashing a fake, malicious smile at Chase.

There's no way I would leave with Deacon, but I also know that making any kind of impression that I intend on going home with anyone else is going to get under his skin—especially given the first thing he said to me tonight was "don't go home with him," wherever that came from. Right now, I'm not sure if I'm just looking to get a reaction out of Chase or if I honestly want him to think I would leave with someone else.

Shaking his head, as if he's unfazed by my empty threat, he chuckles, "Yeah, hate to burst that drunken little bubble of yours, little girl, but it'll be a cold day in hell when I let that happen either."

Turning away from me, like he's about to walk away from me, he pauses and then shakes his head. What I wouldn't give to be able to read his thoughts right now. There's no time to wonder about what could possibly be going through his mind, because without so much as a warning, he turns back around, walks back over to where I am still standing and picks me up, all but tossing me over his shoulder.

Walking us over to the table my dad, uncles, and

grandfathers are sitting at, I hear laughter from the table of men that I assumed would tell him to cut the shit. Instead, Chase tells them all that I have decided I would like to go home, but since I have had "five too many drinks tonight," he will be bringing me to his house for the night.

My father stands up from the table, pats him on his empty shoulder, and thanks him for "always looking out for his favorite girl."

He. Fucking. Pats. Him. On. The. Shoulder.

I am his only daughter, slung over someone's shoulder, being carried like a fucking cavewoman, and my father THANKS HIM AND PATS HIM ON THE FUCKING SHOULDER.

"Daddy! Are you serious, right now?" I yell back when Chase turns and makes his way toward the exit. "CHASE MATTHEW MERRIMACK. Put my ass down."

The entire room is watching as Chase continually shakes his head and makes his way across the room. The time for worrying about causing a scene has passed, as I kick and scream for him to put me down like an angry child not getting their way. I don't even have to see his face to know he has a shit-eating grin on it. Bastard thinks he's won this round.

Ellis, Kinley, and Cole laugh and wave as we walk past them at the cupcake table. When we pass the bar, Davis, Tucker, Travis, and Kenny shake their heads as if they're amused, but not in the least bit surprised by what is going on right now. Mischa grabs his arm, asking to text her when he gets home. My Aunt Grace and Zia Kat chime in with, "us toos" and Chase assures them they'll each get a text, but not one of those assholes step in. Not one of them tell him to put me down.

Through the lobby and the parking lot, Chase still carries me. Unlocking his truck with the key fob, he uses his free hand to open the door and plops me in the passenger seat. Realizing that my entire family and our friends think this is some big joke and that fighting with him is pointless, I cross my arms, pissed, but accepting the situation. Giving me a once over, Chase shuts the door, and I pretend not to watch him as he walks around the front of the truck.

Putting the keys in the ignition, he starts the truck and looks over to me and says, "Put your seatbelt on."

Ripping the belt from the seat behind me, I whip it over my front and click it into the belt. "Just so you know, I put it on because I don't want to die, not because you told me to."

A booming, hearty laugh erupts from Chase's lips and it takes every ounce of willpower I have not to smile in response.

"You stubborn little shit," he chuckles as he puts the truck into reverse and backs up out of the parking space. "You are going to give me a stroke or a heart attack or a combination of both one day. I hope you realize this."

CHAPTER TWENTY-FOUR

CHASE

THE SILENT TREATMENT. That's her next move.

And sure enough, there isn't a word spoken between the two of us the entire fifteen minutes it takes to get from the hotel to my house. As soon as I put the truck in park, she unbuckles her seatbelt and lets herself into my house. Without so much as peep, she heads straight up to the guest room.

Not bothering to shut the door, she opens the bottom drawer of the dresser and pulls out a small pair of shorts and an old t-shirt that she must have left here when she was staying over. With her back to the door, she unsnaps the seashell bra, dropping it to the floor without a second thought. Pulling the gray t-shirt over her head, next comes the sandals. Kicking them off with as much care as the bra, I brace myself as she reaches behind and unzips the green sequined mermaid tail skirt.

There isn't a doubt in my mind that I should leave...that I should walk away, go to my own room, shut the door, let her sleep by herself, and we can have the conversation I've been wanting to have all night, tomorrow. But no matter what I say in my head, trying to convince myself to walk away from her, I can't bring my legs to move. Especially as she shimmies out of the skirt and stands there in the smallest white panties and her t-shirt.

"Fuck."

Muttering under my breath, I fight everything reason is telling me to do and walk over to her. She still doesn't say anything, but finally acknowledges me by raising her eyebrows, unimpressed by my presence.

"Will you talk to me?" I beg, standing in front of her. "Hollis, please."

"And say what, Chase?" she asks, really looking at me for the first time since we left the hotel. "What the fuck do you want me to say? That I can't believe I was stupid enough to believe that I meant more to you than every other girl you've fucked? That I thought, if nothing else, our friendship meant more to you? I fucking trusted you. I gave you all of me, Chase. And you broke my fucking heart. You left me. Dammit Chase, you left me."

Faster than I can catch them, tears stream down her face. I've seen it too many times, this look of hurt and betrayal on Hollis's face, but it's never been my fault. I've always been the one there to fix it. And I can't. All I can do is give her the explanation she deserves and hope that she'll still want me when I'm done.

Taking her hand, I bring her over to the bed, where she sits on the edge. Wiping away the tears, she says something about being a hot mess and needing to wash her face before she stands up again and begins walking out of the room.

"Do you know when I knew you were different from every other girl I'd ever met?" I ask, not expecting a response, just hoping to get her stop and give me her attention long enough to explain myself.

"Chase…" she tries to cut me off, but I keep going, knowing she needs to hear what I was about to say.

"You came over after school one night to help me with a project. I remember my mom was so surprised, because you know, you weren't the normal type of girl I usually brought by the house. And by that, I mean, you were classy, respectful, polite…"

"Anyway," I continue, "I was trying to convince you to just do it for me. Hell, it worked on girls before. I figured it was worth a shot. Until you looked me dead in the face and said, 'You might be able to play dumb with all the other girls, but not me. You're smart enough. Stop being lazy and just fucking do it.'"

"It was an English project," she confirms, knowing exactly what I'm talking about. "On Jane Austen."

"It was the English project, then it was Thanksgiving when we were going to eat alone, and then when my dad bailed on me and Tuck for Christmas and you and your whole family made us feel like we belonged with you guys. Your aunt is my mom's best friend. Your dad and your uncles protected us like we were their own. I thought about going back to Washington after I left the NFL, and even though I applied for the open coaching position at LSU, I could never leave Abbott Hills. I could never leave you. You, Hollis. You are my home. Wherever you are, that's where I need to be."

"But, you did leave," she repeats, not as a question, but as a statement.

"You're right," I shrug, "I left. I left you and all the promises we made to each other in the mountains behind that morning because it scared me. And I have no explanation other than in my head, I was saving you from the bullshit of being with me. I've never done serious, Hol. And who are you supposed to turn to when I piss you off? I do that enough as your friend, never mind something more than that. What if I can't love you the way you deserve? What if we do this, and you realize that I'm not the kind of man that you want to be with for the rest of your life? You told me over and over that night that this changes everything, that we can't go back once we start something like this. What if I lose you, Hol? What if we-"

"What if we have the most epic fucking love story in the history of love stories?" she counters. "What if we spend the rest of our lives being stupidly happy because we're together? What if there is no one else on this Earth that will love you, unconditionally, the way that I love you, Chase? Huh? So, that's all this was? It wasn't me or something I did, but the fear that we could lose something so fucking incredible before it even happens?"

Making her way back over to where I am sitting on the bed, her intent to go wash her wash is long forgotten about. The purpose and intent in her walk give me so much hope. If we can fix this, if I can get her to just see that I was a fucking idiot, I can finally breathe again.

"Chase, I've denied it every single day before now, but I have loved you since the day you saved me from falling on my face in gym class, and I will love you for the rest of my life. If that isn't enough for you, nothing and no one else ever will ever be."

And with that, I know it. She's right. The fear of losing her had sent me running, but how could I spend the rest of my life wondering about the 'what ifs.' Which means there's only one thing left to do.

CHAPTER TWENTY-FIVE

HOLLIS

WITH TREMBLING HANDS, Chase places his fingers under my chin and pulls my face up so there's nowhere to look but right at him. His bright green eyes, full of hope and adoration, search mine as if they have all the answers. When he finds the answer he's looking for, he leans in and my already racing heart beats faster.

When his lips find mine, I pause, wanting it, wanting him, but needing the confirmation that he's in too. Pulling back, while still in his arms, I glance up at him, ready to jump, both feet in, but before I do, I need to know he really means it this time. This cannot be a fleeting emotion. I can't do the back and forth. I cannot relive the last week over again.

"So, we're really going to do this, right?" I ask. "We're going to jump?"

"I'll jump if you jump, Hurricane," he nods against my head, his voice just barely above a whisper.

"You can't run from here, Chase," I remind him, pointing around to his house. "When we wake up in the morning, I'll still be here, and we can't run from this. If you're not in, one hundred percent, I need you to tell me. Right now. I need you to let me go."

"I can't," he starts. "I won't. Ever again."

"Then, what are you waiting for?" I ask, giggling when he looks at me curiously, because I know he has no idea what I'm asking him. "Kiss me."

And he does. Overwhelming love for the man in front of me fills me as our lips slide over one another, slowly and purposely.

"By the way," he laughs, in between kisses. "It was super cute how jealous you got of Bethany."

"Oh, yeah?" I shoot back, poking him in the chest. "Kind of like how you masterminded a plan to have them play Dropkick Murphys so I didn't dance with Deacon? And your comment about 'not going home with him.' What was that about anyway?"

"One, that had nothing to do with whatever his name was and everything to do with knowing the way to your heart is through my mom's blueberry pancakes and your favorite band. Since I couldn't get you blueberry pancakes, I figured Dropkick Murphys was the next best thing," he says. "And two, I heard you came to the gala with one of the guys from your work. I don't know. I just thought the worst possible way tonight could end is you leaving with another guy. So, I said something."

"There is another way to get to my heart," I laugh, tipping my head up to kiss him.

"Oh yeah?" he mumbles against my lips. "And what's that, Hurricane?"

"Well, you're already dressed like a pirate, so how about you take me out on that date you promised me on my birthday?"

"Anytime, pretty girl, anytime," he says.

"How about right now?" I ask. "You have the keys to the Abbott Hills gymnasium, right? Because, I demand a rematch. You cheated."

"Go wash your face and put some pants on," he laughs. "Because it's on, rally girl."

After we've both scrubbed our faces of the makeup from the gala, hand-in-hand we begin to make our way back to where it all started for us. With everything I am, I know this is it.

There are going to be good days and bad ones. But after going through the last week, I know that the bad days with Chase will still be better than the good days with anyone else.

We took the long way and every detour possible to get here, but I guess that's how it always goes, doesn't it?

Soulmates, they said.

Chase Merrimack and our love that came without warning.

THE END.

The Capparelli & Co. gang will return Spring 2019

ABOUT THE AUTHOR

Dee Lagasse is a forever 29-year-old native New Englander. Before anything else, she is the momma to three kiddos – affectionately known as The Minis. When she isn't writing, she can be found eating cheese fries, harassing her family to reach things on the top shelf, wandering a soccer field, or fixing a cheer bow.

Facebook
Capparelli & Co. Reader Group

Made in the USA
Columbia, SC
29 November 2020